Raven Mocker

Also by Don Coldsmith

Trail of the Spanish Bit
The Elk-Dog Heritage
Follow the Wind
Buffalo Medicine
Man of the Shadows
Daughter of the Eagle
Moon of Thunder
The Sacred Hills
Pale Star
River of Swans
Return to the River
The Medicine Knife
The Flower in the Mountains
Trail for Taos
Song of the Rock
Fort de Chastaigne
Quest for the White Bull
Return of the Spanish
Bride of the Morning Star
Walks in the Sun
Thunderstick
Track of the Bear
Child of the Dead
Bearer of the Pipe
Medicine Hat (Norman, 1997)
The Changing Wind
The Traveler
World of Silence
The Lost Band (Norman, 2000)

RIVERS WEST: *The Smoky Hill*

Runestone
Tallgrass
South Wind
The Long Journey Home

Raven Mocker

A Novel

Don Coldsmith

University of Oklahoma Press : Norman

A novel in the Spanish Bit Saga
Time Period: circa 1800

All of the characters in this book are fictitious, and any resemblance to actual persons, living or dead, is purely coincidental.

The Raven Mocker, an original pen-and-ink drawing by Bob Annesley, appears on the title page, and a portion is used as an ornament in this book, courtesy of the artist.

Library of Congress Cataloging-in-Publication Data

Coldsmith, Don, 1926–
Raven Mocker : a novel / Don Coldsmith.
p. cm.
"A novel of the Spanish bit saga"—T.p. verso.
ISBN 0–8061–3316–3 (alk. paper)
1. Cherokee Indians—Fiction. 2. Women shamans—Fiction. 3. Immortalism—Fiction. 4. Aged women—Fiction. I. Title.

PS3553.O445 R35 2001
813′.54—dc21

00–061538

The paper in this book meets the guidelines for permanence and durability of the Committee on Production Guidelines for Book Longevity of the Council on Library Resources, Inc. ∞

1 2 3 4 5 6 7 8 9 10

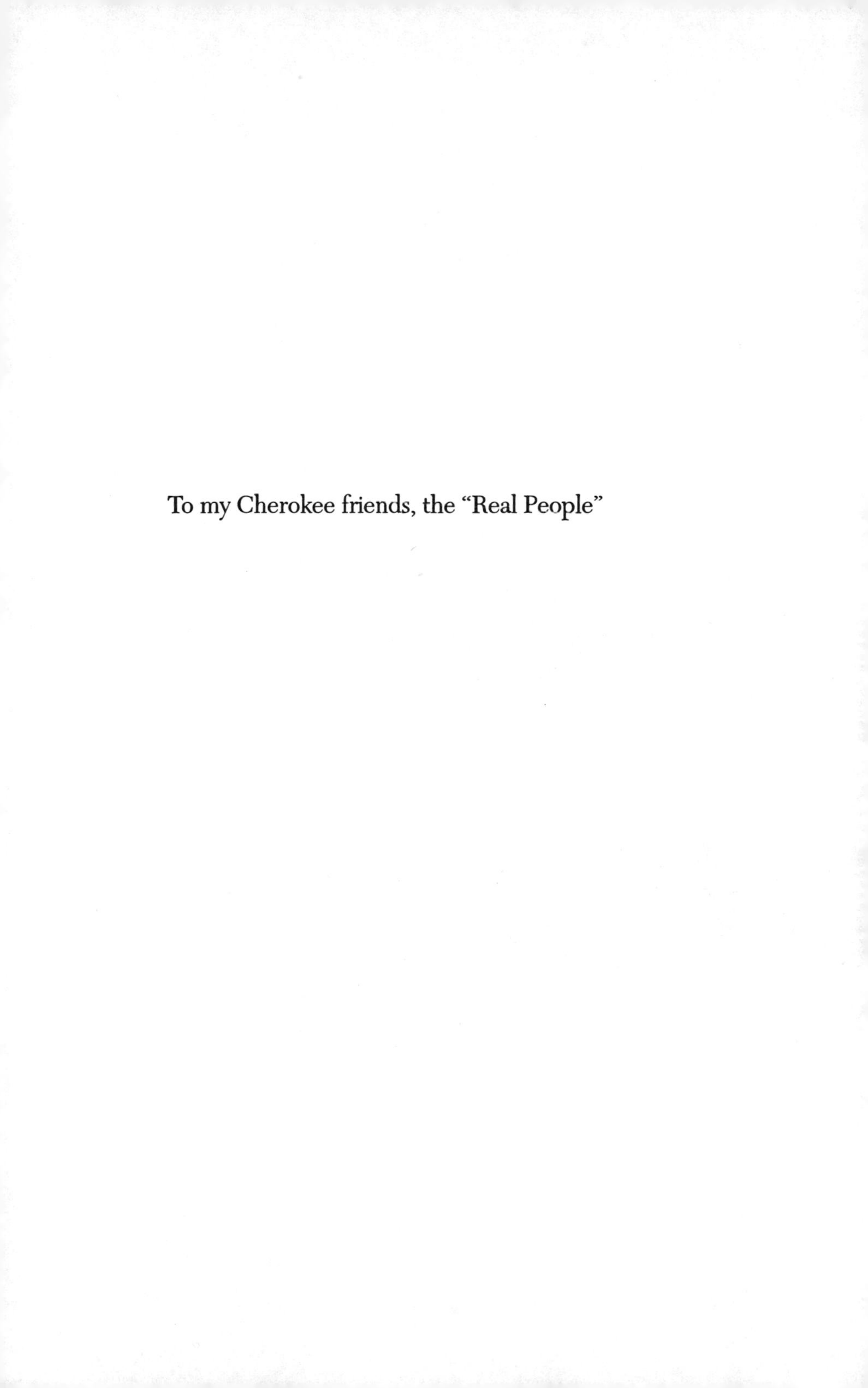

To my Cherokee friends, the "Real People"

Raven Mocker

1

The old woman woke and lay there for a few moments, not quite ready to face the day. It had been a chilly night, and her bones told her so, with the dull ache that seemed to settle nowhere . . . or everywhere. . . . She wasn't sure which.

She'd need to get up in a little while to go and empty her bladder. Maybe she could catch just a little more sleep first. No, better not. . . .

She gave a great sigh and raised to an elbow. It must be almost day, because she could see the outline of objects outside through the doorway of her little hut. She pulled herself up, her knees creaking just a bit as she rose to her full height. That was taller than most, even though she had shrunk down some in recent years. . . . Never thought a body could shrink that much. . . . Yet she'd managed to stay active. That had been a big effort sometimes, but it had worked. *If you keep movin', they can't cover you up,* the old granny had told her.

That had been years ago, when she was a child. The granny woman had been her friend, one of her few. And she realized later that old Snakewater, the granny, had had very few friends either. People had been afraid of the wizened little woman. They came for her spells and potions but left as soon as they could, glancing back fearfully over one shoulder. They wanted and needed Snakewater's medicine but didn't really like her. *Feared* her; maybe even hated her.

So Corn Flower, tall and gawky, a little girl with no friends, had been drawn toward the granny woman, short and wrinkled. They must have made quite a pair, the two of them. She smiled to herself, even now, as she thought how they must have appeared to others. She had spent more and more time with the "witch woman." It was exciting to know that this greatly feared person who had deep secrets, and powers given to few, was her friend. It gave a status and pride to young Corn Flower that she never could have achieved otherwise.

Her mother had died almost before she could remember. Her father, an important man in the town, was usually busy with the other men. His new wife, Frog, had little use for an unwanted stepchild, and no objection at all to Corn Flower's absence, which by now was almost continuous. When, a few years later, Flower's father had been killed in a skirmish with white men, she simply moved her few possessions to the hut of old Granny Snakewater.

That had been long ago. So long, in fact, that she could no longer remember her own age. The seasons seemed to follow each other in a rapidly accelerating sequence that became almost a blur. She had seen many people born, live their lives, and die. There was probably no one older in the whole nation of the Cherokees, she thought. Certainly none in this town. At least none she could think of. And her mind was clear. For that she was grateful.

Corn Flower sighed again and shuffled outside, toward the customary area where she could attend to body functions. A little while on her feet . . . slowly, mobility returned. It was always that way, and had been for a long time. It took a little longer now. That was all.

Granny Snakewater had given young Corn Flower her medicine before she passed on. It was a logical thing, not a decision. The younger woman had learned the use of the herbs and plants, the purpose of each, and the rituals involved in the search and harvest of the most important. Some could not even be gathered until seven had been located and the first six rejected. There had been very little instruction. Mostly merely a comment: *No, not like that. . . . Do it this way. . . .* Little praise either—usually just a nod and a tight smile when something was right. A frown when it was wrong.

The last few seasons of her life, old Snakewater would often turn a request over to the younger woman: *Here . . . Fix a potion for Little Dog, there . . . for the stomach.*

By the time Granny Snakewater died, her understudy was nearly twenty. Corn Flower had never married. There had been no suitors. She had wished, sometimes, that . . . No, there was nothing to be gained by *what if. . . .* The young men were afraid of the witch woman with whom young Corn Flower lived.

Besides, there were plenty of more attractive young women in the town. More eligible females of marriageable age than men, always. Young men were always getting themselves killed in skirmishes with their neighbors.

She didn't care much, she always tried to tell herself. It was apparent that women who had a man also had more problems than Granny Snakewater did. If a young man came along with romance on his mind, she'd think about it. Meanwhile others had noticed that the young assistant to the granny woman had come to look more and more like Snakewater herself. By the time of the old woman's death there was an eerie feeling that the strange and isolated Corn Flower had taken over not only the house and the medicine of the old granny, but maybe even the *person* of Snakewater too. The younger woman had been partly aware of this. Sometimes people would call her "Snakewater" and then show great embarrassment over the mistake. That brought a certain vengeful satisfaction, so she let it happen.

But all that had been decades ago. Now she answered to either name, but was mostly called by that of her mentor, Snakewater. There were few still alive who remembered that she had once been known as Corn Flower. Maybe she *had* become Granny Snakewater after all.

She finished her necessary body functions and went on to the stream. The most important ritual of the day was that of Going to Water, men in one area, women in another.

There were a few people already there when she arrived, wading in as far as waist-deep to fulfill the cleansing ritual and welcome the sacred joy and gratitude of a new day. A few nodded or spoke, and she returned their greetings, but would as soon be alone. She disrobed and followed a narrow gravel bar out toward the center of the stream. As expected, no one else followed her. She made others as uncomfortable as they made her, she had decided. Well, so be it! Still, there was a certain satisfaction in the fact that most of these people, at one time or another, had sought her help. They had been forced to do so. A healing potion, one to attract the attention of a lover, a medicine to correct some ailment—she alone could furnish them, and this brought a perverse pleasure each time it happened. It was better to be feared and respected than to be pitied and loved, she always told herself, though she knew it was a lie.

She dressed, shivering a little, and started back to her house. It had been her house ever since the death of the granny, a lifetime ago. No one else had wanted it, even. It was outside the town, outside the protective wall of logs set on end, which encircled most of the houses. This hut was not really one that most people would consider worth claiming. Old Snakewater had no family, and her successor had been already living in it, so . . . No one had given it much thought, not even Corn Flower. Her most pleasant memories were here, helping Snakewater pound and mix some of the dried roots or seeds or foliage.

There was always an odor around the dwelling. It was a not totally unpleasant mixture of drying herbs, tied in bundles and hung from pegs in the rafters. After all the years the smell was the same as she remembered from her childhood. Of all the senses smell incites the most vivid memories of long ago, and the events connected with it. In this case the scent of the hut was the same, and for the same reasons. The plants for medicine were the same, handled in the same way, for the same purpose, but by different hands.

The old woman strode purposefully up the slope, along the protecting wall, and past the entrance where the wall overlapped. There was a space of a few steps where, entering or leaving, there was only space for one person at a time. This feature had assisted in the defense of the town for many generations. The first few attackers through this cleverly devised chute would face certain death.

She hurried on to the hut, wondering idly what the day would bring. The day was warming rapidly. At this season, early autumn, nights were cool and days warm and sunny. There was a ripe smell in the air, a spicy mix of warm scents and the perfume of flowers and ripening fruits. Maybe this afternoon she'd take a walk and collect some herbs for medicine. She could use some more sassafras. . . . Maybe there would be pecans and hickory nuts, too, to gather, just for her own use. Usually, she had plenty of food, and of good quality: in exchange for the ointments and potions and charms that she could furnish, people brought her things of value. No one would risk giving an inferior gift to someone with as much power as the witch woman. Corn Flower was not quite sure of the limits of her power. She doubted, sometimes, that it was as effective as some people seemed to think. Yet what was to be gained by minimizing it? Let them think what they would.

Publicly, of course, she was always modest: *No, I have no special powers. . . . I do a little medicine, that's all. . . .* Misuse of such a gift would surely be dangerous to the one who sought to invoke it for wrong purposes, and might even be disastrous.

It was nearly noon before she was really ready to go and begin her gathering. Sun had climbed up the inside of the sky dome and was ready to pause at the house of her daughter for the noon meal. Snakewater cocked an eye upward and lifted her basket for gathering plants. *Now, where . . . Oh, yes, there it is. . . .* She picked up her favorite digging stick, and put it in the basket.

"Come on, Lumpy," she said. "I'll need your help today."

Anyone watching would have assumed that the old woman was talking to herself. This, of course, helped to encourage the idea that maybe she was a little crazy.

She had first seen the Little People when she was about twelve, she thought. Old Granny had always talked to herself, or to someone not seen by others. The girl had asked her about it.

"Who are you talking to?"

"Nobody . . . Just the Little People."

"Little People?"

"Of course. You know about them, don't you?"

"I have heard—"

"That they look after children who are unsupervised?" The old woman chuckled. "That they are in charge of lost objects?"

"Well, yes . . ."

"That's true." The granny laughed. "But more . . . I could not do the things I do without my helper here."

"What does he look like?" asked the girl.

"Ah, you try to trick me! You know, child, that if one *sees* a Little Person and tells of it, they die. If you see one, you must say nothing to anyone."

"But you—"

"Ah, I did not say I saw one, did I? I only talked to him. They may be invisible."

"But if I saw one, what would he look like?"

"Who knows? No one must ever admit to having seen one. I am sure, though," she said with a twinkle in her eye, "that they would probably look like little Cherokees."

"But you talk to them. They help you find plants for medicine, Granny!"

"Of course. We can *talk* to the Little People. They are in charge of lost objects, no? Maybe we find a knife in the woods. Somebody lost it; we can claim it. But we must tell the Little People: '*Hey, Little People! I'm taking the knife!*'"

Granny had held a hand aloft to show that the finder must *show* the custodians of lost objects what is to happen.

"What if you don't tell them?" asked the girl.

"Ah, you don't even want to know!" said the old witch woman, rolling her eyes alarmingly.

It had been not long after that, as she now remembered it . . . How often, in an inactive moment, we catch a glimpse of motion from the corner of an eye. We turn and there is nothing there. Sometimes our senses tell us that we *almost* saw it. . . . A flicker of light and shadow maybe. Or a glimpse of something not intended for human eyes. That was how it had happened. Young Corn Flower had turned, and there in the dusky corner of the room was a figure, no taller than her own waist. It was lumpy and indistinct but seemed to resemble a doll or a very short person. In a moment the image was fading and was gone. Oddly, it did not strike her as unusual until after it had disappeared.

"Hey, Lumpy, come back!" she cried with amusement. But there was nothing.

Just then Granny Snakewater entered the doorway.

"Who were you talking to?" she asked.

"Nobody! I . . . Just the Little People," Corn Flower stammered.

"Oh. Of course," the granny said, setting down her basket. Her eyes twinkled. "You didn't see one, did you?"

"I . . ." she began, and paused. "How could I, Grandmother?" she asked.

For an instant she had thought she heard a quiet giggle from the corner, but maybe not. . . .

Now she took the basket and headed out into the woods.

"Come on, Lumpy!" she said, where to any onlooker there was apparently only empty space.

2

Snakewater was tired when she returned. It had been a highly successful day, and her basket was filled with herbs and roots of good quality. But it had been hard work, all the walking and climbing and digging. She reached the hut, set her basket down, and sat for a moment on a little bench that she kept outside the door. It was hot inside in the stillness of late afternoon. Maybe there would be a little breeze later. For now, she'd rest a little, before sorting and tying her gatherings. But the sun was beating down on her bench—that, too, would be uncomfortable. Over next to the stockade wall was a welcoming patch of shade. She rose and moved that way. She considered taking the bench over there, but decided against it. It would be for only a little while.

"Get out of my way, Lumpy," she muttered, and then felt a little remorse for her tone.

"You were a big help to me today," she said to apparently empty air. "What? Yes, I *do* appreciate it."

Leaning against the poles, Snakewater slid to a sitting position with her back to the wall. Yes, it was more comfortable here. She liked the wall. It separated her from the hustle and bustle of the town. Most towns had by now abandoned the use of the stockade wall, but hers was a bit old fashioned. Many of the citizens still held to the old ways of fixing their hair, and more traditional clothing. Not all, of course. There were even a few who wore the white man's shirts and trousers. But only a few. The town was located off the main road a little way, and many traders and travelers bypassed it entirely. There were jokes in other towns about the backwardness of this one. Despite that, or maybe *because* of it, the following of the old ways had become a matter of civic pride. The old stockade wall with the offset baffled entrance was symbolic of their heritage.

Besides, thought Snakewater, it was a good place to rest. She leaned her head back against the heavy posts, settling comfortably. There was a little hollow there, where one of the poles had a slight irregularity, a curve away from the straight growth of the one next to it. It neatly fit the back of her head. She settled in a little, leaning to pillow her head in the hollow. She had done this many times, and did so now without even thinking about it. This was a part of her world, her private world in which she was alone but happy.

She closed her eyes to rest them from the late afternoon sun's glare. Pretty soon she'd sort and tie the herbs in bundles and hang them in the house to dry. But first she'd rest a little.

The sun was considerably lower when she woke with a start at the sound of voices. It took just a moment to realize where she was, and the time of day, even. She had not intended to doze, but apparently she had slept quite soundly for a little while. Maybe more . . . Shadows were lengthening.

She started to struggle to her feet, and then sank back to listen. One of the voices had called her name, and the thought flashed through her mind that the voice was from the spirit world, and that her time had come. Quickly she realized that, no, the sounds were not from the Other Side of existence but merely the other side of the wall. There was a crack between two of the poles where an irregularity left a space. It was the same crooked pole, in fact, that provided her head rest. Such spaces were caulked with clay, but during summer's heat some of the dried clay had fallen out, leaving a crack near her ear. The speakers must be no more than a hand's span away from her ear, and it was quickly obvious that they did not realize it.

Snakewater had clearly heard her name spoken, and now she rejoined the world with awareness of her surroundings. She kept still. . . .

"My mother says she's a witch," said a young girlish voice.

"Maybe so," said another, also young and girlish.

Ah . . . Two girls, maybe more, having found a private, secluded spot, were in the midst of a girlish conversation. Snakewater listened carefully. It did not bother her to be called a witch woman. Actually, she felt somewhat honored. It had never occurred to her that she had been given such a gift. She had merely learned the use of herbs and chants and rituals from the old granny. . . . At what point had she herself received the power? Or had she at all?

Well, yes, now that she thought on it. . . . Maybe there was not one point in time when it had happened. Maybe the transfer had been gradual, so slow that she had not even noticed. Yes, she did know, and did use the incantations and potions to accomplish what she needed. Maybe she had not given enough serious thought to the fact that the people of the town had even transferred the *name* of old Snakewater, the witch woman, to *her*. It was a strange feeling, one that gave her a surge of confidence, of *power*. . . . Yes, maybe so . . . Strange, it had been so many years now. She did not even know how many. *Too* many! But she remembered times when a success with a difficult charm or ritual had made her feel that she was indeed filled with power, and invincible.

Now the girls were talking again.

"My mother says that old Snakewater is good at what she does," one of them was saying, "but I am still afraid of her."

"No need to be," answered the other. "She cannot use that power for evil, can she? It would turn and hurt *her*!"

"Maybe . . . but who knows what she might think good or bad?"

"It would not matter, would it? If it hurt someone, that would be bad."

"But . . . sometimes, the person she is treating dies anyway."

"That is true. . . . Nobody has enough power to stop *all* death."

"But maybe . . . *What if she causes it?*"

"A medicine woman would not do that!" said the other indignantly.

"But what if"—the girl lowered her voice carefully—"what if she is a Raven Mocker?"

There was a gasp and a stunned silence. Snakewater found it hard to discipline herself to remain quiet. She *must* hear this.

"Think about it," said the same voice. "How old is she?"

"I—I don't know. Do *you*?"

"No . . . *No one knows.* She is older than anybody in the town, is she not?"

"I don't know."

"Neither do I. But my mother can think of no one older. So, how does one become older than anyone else? Maybc by stealing a part of the lives of others."

"A—a Raven Mocker . . ."

The voice was tentative and full of wonder.

"Yes! So my mother thinks. How many times has she sat beside the bed of one who is dying? *Many* times. And at the death of a child? Ah! She could steal a whole lifetime and add it to her own. Just think—two or three young persons . . . She might already be a hundred winters old!"

Snakewater did not know whether to be offended or amused. There were some frosty mornings when she *felt* a hundred winters old, but *really*! All in all she was inclined to treat this as a joke.

"My mother told me to stay away from her," went on the talkative one. "She may be able to suck the breath from your lungs to feed her lifetime! She is dangerous!"

Well, so be it. Young people must have shocking stories with which to frighten each other, no? Snakewater had heard stories of the

Raven Mocker as a child. They were exciting and scary, and quite possibly designed to frighten small children into good behavior. Nothing more. *If you don't behave, the Raven Mocker will get you, suck out your breath and steal the rest of your lifetime for himself.* Or, in this case, *herself.* She smiled. She could not believe that there were adults who could take such a tale seriously. She went about her tasks, but even as she did so, she could not stop thinking about it.

On a hunch she found herself at the same spot on the wall the next day. It did not take long. There was the sound of footsteps and the rustling of somebody moving around. Then voices, the same two. . . . This must be a secret place for the children, perhaps a space between a house and the stockade wall.

"Did you tell your mother what we spoke of?" asked the more authoritative of the voices she had heard yesterday.

"Yes. She said maybe it is true. Old Snakewater was present at the death of her uncle, when he was very young."

"Ah, yes, and how many more?"

"But . . . she was making medicine to help him!"

"Are you *sure*? Maybe to help him cross over, so that she could steal his life-years. He had many left, no?"

"Well . . . yes. . . . "

"And almost everybody in this town has lost somebody, sometime. And usually old Snakewater was *there*."

"But . . . Rain, she is usually there when people are sick, to *help* them."

Ah, thought Snakewater. *A name: Rain.* Now she knew who this child was. Summer Rain, daughter of Bluebird and Kills Two.

She had never had any unpleasant dealings with that family. With *any* family, actually. There was no one to whom she felt particularly close either. It was not her way. Thinking back, she realized that she had been a misfit as a child. She had been attracted to the old granny, possibly because both were misfits. Now, she *was* the witch woman, Snakewater. It had taken her some time to realize that. The old woman's medicine, her powers, had been passed down, and now *she* possessed them.

Another thought struck her. To whom would *she* pass them? She had no pupil. She had really never thought about that, about her own mortality. Now the thought caught her by surprise. Why had she just assumed that she would simply go on and on? She felt as she always had. She felt . . . well, middle aged. That concept had changed, of course. She had once considered a person of thirty winters *old.* Now that seemed quite young. To complicate all this thinking, she had to concede that the stiffness in her bones on a cold morning told her that she *had* seen quite a few winters. She had lost track of how many, but she didn't really feel any different than she had at forty. Her mind was the same.

It had been a milestone when she had stopped menstruating, some years ago. There had been restrictions on what she could and could not do during her "moon time." Preparation of the herbs and medicines was prohibited until it was past. Now she could mix potions at any time of the month, simplifying her work considerably. And even that, the cessation of her menses, had been a long time ago now. She could not remember how many years.

But . . . to whom would she pass on *her* powers, her medicine? There was no one. That did not bother her as much as the fact that she had never felt the *need* to pass it on. Did she expect to live forever? Why had it never concerned her?

The voice from the other side of the wall brought her back to reality.

"Well, we should think about it," said the one called Rain. "My mother says that it could be dangerous to be around old Snakewater. Especially if you're sick."

"But when you're sick, you need her medicine, her healing power."

"Ah, yes," Rain answered. "That is what she *wants* us to think, so that she can steal our life-years. Clever, isn't she?"

3

It was quite a shock to Snakewater to realize that some people thought along such lines. She had never cared much what anyone thought. She was content to prepare her medicine and to respond to those who wanted her help. Now this . . .

She thought briefly of going directly to the parents of the girl, Rain, and explaining what she had heard and how. But Rain's mother, Bluebird, already had her suspicions, judging from the girls' conversations. To make that contact might not be wise. It might even come down to whether Snakewater had actually *heard* the girls talking through a chink in the wall. Maybe Rain's parents would assume that some mystical ritual had allowed Snakewater to learn of the conversation. No, it would be better not to reveal what she knew.

Instead she now tried to recall all that she knew about the Raven Mocker. It had been many years since she had heard anything about such an entity, or even thought about it. An old story, told with those of Creation, and of the time when all men and animals spoke the same tongue. Tales of Rabbit, Fox, and Bear, and of Brass, the bad deity. Brass was so evil that the other immortals wanted to kill him to protect the human race. But they were unable to do so, because of his immortality. At last they had tricked him and weakened his power, enough to take him to the bottom of the sea. There they drove a great pole through his body and staked him to the ocean's floor. He remains there yet. . . . Her mind had wandered and she drew it back.

What about the Raven Mocker? It was a scary story, told by firelight, of a kind used to frighten children into good behavior. *If you don't behave well, something bad will happen.* Fear of the unknown is a forceful thing. The threat of a mystical entity, ready to steal your very life to feed its own, was a more threatening story than most. He (or *she*) would literally laugh at the carrion eater, would "mock the Raven," and live forever. Or for as long as he was able to steal a few years, even a few moments, from the lives of those around him, to add to his own disgusting lifetime. It would be a sort of artificial immortality at the expense of others, a parasitic existence.

She had been just a bit amused at first, to hear the girls talking. Children often try to frighten each other with stories. But there was something different here. Parents were involved. At least the mother of the one girl, Rain. . . . Possibly, even, the woman had *started* the rumor.

Snakewater was still not fully convinced that this was a serious problem. After all, who would believe such a tale? Well, yes, there might be a few who were gullible, but surely most would have the common sense to understand. . . .

She wondered, though, what might come of this, beyond talk. She could not remember any part of the story that dealt with attempts to *prevent* Raven Mocker's activities. People feared, sometimes detested, the person, but what could be done? Surely someone would wonder if it were possible to kill the Raven Mocker. Yet he is immortal, or nearly so. Anyone attempting such an assassination would be in great danger, probably. The Raven Mocker, with all the accumulated powers of stolen lifetimes, might add the life-years of the erstwhile assassin to his collection. All in all the Raven Mocker would be a very dangerous neighbor. If, of course, one believed the story. Snakewater was not certain that she did. It was all pretty imaginative.

Another thought fluttered through her mind. Could it be that belief and acceptance of the story was necessary for the Raven Mocker's success? If one did not believe, for instance, would it be possible for the stealer of lives to accomplish the theft? Here was another variable to ponder. Would one who did not believe be safe? Maybe . . . Unless, of course, at the last moment, when the Raven Mocker approached, the resolve weakened. . . .

Yet another angle occurred to her: What use are unused years to a dying person? Wouldn't the Raven Mocker merely be utilizing something of no use to the previous owner? In a way, preventing waste, as the scavengers do after the butchering of a large animal. Buzzards, coyote, maybe others . . .

She gave a great sigh. This was a very complicated puzzle.

It rained the next day, and the next. She did not even try to listen at the wall. She knew that would be futile. The girls would not come out and sit in the rain just to exchange outlandish suspicions. Snakewater had all but decided to regard the whole thing that way. It was ridiculous to worry about it.

On the third day the skies began to clear. It was good to see the sun. The Going to Water was observed, made somewhat more difficult by the rise of the rushing stream. The ritual of thanks for a new day was modified to allow for the muddiness of the bank and the water. As usual there was little conversation between Snakewater and the other citizens. A formal nod of greeting, a remark on the coldness of the water, or the foggy morning.

Snakewater finished her ceremonial cleansing, dressed, and made her way back toward the hut. She was thinking about what the day might bring. It would be too muddy, probably, to do much harvesting of herbs, but in another day or two there should be a good crop of mushrooms. Some varieties were useful, and rare at the season.

"What's that, Lumpy? Oh, yes. . . . A day or two. . . ."

A woman nearby noted the old woman's conversation with herself and shook her head, half amused, half afraid. She altered her course

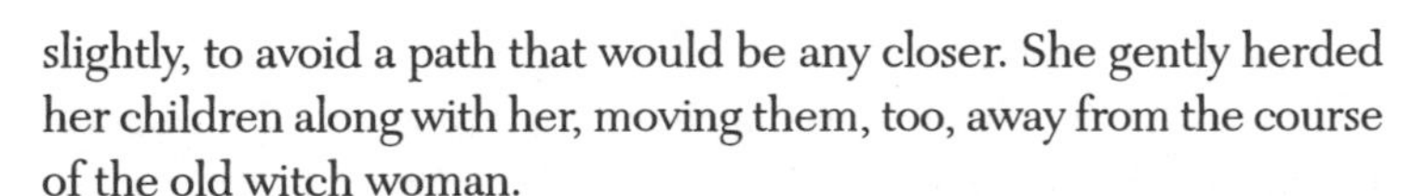

slightly, to avoid a path that would be any closer. She gently herded her children along with her, moving them, too, away from the course of the old witch woman.

Snakewater noticed, of course. This was not unusual. Such actions were expected. It had always been so, even when as a child she had gone to water with her old mentor, whose name she now bore. It was a part of her status and position and, in a way, a form of respect and honor. At least it had always seemed so to her. This morning, though . . . Was there something a little different about the woman's attitude, the sidelong glance over her shoulder? A slightly different look, of fear and dread, in her eyes? Ah, maybe not.

She reached the little house and began to think of some food to begin the day. Hmm . . . Not much in her larder. . . . A couple of rings of dried pumpkin, a pouch of corn, another of beans, a couple of onions.

It had been some time since there had been much illness. There had been little need for curative medicines. Possibly the change to rainy weather would alter that. She hated to think along such lines. It was much more rewarding to think of love potions and romance. But no one would bring her *any* supplies unless they wanted something, some spell or charm or . . . Maybe she could take the blowgun and hunt just a little for herself. Squirrels should be active at this time of year, especially after their work had been hindered by the rain.

She looked over at the weapon in the corner, unused for a long time now. Any darts? She rummaged for a little while and discovered a half dozen of the projectiles, sharp pointed and as long as a finger. Two would need new tufts of fluff, but that was easy. Milkweed pods were plump with their cottony fiber.

Snakewater lifted the long tube and wiped dust off the mouthpiece end. An experimental puff proved the bore to be clear. At least, air could pass through. Lifting the blowgun, she peered through it at the sky outside. It might be that mud daubers or spiders had chosen this place to build their houses. But, no, it was clear and clean. A good sign . . .

"Lumpy," she said, "we are going hunting."

She tucked the usable darts in the thong around her waist, and started away from the town.

Never shoot a barking squirrel was the hunter's motto. The one doing the scolding is the lookout, and his barking keeps the others informed. If he stops, something is wrong, and all activity ceases. The hunt is over for the day.

Snakewater's quest was a little different. Most hunters were interested in numbers. The more kills, the more food for the family. She needed only one, for herself, for today. Yet she hated to depart from custom. She had watched the barking gray creature for some time now, from her place in the thicket. She knew that this one was aware of her presence, but she was looking for the next squirrel to happen by, curious as to what the scolding was about.

But no *next* squirrel appeared. . . . Maybe this area had been hunted heavily by the young men, and squirrels were scarce here. Maybe she should look elsewhere. There were nut trees in several places near the town. Pecans, chestnuts, several kinds of oaks. Squirrels would be busy gathering and storing. But she hated to spend the whole day looking for one squirrel. The only reason not to shoot a barking squirrel, as far as she knew, was that you wanted *more,* and she needed only one. With what she had, she could put together a stew that would furnish several meals. She could do the stew without the meat, but it would not be the same.

Her heart was set on a squirrel now. The one on the sycamore limb above her seemed to be taunting her, as if he knew the custom. Twice she raised her gun and then lowered it again, hoping for another target. Finally she could stand it no longer. She raised the weapon, selected the best of her darts, and inserted it into the mouthpiece. Carefully she aligned the tube and placed her lips on the opening. It had been a year or two since she had used the blowgun, and she was unsure. *I should have tried a practice shot or two,* she thought. Too late now. . . . A deep lungful of air, a puff . . .

She knew as the dart left the tube that it was an accurate shot. When it feels right, there is no doubt. There was only a glimpse of the speeding missile, and the barking squirrel ceased to bark. He tumbled from the white branch and struck the ground with a thud, kicking feebly. The woods were silent as she shuffled forward to claim her prize.

Snakewater pulled out the dart, wiped it on a leaf from a nearby bush, and tucked it back in her belt. It was apparently undamaged.

She took a thong, looped it around the creature's neck, and suspended it, too, from her waist. Now she was ready to start home.

She looked up to see a young man rising from the bushes a few steps away. She had been unaware of the other hunter's presence.

"I am sorry," she said. "I did not see you. I thought I was alone."

He nodded slightly but did not speak. The expression on his face, though, told much.

"I only needed one. . . ." She realized that she must sound ridiculous.

"Here, take it," she offered.

The youngster shook his head. He still held a look of mixed puzzlement and disbelief. She had spoiled his hunt, and his wordless resentment came at his with great force. *You shot a barking squirrel!* his eyes accused.

4

She regretted the confrontation with the young squirrel hunter, and his odd reaction. She had not been aware of his presence and would have gladly given him the squirrel. His actions were strange, it seemed. It was doubtful whether he had been aware of *her* presence, until the squirrel tumbled out of the tree. She had spoiled his hunt, probably. He would have waited for other squirrels, and shot at *them*. He might have procured two or three by waiting. Now he had none. But she had apologized, as common courtesy would demand, and had offered the results of her own hunt. That should have been sufficient.

There was something else here, something vague and poorly defined. It was like something seen through an early-morning fog, identified but with little clear detail. What she had seen in the eyes of the young hunger was a mixture of several emotions: surprise, disappointment, maybe a little indignation, even an accusing tone. All of these emotions could be expected under the circumstances. But she had seen something else, something that not only puzzled, but alarmed her a little. *Fear.* It was there, in the youngster's face. But what had he to fear from an old woman?

It was several days before she chanced to overhear another conversation through the wall. Actually, it was not by "chance," though

Snakewater may not have realized it. Her spot against the wall, with the curving post that just happened to fit the curve of her head and neck, was a convenient place to rest, nothing more. If someone on the other side of the wall happened to have found a convenient place, too, so be it. That was no concern of hers. Sometimes she almost had herself convinced.

Those were her thoughts as she settled down in her resting place against the wall. There were two things that bothered her, both linked to the attitude of others toward her. One was the strange reaction of the hunter when she shot the squirrel; the other, the ridiculous game that the two girls were playing, scaring each other with stories of the Raven Mocker. Maybe it was just her imagination that the glances of people on the street were suspicious, angry, and threatening. No, not threatening as much as resentful. Maybe she had *three* concerns, somehow, or were they all *one*?

She had never cared much what anyone thought of her. The old granny woman had taught her that. There would always be those to laugh and ridicule others who are different. Granny Snakewater had taught her to ignore them. *You know who you are. Nothing else matters. Their ignorance is their problem.*

But now, in some mysterious way, things were changing. She still did not *care*, but was being forced to evaluate her situation. It occurred to her that it had been some time since anyone had requested her assistance with anything. Well, it had been rainy. . . . People were not out and around as much. . . . In her heart she knew that the rain would make very little difference. Could it be that another medicine-doctor had arrived from another town? No, it did not seem logical.

She was dozing in the warm afternoon shade when the girls' voices roused her.

"My mother says there are others who wonder too," Rain was saying.

"Wonder about the old witch woman?"

"Yes! Whether she is the Raven Mocker. She has always been strange, you know."

"Since she was a child, you mean?"

"No one knows," said Rain, a tone of conspiracy in her voice. "Do you think she was *ever* a child, a girl like us?"

The other girl giggled. "It doesn't seem likely, does it?"

"There is nobody in the whole town who remembers her as a child."

"Yes, but that is only because she is older than anyone."

"Exactly! That is the point, Doe. How does it happen that *she* still lives?"

"I—I don't know."

"Yes, you do. The Raven Mocker steals one lifetime after another. Old Snakewater could be a hundred years old . . . *five* hundred, maybe. And you agreed, before, she always hovers around the dying."

This was becoming a bit frightening. Snakewater had not taken it very seriously at first—had almost found it amusing, in fact. But the tone of the conversation she had overheard today was different. It carried an urgency that she did not understand. If the whole town was talking like this, it could account for all of the puzzling questions she had been pondering. The sidelong glances, almost angry . . . the look of fear on the hunter's face . . . the scarcity of requests for her help. People were *afraid* of her. It was a far different emotion from the awe of her powers that she had always felt—and which she had enjoyed, she was forced to admit. This was a completely different attitude on the part of her people, the Real People.

She lay on her pallet, unable to sleep.

"Lumpy, what am I gong to do?" she asked into the darkness. Then, after a short time, "Yes, I know it's not your problem. It is mine, but not of my making. Or is it?"

The suspicion that she had been trying to avoid now reared its ugly head, intruding into her thoughts: *Maybe it is true!*

She could not remember ever having heard how a Raven Mocker *becomes* one. She had always assumed that a Raven Mocker has existed since Creation or before. Or maybe there is a ritual of some sort that results in a person's conversion to whatever mysterious status is implied here.

Or possibly . . . She sat straight up in bed, alarming thoughts swarming into her mind. Could it be that a person could become a Raven Mocker *without even knowing it? Maybe they're right!*

"What?" she said aloud. "Yes, Lumpy, I know you can't help me."

Let me see, she mused, running a couple of different possibilities through her mind.

She had inherited many powers from old Granny. Could one of them have been the Raven Mocker identity? Could the granny have become weary of immortality and transferred it to her pupil? *But wouldn't I know?*

That brought the other thought: Could it be that the acquisition of unused lifetime years happens without the knowledge of the recipient? Is the Raven Mocker *aware* of what is happening? She had been present at the death of many people, old and young. She had been affected deeply by all of them, but the worst had been those of children. What a pity, a young life spent before it begins. . . . Maybe her very sympathy had somehow given *her* those years without her knowing.

She took a deep breath. This was a very disturbing line of thought. She had always envisioned the Raven Mocker as evil, scheming, perhaps even causing death to steal the life-years yet unused. Now, this was an entirely different possibility.

Maybe I am a Raven Mocker!

It was not a comfortable conclusion.

That had been a sleepless night, as she struggled with such a dreadful possibility. How could one escape this fate?

By light of day the idea seemed less logical, and she was tempted to scoff at it. She was unable to completely refute it, however, and it remained a gnawing worry as she went about her daily routine.

She could not avoid the fact that her services were rarely requested now. She had always been able to eat well, supplied by the gifts of the grateful recipients of her skills. Now these were growing fewer and fewer.

Ultimately she decided that there was nothing much she could do about it. To try to protest against what seemed to be growing public opinion would only call more attention to herself—attention that was unlikely to be favorable. No, she must remain aloof, watch closely for further information, and try to provide more for her needs by her own efforts. That should not be too difficult. She could hunt and gather. The woods were full of nuts. . . .

That made her think of squirrels, and that, in turn, of the disappointed young hunter. The incident still bothered her, but she knew nothing that she could do to mend matters.

She had finished the last of the stew she had concocted of squirrel, corn, beans, and onion. With each time she reheated it, she had felt remorse over that scene. Now she must obtain provisions of some sort. Maybe just an afternoon gathering nuts. She could take the blowgun along in case opportunity offered.

As it happened, it was a thoroughly enjoyable day, warm and still, typical of "second summer." There were nuts and acorns in great profusion, and the squirrels were busy. She saw no one all afternoon, filled her sack with the bounty on the ground, and in the process paused three times to harvest squirrels. There was one miss, and she couldn't find her dart. Well, she'd have to make a few new ones, while the milkweed and thistledown was still available before the weather changed.

Shadows were lengthening as she headed home. Her sack grew heavier, and she stopped to rest. The evening was still quite pleasant, the western sky turning the unique fleeting reddish-gold hue of autumn. She drank it in with enjoyment, and listened to the distant call of a hunting owl, and its mate's answer. Down toward the river a whippoorwill sounded its eerie cry. It was all good and right with the world as she lifted her heavy sack and headed on toward the town.

Darkness had nearly fallen as she headed up the slope toward her hut. Suddenly a sense of foreboding swept over her. Danger of some sort. She paused, puzzled, and then stepped on through her doorway, still anxious.

"Yes, Lumpy . . . what is it? Someone here? I—"

Her thoughts and her question met with a quick answer. Not in words, but in a dry, buzzing sound that she recognized easily. It was the warning of a rattlesnake's vibrating tail, and judging from the intensity of the tone, her visitor was a very large one.

5

Anyone is startled by a rattlesnake's warning, and it was no different with the old woman. Her response was conditioned, however, by culture and tradition.

She froze in position, not taking the next step, and stood in her doorway, peering into the darkness. The buzzing rattle continued as she tried to understand this quite unusual situation. At this season a large snake might spend an afternoon sunning in some warm clearing or among the rocks. With the coming chill of night it would be seeking shelter in a crevice or cave, Probably the place it had already selected to winter in. A den might contain dozens of the reptiles, their movements slowed during the moons of winter hibernation.

But by no stretch of imagination could she understand what a big snake could be seeking in her hut. Certainly not food, she thought wryly. And not a place to winter, it seemed. It was illogical, a poor place for the snake to consider. A specimen this large, judging from the sound of its warning, had seen many winters. It would know quite easily that this was not a likely place in which to winter.

Calmly she began to talk to the unseen visitor.

"My brother," she began, "let us consider this meeting. I do not know how you happen to be here. You are welcome, of course, in my simple lodge. It has been so since Creation, among my people and yours. My people, the Real People, called Cherokee, promised at that time that we will not kill your people, the Rattlesnakes. If it happens, we die, because of the broken vow. And in exchange you do not kill us. Is it not so? I hope you remember these things."

There seemed to be a change in the tempo of the rattling. No longer an angry buzz, but a calmer rustle, rising and falling in tempo, much less threatening than before.

"Ah, I see that you understand," she told the visitor. "Now, how do we solve this problem? As I said, you are welcome, but I think that you would be more comfortable in your own lodge, no? I cannot take you there, because I do not know where it is. And I cannot use my own lodge just now, because I might step on you in the darkness and cause you harm."

She had not moved a muscle in all of this time, lest the motion provoke a strike by instinct.

"Now, here is may plan," she continued. "I will back away and rekindle my cooking fire outside here. By its light I will be able to see you, to avoid injury to you under my foot. This avoids danger to us both, no?"

There was no answer, of course, but the sound of the rattles did seem to be slowing.

"It is good," she crooned. "Now I am going to take a step backward."

Her tone was calm and reassuring, but cold sweat moistened her palms. The middle of her back, between the shoulder blades, had developed an itch, and her leg muscles ached from being held in the clumsy position in which she was frozen. Very slowly she raised the foot nearest the visitor. The buzz intensified, but she continued her motion. It was not easy, standing on one leg while she moved the other, ever so slowly, so as not to alarm the snake. The warning rattle seemed to calm again. Finally she was able to place that foot behind her. As she stepped back, the rattling ceased.

"Ah, that is better," she said calmly. "Now I light my fire."

She placed a few small sticks and a handful of dry grass on the red coals that nestled in the ashes, and leaned over to blow gently on the tinder. White smoke grew and thickened. In a few moments the grass and sticks burst into flame with a sudden puff, lighting the whole area. Quickly she added larger sticks, and her fire began to broaden the circle of light around her. She looked at the door of her dwelling, watching carefully.

It was still a little while before she saw movement there, the sinuous motion of the snake. It moved to the opening and peered out, one way and then the other, seemingly undecided. Its black, forked tongue flickered in and out and from side to side like the flicker of the tiny flames in the cooking fire as it grew. Then, apparently decided, the creature started out into the open space and turned to its right. *Good,* thought Snakewater. *That is the way . . . rocks, brush, and trees. May you find your way home!*

The broad head of the snake, with its pointed and upturned nose, was followed by a slender neck, which led to a thicker and fatter body. Now the portion of the snake that was sliding through the doorway into the light was as thick as a man's arm, and much longer. This snake must be as long as her own height, Snakewater thought. The colors of its patterned body were startling. The base color was black or dark gray, with symmetrical squares of white placed corner to corner, the length of the body. Along the sides the dark color gave way to brighter reddish and russet shades. Lastly, the tail, not vibrating now. She counted at least a dozen rattles. . . .

"Good hunting, my brother," she murmured. "Now, I hope you brought no friends."

She lifted a torch from her now bright fire and stepped into the house to look around.

"It is good," she said, when no other snakes made an appearance. "Don't laugh, Lumpy!"

She set down her sack of nuts and prepared to skin and dress out her squirrels. Maybe she'd broil one for supper before she retired.

It was much later now. She had skinned and gutted her squirrels and was relaxing, sitting on her bench to watch the three-quarter moon rise beyond the trees. She smoked her pipe, enjoying her personal mix of *kinikinnick.* She liked the taste and aroma of a bit of sumac mixed with tobacco, just a hint of cedar, and a few leaves of catnip. Relaxing this way before retiring helped her think. It had been a big day. Very satisfying, in proving her ability to gather for the winter. She had cooked all the squirrels for better keeping qualities and would shell and leach the acorns later, when she had time. There had been more time, lately, with fewer people requesting her services. She was still puzzled over that.

Even more puzzling was the incident with the snake. She could easily have blundered into her house in the dark and been bitten before she realized it. She had been fortunate to avoid that, through no great credit to herself. The spirits must have been looking after her welfare.

Even so, the mystery remained. Why had the snake come there? It made very little sense. No reason for it to seek out her house. . . . And then, when the confrontation occurred, it had seemed happy for the opportunity to leave. There had been a considerable chance of an accident, a risk to either or both parties. Try as she would, Snakewater could think of no reason why the wise old snake would have come there.

Well, it was time to seek her rest. She knocked the dottle from her pipe and tossed it from her palm into the fire, now dying to a bed of coals. She started to turn away. . . . No, maybe a torch for a last look around the hut. If it was illogical for one snake to be there, how much more so for two. But it would do no harm to look.

She thrust a torch into the coals and, when it blazed to brightness, walked to the hut. A quick look around . . . Nothing unusual . . . Wait! What . . . ? A sack, similar to that containing the nuts . . . It was lying against the east wall, as if it had fallen there. But how could that be? She looked to the peg from which it must have fallen, but the mystery deepened. *There was no peg above that spot.* Nothing could have fallen there from a hanging position above. She hated to accept the implied answer that she must now ponder: If the sack had not fallen from above where it was lying, *it must have been thrown or tossed.* She did not recall . . . No, she would not have done that. Someone else, daring her absence? But *who*? And *why*?

She carried the empty sack outside to examine more closely by the firelight, building it up with a few sticks. It was not a sack of her own, but one she did not think she had ever seen before. Its weave, its pattern and size . . . No . . . not familiar. She felt its texture, then lifted it to her nose to smell, for no reason she could have explained. There was a slight musky odor about it, familiar, yet not one she recognized. Then suddenly it came to her, and she knew. She had smelled it before, at the opening of a winter den of snakes. The *snake*! It had been in that sack. . . . Someone had passed the door of her house sometime during her absence and tossed the snake, still in the bag, into the room for her to encounter when she returned.

It was a frightening thought, as she reached the inescapable conclusion. Someone had tried to kill her, either by the snake's bite or indirectly, if she injured or killed the snake, breaking the covenant of the Real People. But again, *who* and *why*?

"Lumpy," she said slowly, "I know you can't help me with other humans, but I rather wish you could."

It was a sleepless night, and much later, as she lay staring at the darkness, another thought struck her.

The person who had tossed the snake into her home had taken a considerable personal risk. Not only the risk of discovery, but the risks of finding, capturing, placing in the sack, and delivering the huge snake. It was one of the largest that Snakewater had ever seen. What motive would drive anyone to take such risks? She knew of no one she had ever harmed. Even the incident with the young squirrel hunter would not have seemed to call for such vengeance. The person who had made this attempt on her life had risked the same fate. He could have been bitten, or could have harmed the snake in violation of the covenant.

She could not understand such a massive hate.

6

Log Roller, the War Chief, sucked thoughtfully at his pipe and wondered what the approaching duo might want. He hoped that it wouldn't be anything of great importance. Things had been quiet for a long time, and he had no desire to have it otherwise. There had been at time when he relished excitement, but he had been younger then. Now he much preferred the quiet stability of a peaceful town. His was the best of both ways—the prestige of his office and the solid reassurance that nothing much ever happened around Old Town. Travelers more often used the road through Keowee, the town to the north, and Old Town had become almost isolated in its following of the old ways. There were occasional traders who stopped by. Enough to supply their needs and to bring news of the outside world. He had not even been over to Keowee for several years. He liked it this way.

There was a sense of foreboding about the two men who approached his house. Log Roller had a bad feeling about this. He knew these men, of course, Red Dog and Hominy, the latter known for his ability to eat the staple food that gave him his name. The looks on their faces suggested that it was a very serious matter that had brought them here.

"*Osiyo,*" said Red Dog by way of greeting. "May we talk with you?"

"'*Siyo,*" answered Log Roller. "Of course. Want a smoke?"

Without waiting for an answer he knocked the ashes from the pipe and refilled it, as the two visitors settled themselves. He called inside, and his wife brought a burning stick, nodding pleasantly at the visitors. Log Roller took the light and applied it to the fresh tobacco, handing the stick back when the task was accomplished. After a few puffs he handed the pipe to Hominy, who took a few puffs. Hominy passed it on to Red Dog as indicated by its owner's lazy gesture.

When this informal ritual of hospitality had been completed and the pipe returned to Log Roller, he cleared his throat.

"You wish to talk?"

"Yes," said Red Dog. "There is a problem in Old Town."

Log Roller was greatly relieved. Dog had plainly said *in Old Town.* That would clearly make it a matter concerning not the War Chief, but the Peace Chief. But he must hear the rest.

"It may be," he said thoughtfully, "that if it concerns only the town, it would be in the responsibility of Three Fingers, the Peace Chief. His is the concern of matters *in* the town or among the townspeople. Mine is in dealing with others. Outsiders."

"We understand," said Red Dog, "but we were made to think we should talk to both."

"What is it, then?" asked Log Roller, perhaps more irritably than he had intended.

"You remember the story of the Raven Mocker?" asked Hominy.

"Of course. He cheated the Raven, the carrion bird, in the Creation story, by not dying. Only a story, no?"

"Well . . ." said Hominy.

"Maybe," said Red Dog, "but this is our problem: My wife, and the wife of Hominy, here, say that the women are talking. There may be a Raven Mocker here."

"Here? In Old Town?" asked Log Roller.

"Yes, so they say."

"But—but *who*? How do they know?"

"Snakewater," said Red Dog. "The medicine woman."

Log Roller's first inclination was to laugh, but he saw that the men were serious.

"Think about it," said Hominy. "Nobody even knows how old she is. She just goes on and on. And she has been present at many deaths."

"Well, so have I," observed Log Roller. "Does that make *me* a Raven Mocker?"

Both of his visitors appeared very uncomfortable.

"The women have talked much about this," said Hominy.

"What clan?" asked Log Roller

"Mine, Bird Clan," said Red Dog. "Hominy's, Deer. Both have talked of it.

Log Roller nodded. "And mine, Wolf Clan." He raised his voice to call through the doorway. "Cat, are the women in your clan talking about the Raven Mocker?"

"Well, I heard something," she answered, coming to the door. "I did not pay much attention. Foolish girl-talk, I supposed."

Log Roller nodded. "*Wado,* Cat." She turned away and addressed the other men. "So . . . the women of at least three clans talk of it."

"Maybe others," added Hominy.

"It seems likely," said the War Chief. "What is Snakewater's clan? Does anyone know?"

There was silence for a little while, and then Cat spoke from inside the house.

"Paint, I think. No one seems to know for sure."

So, thought her husband, *the Wolf Clan women have talked of it more than we realized.*

"But it would still seem to be a matter for Three Fingers, the Peace Chief," he said. "It is within the town."

"Well, " said Red Dog, "you should know that someone tried to kill her. Put a rattlesnake in her house."

"*Who?*"

"I am not at liberty to say," said Red Dog smugly.

"Is this true?" Log Roller asked Hominy.

"I heard it too."

"A clumsy effort," Log Roller observed. "Not successful, I assume."

"That is true."

"Nevertheless, it would seem to be Three Finger's problem."

With that he rose and went inside. The interview was over.

Privately he wondered much more seriously about this. How could it be decided? Could it be proved that the person in question was actually a Raven Mocker? Even if so, what could be done? He knew of no rule or law that would apply. It would be up to the Council anyway.

Yes, that would be the logical sequence. A hearing before the populace of Old Town.

He still thought that the one to call for a council should be the Peace Chief. Well, he would talk to Three Fingers and offer his help in any way that he legitimately could.

"You talked with the young men?" Log Roller asked conversationally.

He had gone to see his friend Three Fingers, and the two had exchanged greetings and smoked. Now the pipe was finished and it was time to talk.

Three Fingers sighed deeply. "Yes, my friend. My heart is heavy. They said that they had been to talk with you."

"Yes," replied Log Roller. "I told them that it was in your area of concern."

"That is true, much to my regret."

The two men chuckled.

"I also told them," Log Roller went on, "that I would talk with you and help in any way I can."

"*Wado.* It is good. Of course, it is the women who will decide. But for the hearing, we should both be there. And, my friend, I do appreciate your support."

"It is nothing. . . . You would do the same for me."

"Do you know the clan of old Snakewater?" asked Three Fingers.

He had refilled his pipe and was tamping the tobacco mixture with one of the stub fingers that gave him his name. That accident had taken place long ago in his youth, as he was loading his musket. The ramrod had never been found.

"Those young men asked about that," Log Roller answered. "I was thinking Paint Clan, maybe. She was older than I, by several seasons. She was called Corn Flower, as I recall. Her mother died, and her father remarried. That wife was Deer Clan, I'm almost certain. But the girl, she who is called Snakewater now, was something else. I remember my parents talking of it. That was one of the differences between the girl and her stepmother. Her father had to move to the other clan."

Three Fingers nodded sadly. "Too bad. I don't remember any of this."

"You were just enough younger not to understand."

"You think she is Paint Clan, you said?"

"Maybe. I don't know. I don't know whether she attends clan functions at all," said Log Roller.

"Probably not. She has never married, so she had no potential husband to be considered by her clan," Three Fingers said.

"Well, the old women will know. I am made to think that this will be mostly their decision anyway. If it seems that there is any need for action, that is."

"I would think so," Three Fingers agreed. "An open hearing before the council, to determine whether there is an offense?"

"That's how I do it. There may not *be* one. Even if there is, it could probably be handled within her clan, don't you think?

"My thinking, also," said Three Fingers. "Even if the Council agrees that someone has been wronged, it could be worked out between the two clans. Her clan would carry out whatever action is decided."

"Good thinking, Fingers," chuckled Log Roller. "I hope it works out that way."

"But what if it seems to be that old Snakewater *is* a Raven Mocker?" asked Three Fingers. "Is there any action that should be taken, or must be?"

"I don't know," answered Log Roller thoughtfully. "I can't remember when this might have come up before, in the entire Cherokee Nation. Surely we would have heard."

"One would think so. Maybe we could inquire of other towns."

"Maybe. Let us call the Council first, though, to see if we need to go farther. And a decision could be deferred, of course."

"Yes, that's a possibility," agreed Three Fingers. "Well, I'm hoping it can be handled at the clan level. But if worse come to worst, I wonder if the Council could banish her?"

There was a long silence. Both men realized that they had been avoiding any specific possibilities.

"That could be dangerous," Log Roller observed. "Especially if she really is a Raven Mocker. We don't know *what* powers she has. And would it be within our laws?"

"I don't know. But first we must call the Council, no?"

"Yes, but let's wait a few days, try to learn all we can about how this started. We should talk to the young men who came to us. Red Dog and Hominy, wasn't it?"

"Yes. And, as much as it pains me to say it, I fear that I, as Peace Chief, must be the one to call for the Council. It is a matter for Old Town, not for the War Chief. Let me inquire a little further. I will talk to you again before announcing the call to Council. Let me know if you learn anything."

"It is good," said Log Roller as he rose to depart, then he chuckled. "Well, not really. The *plan* is good. Not the situation."

The Peace Chief smiled wryly. "Easy for you to say! But thank you again for your support, my friend. I will probably need it."

7

Snakewater knew that there was something going on. There was a feeling of excitement in the air. For some time she was inclined to attribute it to the season. Warm days, cool nights, the "second summer." There had been a hint of frost a few days ago. Not a hard freeze, merely a rim of white along the edge of the river as they went to water.

The geese were passing overhead, high in the clear blue. . . . Shining white lines of the birds made a yelping sound like a myriad of small dogs, as they headed south for the winter. She wondered where. She had always wondered that. It stirred a restlessness in her, and for some time she thought that the subdued excitement in the town was the same reaction in others.

Odd, she thought, *they have never seemed to feel it before.*

Her questioning was partly answered by a conversation heard through the fence. It had been several days since the young girls had come to their secret place to hide, play, and visit. Snakewater had been dozing in the sun and was wakened by the voices.

". . . and my mother says there will be a Council soon," one was saying.

Her nap interrupted, Snakewater almost drifted back into sleep. It was of no concern to her whether the chiefs called a Council. She seldom attended anyway. They would do what they decided. She knew that there was no major threat to the town from outside. If there were, she'd have heard, because there would have been much more excitement. That meant that it was some problem *within* the town. Maybe somebody wanted to marry, and the clan structure prohibited it, because a man must marry into a clan not his own. . . . Some other technicality. Such things were usually evaluated and decided by the women of the two clans involved. Never having been through a courtship, Snakewater had no such experience, the seeking of approval for the marriage. It might have been interesting. She wondered how it would have felt to be with a man. She used to dream sometimes, and that was good. Her body's call to such contact was fainter and more seldom now.

She wondered, too, how it might have been to bear a child, to hold and rock it and put it to breast. She loved children but had seldom had opportunity to hold one. Even then it was always because it was sick, and she picked it up as part of her ceremony. If it had been different, if her ties to family had been better, she could have held the babies of her sisters. But she hardly knew them, because of the enmity of their mother. And of course, they were of a different clan. Deer Clan, as nearly as she could remember. Her own was Paint Clan. It mattered little now. She drifted back to sleep.

It was a day or two later, as she returned from gathering wood for her cooking fire, that a man approached. His manner was serious, and it was apparent that he was seeking to talk to her. She recognized Three Fingers, the Peace Chief. She was glad to see him. It had been some time since anyone had requested her services. It was seldom, in fact, that she'd had to gather her own fuel. Those who had successfully sought her help kept her supplied. But not now.

"*Osiyo!* How can I help you?" she asked cheerfully.

There was a troubled look on his face. What could it be? Three Fingers appeared healthy enough. Maybe his wife was ill, or one of his children, although they were all grown. At least, she thought so.

"You are Snakewater, of the Paint Clan?" he asked formally, without changing his stern expression.

"Of course," she answered, puzzled. "Once called Corn Flower when I was young. But you know that, Three Fingers. How may I help you?"

"It is not that," he said formally. "You are requested at a Council tomorrow at the town house. You must attend."

"But . . . what . . ?" she stammered, confused.

Now the expression on the face of the Peace Chief relaxed somewhat, to be replaced by one of genuine concern.

"My heart is heavy over this, Snakewater. You have been accused."

"Of *what*?" she demanded. "I have done no crime."

"It is not that," he said. "This is a most unusual thing. Snakewater, are you a Raven Mocker?"

There was a hint of fear in his eyes, as if she might become violent, or try to forcibly seize his unused life-years on the spot.

"How could I be?" she demanded. "Three Fingers, you have known me since you were a child. Since before you *lost* those fingers. I helped you with the healing of them!"

"That is true," he said uncomfortably. "But it is the duty of my office to . . . Well, you know. . . ." he finished lamely.

She almost felt sorrow for the man. "Do *you* think that of me?" she insisted.

"I—I don't know what to think, Snakewater. I know very little of your medicine, and nothing of the Raven Mocker, except as part of the Creation story."

"Who has brought this complaint?"

"I cannot tell you. You will learn at the Council."

"Is this not unusual?" she asked.

"Yes, the whole thing is unusual."

She became defiant. "And what is the procedure to deal with one who is a Raven Mocker?" she demanded. "And how would you know?"

"I am not your accuser, Snakewater. As to what happens . . . that is why we have the council. A request has been made, a complaint stated."

"It is ridiculous," she sputtered. "What if I refuse to attend?"

"Then men of the warrior society would be sent to bring you."

"How many would it take, to drag a poor old woman?" she taunted.

Three Fingers sighed deeply. "Don't be this way, Snakewater. Listen to her complaint, answer it. . . . That may be all."

"Ah! A woman! Does she think I would steal her husband, and she wishes to get me out of the way?" she sneered. Then she relented. "Well, I will be there. I would not dignify such stupidity by making a big thing of it. In public, of course."

"Of course. *Wado,* I thank you, Snakewater."

He started away and then turned. "There are many," he said haltingly, "who consider you a fine woman. I want you to know that I am one of them. This will pass."

She watched him go. She was not so certain.

"I don't know," she said, half aloud. "What do you think, Lumpy?"

The town fairly sizzled with excitement, as the people began to gather at the town house. Its unique seven-sided architecture was for a purpose. Each clan held an official position around its own section of the wall. Sometimes there was a fire in the center, vented through a smoke hole in the roof, but not today. It was warm and sunny, and the opening cast light instead. There was a shaft of sunlight that shone almost in the corner between the Wolf and Bird clans.

Snakewater arrived and smiled at the women of her Paint Clan. She knew most of them but had seldom sat with them in council. Still, if a verdict ensued that called for some penalty to be meted out, these were the women who would administer and oversee it.

I'm getting ahead of myself here, she thought, as she took her seat.

There was little formality. Three Fingers quieted the crowd and opened the meeting. Log Roller sat near, in his designated seat as war chief. Something might develop that called for his opinion, though it seemed unlikely.

"We are gathered to hear a complaint," Three Fingers began. "I am sure that you all know what it's about. Who brings the complaint?"

"*I* do!" said a woman in the section reserved for the Long Hair Clan. *"There is among us a Raven Mocker."*

A few gasps indicated that not everyone in the town was aware of the topic under discussion.

"And who . . . Please state your name, and that of him whom you accuse."

"Not *him,* but *her*!" The woman pointed to Snakewater.

"*Your* name," persisted Three Fingers. He wanted no misunderstanding.

"Spotted Bird," the woman retorted. "This woman stole the life-years of my baby."

Snakewater remembered her now. A tragic death . . . She had felt it deeply herself. . . . A beautiful child. Only a few moons old, dying, lungs filling, and coughing with no effect. She could well remember the look of panic in the child's eyes. She had even tried to breathe the life back into the tiny chest.

Spotted Bird was talking ". . . and I *saw* her suck the life from my daughter's nose and mouth," she finished.

"I tried to *save* her!" protested Snakewater.

There were several derisive hoots from the crowd.

"She was present at my brother's death!" shouted another woman.

"He was killed by a bear!" Snakewater answered indignantly.

Three Fingers quieted the crowd and spoke firmly.

"Let us be reasonable," he insisted. Snakewater has been present at many deaths. She has been asked there because of her medicine, is it not so? Now, let me ask you . . . How many are *alive* today because of the powerful medicine of this woman?"

There was a moment of stunned silence.

"I am!" called a burly warrior.

"And I!" added a young woman.

There was a ripple of agreement.

"So . . . ?" said Three Fingers in mock surprise. "It seems we can prove little here. And let us think on this: No matter how powerful a medicine may be, eventually it fails. Otherwise everyone would live forever, no?"

Silence was heavy in the town house for a moment. Then . . .

"Except for the Raven Mocker, who *does* live forever!" called Spotted Bird, the complainant.

"Wait!" said another woman. "That is only a story, like that of the Giant Leech, to frighten children into obedience."

"How do you know? Are you *sure*?" asked someone.

There was a babble of voices, and the Peace Chief was forced to quiet the crowd again.

"This is going nowhere," he stated firmly. "I have heard nothing but opinions. Let me ask: Does anyone have any *proof*, one way or another?"

There was silence, and he continued quickly, before anyone could break the ribbon of this line of thought.

"Does anyone have any proof that the Raven Mocker is more than a story?"

Again there was silence.

"Let us think on this, then," said Three Fingers. "Let us consider, and meet again in seven days. That will give us time to seek visions for guidance. It is good to sleep on such matters. And one other thing: For most problems we have solutions. Laws. It is the way of the Real People. Does anyone know of any precedent here? Did anyone ever hear of how a Raven Mocker case was handled? Did we ever *hear* of a real Raven Mocker?"

In the ensuing silence one voice was heard. It was quiet, but effective.

"Not until now!"

8

Worries hung over her in the ensuing days. One was the awareness that someone had tried to kill her with the snake. At least it seemed so. Another, the disquieting events at the Council, and the knowledge that another Council hearing was pending. Still another, perhaps worse, was the suspicion that the accusation might even be justified in some way. *Maybe they are right. I could be a Raven Mocker.*

With the next breath she would think such an idea ridiculous. Surely it could not happen to a person without his or her knowledge. *When* could it have happened? But close on the heels of that thought, another . . . *Maybe I was born with it.*

She had always been different in many ways. She knew it. Everyone knew it, from the time she was small. Perhaps that was the difference. The Raven Mocker, born among ordinary humans, of human parents, but with the ability to transfer and absorb the unused life-years of the dying. . . .

But if that were true, where did the old granny, her namesake mentor, fit in? The two of them had always seemed so close, so similar . . . not in appearance, of course, but in spirit. To others, so similar that she now bore the same name: Snakewater. Had the witch woman, too, been a Raven Mocker? *Is that how it works?* she asked herself. Was the understudy already born a Raven Mocker, or was such status bestowed by the teacher when *that* Raven Mocker became tired of the false immortality?

No, she told herself, that was making it too complicated. Her mentor had been kind and generous and had helped many people, as she had herself. They had been gifted with certain powers, which required some knowledge of how to use them to the good of others. That the old granny had given to her. *It cannot be evil to help others,* she assured herself.

She tried to shake off the fantasy that had begun to depress her. There were times when her heart was so heavy that she even considered suicide, though not for long. Such reflections might interfere with what she was intended to do. She wished that she could talk to her teacher. She shrugged off the angry thought that *Granny left me.*

Maybe she could talk to someone else. . . . No one in her own village, of course, but was there not a conjure woman in the next town, Keowee, a day's travel to the north? Yes, she was sure of it. Possibly . . . What was her name . . . Frog! Yes, Spotted Frog. No sooner had she thought of this possibility, than she began to plan her journey. It did not take long. She gathered enough food for subsistence, blankets for the overnight stay, and chose a small but well-made basket as a gift. She would start at daylight.

Her heart was light during the journey. The day was pleasant, the road easy. She nodded cheerfully to the few travelers she met, and they returned her greeting.

She was surprised at the changes since she had last visited here. There were fields and farms and houses and herds of cattle grazing. She shook her head in disapproval. The Real People were living like whites.

Reaching the outskirts of the town, she made her campfire and settled for the night. She would go in when morning came and ask for Frog, the medicine woman. She was tired and slept well.

In the morning she rose, went to water at the stream, and redressed, combing her hair to appear presentable. Entering the town, there were more changes—a store, a blacksmith preparing his forge for the day's work . . . Times were changing. She had no difficulty inquiring her way to the house of Spotted Frog, and knocked at the door.

"Who is it?" a voice called.

"I am called Snakewater," she answered. "I come from the town to the south of here. Old Town. The one with the wall. I would talk. . . ."

A woman appeared in the doorway. She was heavy, of medium height, and she might have been of almost any age. The lines in her face belied the jet black of her hair. All in all, though, the lines were those of a happy disposition.

"I have heard of you," she said. "Come in. Let us smoke."

Snakewater offered her gift.

"It is beautifully made," said Spotted Frog. "Your work?"

"No, no. A woman in our town makes them."

"*Wado!* It is good! Come . . . let us sit outside. The day is pleasant."

They sat on a bench, and Spotted Frog brought a pipe and a burning stick with which to light it. They smoked in silence for a little while, and finally Frog spoke.

"How may I help you?"

"I—I don't know," said Snakewater truthfully. "There are things that I do not understand."

The other woman smiled. "There are many things like that, no? What is it, Snakewater?"

"Well, I . . . What do you know of the Raven Mocker?" she blurted.

Several emotions flitted across the face of Spotted Frog. Suspicion, fear, defensiveness, maybe even anger.

"Why do you seek of this?" she asked carefully. "Has your town a problem?"

"No . . . Well, maybe. There are suspicions, talk. There have been accusations."

The other woman was quiet for a little while.

"You have heard the stories of the Raven Mocker?" Snakewater finally prompted.

"Of course. He steals unused life-years at the death of a young person. Or any person. Adds them to his own, to become immortal."

Snakewater nodded. "Did you ever hear how he *becomes* a Raven Mocker?"

A look of alarm, almost of horror, settled on the face of Spotted Frog. "You want to *become* a Raven Mocker?"

"No, no! Not that at all! It is only . . . Ah, how can I say it? I am the one who has been accused."

The woman rose and stepped back, as if there was a danger in the nearness.

"I cannot help you!" she snapped.

"Please!" pleaded Snakewater. "I mean no harm to anyone. I do not know how this started. There has been an attempt on my life. There was a hearing in our Council."

Quickly she told about the snake, the outcome of that episode, and of finding the sack in which the snake had been tossed, and of the details of the hearing.

Spotted Frog's face softened. "I am made to think," she pondered, "that your heart is good. Yet I do not know how I can help you."

Snakewater's eyes welled up with tears. "Could I be a Raven Mocker without knowing?" she blurted.

"Who knows? But I would not think so. No, surely one would *feel* the change when new years were added, no?"

"*Wado.* Thank you. That was my thought too. But I have no one to talk to . . . no one to understand."

"Ah, we may never understand. Maybe it is not meant that we should. But I have heard that your medicine is good."

"I have thought so. I have tried to make it so. But no one comes to me now. They are afraid."

"Yes . . . afraid enough to try to kill you, no?"

"I fear that is true."

"You may have to move, Snakewater. Another town?"

"I had not thought of that. I have never lived anywhere else. Never *been* anywhere except here."

Frog nodded sympathetically. "I will conjure a spell for you. I wish that I could do more."

At least it was comforting to know that there was someone who could understand. Even if she was no closer to understanding the whole thing, here was something to cling to. Spotted Frog, a powerful medicine woman, did not believe that she, Snakewater, could be a Raven Mocker. That was reassuring.

As she walked along, she fingered the protective amulet that Frog had given her. It was a medicine bag on a thong, a tiny buckskin pouch no bigger than her thumb. The woman had placed tiny pinches of several substances in it. Snakewater did not know what. . . . She preferred not to know, and her trust in Frog and her medicine was strong.

She was somewhat stiff and sore from the long journey yesterday. That, she thought with wry humor, was probably good. If she were really a Raven Mocker, her limbs would be young from the young lifetimes she had absorbed. It amused her to think so. It had been a good thing, to share her concerns with another medicine woman, and she was thinking more clearly now.

It was a matter of concern that Frog had suggested that she move to another town. Such an idea had never occurred to her, but it might be the most practical solution. Another town, a fresh start. It was something to think about.

She knew that there were Cherokees moving westward, building towns in a place called Arkansas. There would be need for a person with the medicine gift. But how could she find the town where she could settle, one with the need for the skills she could offer?

It was well after dark when she reached home. She had refused Frog's kind invitation to spend the night. She had been away for two days, and it would be good to be home. This thought made her uneasy again about the possibility of moving. Well, she'd think about that later.

The town was quiet and dark. The moon had risen to help her find her way, and the squat outlines of her modest dwelling had never looked so welcome. She was tired, as she shuffled the last few steps to the doorway. She paused, hesitating to step into the darkness where—

The familiar buzzing rattle sent cold chills over her. Was it starting again? This time she was not close enough to be in real danger. She stepped back, and the rattling ceased. She must have some light. . . . The fire was surely dead, after two days. . . . She would have to make one. With a sigh she set her pack against the outside wall of the hut and drew out her flint and steel. It took a little while to arrange her tinder and the charred cloth that would catch the first spark. She knelt, striking the metal with her flint, trying to catch the spark she needed. . . . There! She lifted the handful with the spark and blew gently until it glowed, then burst into flame, lighting the area in front of the hut. . . .

She fumbled with some of her fuel, stacked against the end of the structure, and quickly fashioned a torch. Carrying it for light, she approached the doorway again. The rattle sounded. . . . Very cautiously she peered around the opening and drew the hanging doorskin aside, to see . . . *nothing.*

The startling sounds ceased, and Snakewater could have sworn that she heard a suppressed giggle.

"Damn you, Lumpy!" she exploded. "Where are you? That wasn't funny at all!"

She tossed her pack inside, followed it, and quickly sought her pallet. It had been a long and eventful day, and she was exhausted.

9

Three Fingers spent a very uncomfortable few days, waiting for the next meeting of the Council. There were several things he did not really understand. It was still a mystery to him, how rumor and accusation could have divided the town so quickly and so bitterly. As far as he knew, Old Town had experienced no more illness or unexpected death than any town does. People are born, live, and die, like the leaves on a tree. Death is a part of the cycle, just as autumn leaves grow ripe and fall in their multicolored splendor. That was an analogy which appealed to him.

He regretted the losses, some more than others. The death of a child is always hard, even beyond the loss to those most closely involved. Such concern Three Fingers felt quite personally, as part of the responsibility of his office. Still, death happens. To look for causes beyond the obvious seemed fruitless to him. There are things not meant to be understood by mere mortals.

It seemed infinitely more ridiculous to him that anyone would attempt to assign *blame* for such an inescapable event as a random death. He was concerned that this conflict threatened the town. Already there were friends of the Spotted Bird woman, sympathetic to her loss, who were loud in their denunciation of old Snakewater.

The situation might deteriorate to the point where they began to demand action. And in turn the council might find it necessary to make some sort of decision, simply to avoid violence. That was a hard thing to imagine, in a law-abiding setting such as Old Town. The Real People had respected the authority of duly chosen leaders for many generations.

Sometimes he wondered, though, how he had allowed himself to be selected for his present position. And *why* would he have accepted it? For the prestige, he had to admit.

But in the years since he had been Peace Chief of Old Town, there had certainly been no crisis to compare with this. His greatest fear was that friends of the woman who had brought the accusation would try to take action on their own. That in turn could trigger a defensive reaction by the supporters of the medicine woman. Such a thing could tear Old Town into two warring camps, and he doubted that the town could survive such an internal war.

It was a welcome distraction, then, when a trader and his wife arrived at Old Town. They sought out the leaders of the town, Three Fingers and Log Roller, to pay their respects, as was customary and proper. It was always pleasant to have traders visit. They carried not only trade goods, but news and stories. Many traders did not include Old Town among their stops. It was somewhat off the main road and had a reputation for being a little slow to accept change. Such a town is likely to acquire also a reputation for slow trade. There is a reluctance to try new things.

Such a reputation did not bother the citizens of Old Town, or its leaders. It was apparent that its citizens were content to follow the old ways. The crops were planted outside the walls, in small plots and fields. Few people had livestock, beyond a horse or two. By contrast, some of the Real People in other areas had adopted many of the white man's ways. Three Fingers was aware that over beyond Keowee there were larger farms and fields worked by black slaves, and plantations with big houses, herds of cattle, pigs, and poultry.

The traditional walled towns of the Real People, as well as their houses and clothing, were becoming more and more like those of the white man. A strange thing: The whites had never seen crops such as corn, pumpkins, beans, or potatoes until a few generations ago. But they had learned to plant and grow these crops from the Real People and other tribes, changing the whites' ways to meet new conditions. Now the change had come full circle. The Real People were adopting white ways. Ah, it made his head ache to think about it.

But now Three Fingers was glad to see the trader. He would have a variety of new goods. More importantly, news of other towns, maybe even new stories. But above all the presence of the trader would provide a distraction for Old Town. People would not be brooding about the question of the Raven Mocker. At least not so much. It was another three days until the time for the council to reconvene.

This trader, a Choctaw, had been here before and was known to Old Town. Trading was brisk, and the time around the story fire in the evening an enjoyable distraction.

On the first evening the trader began by relating all the news from the places he had been. A fire had destroyed the council house in one town, and it was being rebuilt. The Peace Chief in another town had been killed by a tree he was cutting. It was an accident—a sudden shift in the breeze just as the trunk spoke its characteristic crack and began to fall. The tree twisted, spun at an awkward angle on its stump, and fell directly in the preplanned path of retreat. But such things happen, no?

Three Fingers hoped that Old Town's people would not see a similarity in this, the unexpected death of a young man, with their own Raven Mocker problem. Or maybe it would be a *good* thing. No one can ever be sure of anything, except that he can always expect the unexpected. He smiled to himself at this contradictory thought. Ah, well . . .

There was good news, of course. Crops were good and hunting productive. In several areas the Real People were raising pigs, which seemed to thrive on the abundant crop of acorns this season. The pigs met with mixed reactions, but there was much to be said for an animal that required little hunting. Cattle, too, were becoming more common, for meat and milk, and ox teams were replacing horses and mules for hauling wagons.

There were also, said the Choctaw, more Cherokees heading west to join their relatives in Arkansas. Several towns had been established already. It was good country, he said, beyond the big river, the Mississippi. All new country, with few white men yet. The French had been there earlier, trapping furs, but had been replaced by a few of the English-speaking whites.

"These are the ones we know," he explained. "We called them *Yen gleesh,* before. They call themselves Americans now. You know them."

The crowd nodded, murmuring.

"Not many of them west of the Big River yet," the Choctaw went on. "But lots of room out there. I am thinking of going there to trade."

"You go there now?" someone asked.

"No, no. Not this season. We are not prepared for it. Maybe next season. But some of your people are going."

"Ours? The Real People?" someone asked.

"Yes, so they call themselves, as you do—Cherokees. They are only a day or two behind me, maybe."

"How many?"

"I don't know. Two wagons, maybe three. Two or three families."

"Will they come this way?"

"I could not say. Maybe they follow the main road, through Keowee. . . . Yes, that's most likely."

It was about this time that Three Fingers noticed Snakewater, out on the fringe of the crowd. He wasn't sure for a moment whether his eyes were deceiving him. The old woman was at the farthest edge of the circle of light. She was not doing anything in particular, just quietly listening.

Interesting, Three Fingers thought to himself. *She seldom attends the story fires.*

It was three days until the Council would meet again. Snakewater was doing a lot of thinking. Her conversation with Spotted Frog had been useful in providing new ideas. Until then she had not even thought of leaving Old Town. Now it seemed like a worthwhile option to consider. She had never run away from trouble. It was against her nature.

Yet this current problem was different in many ways. She had been accused of things over which she had had no influence. Even if she *were* a Raven Mocker, she told herself, she would have little control over whether someone lived or died. She used her potions and teas and ceremonies to try to *help* the sick or dying when requested. As her mentor had reminded her many times, to misuse such gifts would be quite dangerous to herself.

Even so, the thought occurred to her that maybe, somehow, she *had* misused her gifts. No . . . On reflection she did not think that was possible. Besides, this was a unique situation. The attempt on her life was a very unsettling thing. Would it ever be that she could feel confident and at home in Old Town again? It seemed unlikely. Someone's hate was deep and powerful, to make him (or her) take the personal risk required to handle that snake and put it in the bag. The idea of leaving began to look more and more attractive. After all, even if the decisions of the Council were favorable to her, some unknown person would be out there with a powerful hate . . . powerful enough, maybe, to try again to kill her.

The arrival of the trader, and his news of other Cherokees moving west, stimulated thoughts of leaving. She might be able to join such a party and travel with them. Maybe she could inquire of the trader before he left. Yes, that could do no harm. . . . She'd talk to the trader or his wife. . . . Yes, the *wife*! That was it! They were expected to leave tomorrow, but she would rise early and talk to the wife, learn more if she could. More about the travelers who were coming along behind them. There might be a good chance that she could join the travelers.

But what about the Council? It seemed that no one was certain as to what action would be appropriate if it *was* determined that she was a Raven Mocker. Maybe, she thought, that was the reason for Three Fingers's delay. The Peace Chief himself was unsure. Now, what if she approached Three Fingers and offered to solve his problem by leaving? Yes, that might be the answer. She would talk to him tomorrow too.

She fell asleep with a sense of satisfaction. She was ready, at least, to take some action toward solving her problem, and that of Old Town.

Sometime later she awoke with a sense that something was wrong. It took her a moment to orient herself to reality and to realize that she was awake and not dreaming. Yes, she was in her own house, in her blankets. The familiar scents of her drying herbs were there. But something was *different* somehow. What had wakened her? Some primitive instinct, a warning of danger?

Snakewater lay unmoving, waiting. . . . She could see the familiar outline of the doorway by the pale starlight that leaked in around the doorskin that served to close it. Then she sensed a presence somewhere near. Just outside the door curtain, maybe. Surely not *inside* the hut. No, outside. She could hear someone or some*thing* shuffling along the outside wall, coming toward the door. Quietly she reached out and picked up a knife that lay beside her pallet. She had placed it there with no real purpose in mind; just her general sense of uneasiness over the situation at Old Town.

Now she shifted it to her right hand in a position of defense. An assailant attempting to surprise her would find what it meant to experience surprise.

The approaching visitor paused, and Snakewater realized that whoever or whatever was there may have been listening to her breathing as she slept. A change in the rhythm might have signaled that she had wakened. Instantly she resumed the deep, slow breaths of a sleeper, even adding a light snore as she inhaled. The invader moved on toward the doorway and paused again. Surely a human, she thought. Then, to her amazement, a voice spoke softly.

"Snakewater!"

It was the voice of a man, urgent yet secretive. She paused a moment, and he spoke again.

"Snakewater! I mean you no harm. I would speak with you."

She was astonished. She did not recognize the voice, but there were many in Old Town with whom she had never had a conversation.

"Who are you?" she demanded.

"It does not matter. I come as a friend. May I come in?"

"No! Have your say from where you are!" she demanded.

She was still trying to identify the voice. It seemed to be that of an older man, and carried a tone of authority. It was definitely not Three Fingers. She knew him well. Not Log Roller, the War Chief, either. No, this must be a person whose authority derived from his wealth or prominence in the town. She had little contact with such persons.

"Well . . . I would rather speak face to face!" the visitor said.

"No! Talk, now!"

"I—I want to help you, Snakewater. I can make you wealthy."

She snorted with laughter. Why would she want such a thing?

"How?" she asked, trying to control her indignation. "What would I have to do?"

"Very little," the visitor said, more confident now. "Just teach me how to do it."

"Do *what*?"

She was completely puzzled now.

"To become a Raven Mocker, like yourself!"

10

Snakewater was tempted for a moment to leap from her bed and attack the intruder with her butcher knife. She took a deep breath to regain her composure, and to think. She was furious, but a wrong reaction to the situation might carry consequences.

It was tempting to play along, to learn more about this person who skulked around in the dark with such a revolting proposal. Yet doing so would imply that the accusations against her were true. *Wait*. . . . This might even be a trap. She must not even suggest a willingness to negotiate such a bargain. To do so would virtually be an admission of guilt.

Either way the person outside her door was dangerous. For a man actually to seek such a thing was completely foreign to the customs and ways of the Real People. He might be dangerous to her or to others, with such a bizarre goal in life. If it was a trap, there was also great danger to her. Her answer would be critical.

"Snakewater," the voice said in a loud whisper, "are you still there?"

"Where else would I be?" she snapped. Then she tried to take control of her temper. "I was only wondering," she said more calmly, "how anyone could think such a thing possible. I know nothing of the Raven Mocker, beyond the old story."

"Huh!" came a sarcastic grunt from outside. "Of course you would have to say that. But think about it. I will be back."

"Who are you?" Snakewater demanded. "Why do you bother me with this?"

She waited. . . . There was no sound outside. Quietly she rose and stepped to the doorway, knife still in hand, and flung the doorskin aside. There was no one. Not even a retreating figure in the dim starlight. Had she dreamed it? No, it had been too real. She glanced at the position of the stars as they rotated around the one fixed star in the north. Yes, a long time until morning. Well, when morning came, she would look for footprints in the dust outside the door. For now . . . She let the leather curtain fall back into place and sought her bed. There would probably be little sleep, but she would try.

"*Wado,*" she said into the dark. "Thank you, Lumpy, for waking me!"

Despite her doubts she quickly fell asleep.

The next morning the whole episode seemed like a dream. She lay there a moment, then rose to look outside. It was barely growing light. Dew that had collected on the roof dripped from the edge and spattered in the dust below. And, *yes*! It spattered in the footprints that she saw along the front of the house. And, yes, *there* was the spot where he had stood, shuffling a little with nervousness as he had talked with her. Now she had a strange feeling that it had *not* been a trap. The misguided man in the dark had actually believed that she could teach him to be a Raven Mocker. She shook her head sadly at the thought of such a sick mind. However, a person with such a belief could be very dangerous, especially to her, with the Council ready to further discuss the problem that faced both Snakewater and Old Town.

There was yet another question that now occurred to her. The visitor in the night, having been rebuffed, might easily turn against her completely. He would not be certain whether she could identify him. Possibly he might fear she would go to the Council, putting him in jeopardy. What recourse would he have? A cold chill crept up the back of her spine. In that case she could see no alternative for him except to kill *her.* It was not a pleasant thought. If he did kill her, of course, it would prove her innocence before the Council—a hollow victory, one she would not be alive to enjoy.

After worrying for half the morning she came to a conclusion. She must talk with someone, a person who would be aware of what was going on, in case something happened to her. Better a person with authority. . . . Of course! Three Fingers . . . Why had she not thought of it before?

It was not easy to find a way to talk privately with such a person as Three Fingers. But it was still early. People were just beginning to go to water, stumbling around sleepily. Men and women used different sections of the river, of course. If she hurried over to wait, partially concealed, along the path the men took to the river . . . No sooner had the idea formed than she was hurrying in that direction. She encountered a man or two and, when appropriate, nodded a greeting. Mostly she kept a little way off the path, making use of bushes and patches of fog to remain as inconspicuous as possible. It did not occur to her that this would lend an ethereal nature to any encounter with a sleepy citizen.

She concealed herself behind a clump of shrubs and waited. Younger men, having completed the morning ritual, were drifting back toward the town by twos and threes, visiting about the weather. Older men, rising more slowly, were mostly headed toward the water. She had no idea where Three Fingers might be. It was possible that he had finished the morning ceremony and returned to his house, but she thought not. The sun was barely peeking under the sky dome, and Three Fingers was, above all, a deliberate and thoughtful person. No, he would be among the later persons to go to water. . . .

Snakewater was almost convinced that her guess was wrong. The sun was fully up, starting to crawl up the dome, and the men were no longer heading toward the river, but back. She had nearly decided that she must forget the secrecy and go to the house of Three Fingers, when he appeared from the direction of the town. He looked very sleepy and undignified, his hair awry, yawning and scratching his belly. She had guessed right after all. Three Fingers was a late riser.

"Ssst! Three Fingers!" she called.

The man nearly jumped off the path in his surprise.

"It is Snakewater," she said hurriedly. "I must talk with you."

"I—I . . ." he stammered, trying to regain his dignity. Irritation and embarrassment showed plainly in his face. But after all, talking to citizens was part of his responsibility as Peace Chief.

"Wait here," he said irritably. "I am going to the water."

When he returned a little later, his dignity was restored. He appeared alert and confident, well dressed, and his turban was carefully wrapped. The irritation was gone from his face, replaced by his usual look of friendly concern, which befitted his position and office.

Snakewater rose from her concealment and motioned for him to follow her into the woods a little way. He did so, although she was certain that the situation was not to his liking.

"What is it, woman?" he asked almost irritably as she stopped and turned. "This is most unusual!"

"That is true," she agreed. "But, Three Fingers, the whole thing is unusual. A man came to my house in the night."

His eyebrows rose in surprise, but she continued.

"No, not in that way! Be sensible, Three Fingers! He came about the Raven Mocker."

"Ah! How so, Snakewater?"

"He wanted me to teach *him* to become a Raven Mocker. He offered to make me rich if I would do that."

"I see. . . . This is a serious thing. . . ." he mused.

"I thought you should know of this."

"Yes, yes . . . I had no idea that there were those who . . ." His voice trailed off. Then he seemed to regain the authority of his office. The confusion was gone, shrugged aside, and he was again the dignified Peace Chief of Old Town.

"Let us consider," he began, firmly now. "The Council is to meet tomorrow. I have given this much thought. There are two or three families who will back your accuser. Mostly the people will support you. Some are unsure. But this . . . You have no idea who this was?"

"None. I did not recognize the voice."

"Mmm . . . And he would make you rich?"

"So he said. But I could not do so."

"Yes, yes, I know this." Three Fingers waved her protest aside. "But *he* does not, it seems. There are few men in Old Town with the wealth to offer. I can think of none who would consider such a thing. But there may be those who could *not* have the wealth, but would try to cheat you. Yes, this would be one of those. . . . "

"I had not thought of that," she said. "I had wondered, since I refused, that he might fear I would tell of his offer."

"But you do not know who he is."

"True. But he does not know that. Oh, yes . . . He said to think about it, and that he would be back."

"Ah! Now we have him!" Three Fingers chortled.

"How so?" Snakewater was puzzled.

"The Council meets tomorrow. He would want to know before then, so he will come tonight!"

"Three Fingers, I am sick of this whole thing! I have decided to leave, to go west. The trader said there are others of the Real People moving west, building towns."

The Peace Chief nodded. "I can understand, Snakewater. I would hate to see you go, but for you it may be best. It is yours to decide. Still, that is another matter. I am concerned about this attempt to buy your powers. That cannot be done, can it?"

"I *have* no such—"

"I know, Snakewater. But your medicine gift, the conjuring. That cannot be misused, can it? If you used such a gift to harm someone, what would happen?"

"It would kill me, I suppose."

"Yes. Even more so, with the Raven Mocker secret? *If* you had it, of course?"

"I would think so. I do *not* have it, though."

"Yes, yes. Mmm . . . When did you intend to leave?"

"I don't know, Uncle. If I left before the Council, there would be no need for a Council, no?"

"I had thought of that. The trader said that the travelers west would be taking the other road, through Keowee, instead of Old Town. They should be there tomorrow."

"So I understood," she said. "I had thought, maybe, to join them there."

"Snakewater," he said seriously, "you don't *have* to go, you know. The Council will clear you."

"I know. But still, I think it might be best. Besides, I am tired of thinking about it."

"I can understand that. If you try to join the travelers, though, you would leave today?"

"Maybe. I had not thought through the whole thing. My visitor came just this past night. But I *have* decided to leave."

"You would walk?"

"Of course."

"Could you ride a horse?"

"I have no horse."

"That was not my question, Snakewater. It would make your travel much easier."

"But I—"

"Let me see about a horse for you," said the Peace Chief, waving aside her protest. "Now, here is what I'm thinking, about your visitor last night. I want to catch him. A warrior or two, hidden near your house when he comes. . . . We can do that, whether you are still here or not."

She thought for a few moments.

"I am made to think," she said finally, "that I would rather be gone."

Three Fingers nodded. "I can understand that," he agreed. "But let us plan how to accomplish this."

11

It was a busy day, trying to prepare her departure without appearing to do so. Much of the preparation could be done inside her house, of course. It consisted largely of packaging her plant medicines for travel. A major problem was trying to decide what to take and what to leave. She wanted to take everything. The bundles and bunches of herbs, selected carefully, prepared and dried and now hanging from the walls and ceiling, represented many days of search and collection. Some were already pounded or ground, and stored in gourd containers or packets of well-tanned buckskin. These could be easily carried on the horse that Three Fingers had promised. The dilemma that she faced was what to do about the array of hanging clumps of plant material. She hated to leave any of it behind, but it was obvious that she must. Some of the rarest and most valuable specimens she partially processed and packaged. It was hard to estimate how much she could carry on a horse. Three Fingers had managed to bring her a pair of pannier bags, which could be prepacked, ready to toss over the animal's back and tie to the saddle.

Almost too late, after the panniers were nearly full of her herbs and medicines, she realized that food, too, would be important. She gathered the most nutritious and least bulky of her supplies of dried meat, corn, and other vegetables, as well as nut meats. She must abandon a large supply of nuts and acorns still in the shell, but they would be too bulky and heavy to take. . . . No time today to pick out nuts. . . . She added to her pile of plunder a favorite cooking pot, obtained a few seasons ago from a trader. It was of shiny metal, one of her few concessions to white man's technology.

By evening she was ready, or at least as close as she could manage. Her fire outside the door had been fed slowly, a little at a time, and she had intentionally moved around as she usually did in the evening, showing herself to any who might be interested in watching. Just after it was fully dark, Three Fingers and one of his grown sons approached quietly.

"Are you ready?" he whispered.

"Of course!"

"It is good. . . . Come . . . your horse is in the trees there. Corn Plant will carry your bags. You have food, weapons?"

"Three Fingers," she scolded, "I was using such things before you were born."

"Yes . . . yes, of course."

She picked up her short bow and its quiver of arrows, and the blowgun, a dart already in place. A last moment she stood in the darkness of the familiar room. She could see nothing, but the feel of the place, the smells of herbs drying, of fires and cooking, of habitation, she would want to remember.

"Good-bye, Lumpy," she whispered. Then, to the others, slightly louder, "Well, let us go."

They reached the horse, a steady old mare, concealed in a clearing in the woods, and the three quickly loaded the packs.

"You know the road to Keowee," said Three Fingers. "You should have no trouble. The moon will be up soon."

"*Wado!* I thank you for your help, Three Fingers, Corn Plant. . . . How will you do this, now?"

"Hide near your house," said the Peace Chief. "Build up the fire a little. See who comes."

"What if no one does?"

"Then I will announce at the Council that you are gone, and there is no problem anymore. But I think he will come, don't you?"

"I am made to think so," Snakewater answered. "He will want an answer to his bargain before the Council meets."

She mounted the horse, a bit clumsily. It was hard to swing a leg over the bulky baggage. And it had been a long time since she had been on a horse. But she'd manage, she told herself.

"If you can," she said, "you might send word what happened here. . . . No, that would be hard. I may learn someday. . . . Or not. But never mind."

She pulled the mare's head around and clucked her forward, flapping the reins gently.

"May it go well with you, Snakewater," said Three Fingers softly, after the retreating shadows.

Whipper waited until the night was more than half gone. Old Town was sleeping as he rose, leaving his wife softly snoring and the children quiet. If they woke, they would think only that he had gone to empty his bladder. That would be his story, regardless of how this meeting turned out. He was sure that the conjuror would be expecting him tonight. He had told her that he would return, and this was the last night before the Council was to meet. Snakewater would not allow the Council to convene without having resolved her business with him.

This was probably the best thing ever to happen to him in his entire lifetime, he thought. He knew that he was not well liked or even respected. It was not his fault that people were so unreasonable. Everyone went out of the way to find bad things to say about him. Even his name . . . *Whipper.* He had been only about twelve summers when the other boys found him whipping the dog. The animal was tied, and he was simply punishing it. The dog had defecated, and he had stepped in the dung with his new moccasins. But had it not been his dog anyway? He could whip it if he wished. The other boys had run to tell adults, claiming that he had beaten it half to death. That was untrue, of course. . . . Not nearly half.

But the adults had believed the troublemakers, and he was severely scolded. The dog did limp for a long time, and the incident earned him the name "Whips His Dog" . . . Whipper. He had protested, but the more he complained, the more they used it and more they laughed at him. He finally stopped complaining, but it was too late. The name stuck.

There was the incident of his first kill. . . . He had found a dying deer in the woods and shot an arrow into it just as two other hunters came into the clearing. They claimed that it was a deer they had been tracking, after wounding it with an arrow. Whipper responded with indignation, stating unequivocally that he had been waiting here, still-hunting, for half the day. He was a big young man, his voice loud and dominating, and the others had backed down. They sat to watch him skin out his prize. They seemed quite amused when he rolled the carcass over, to reveal the arrow of Black Otter protruding from just behind the ribs.

There were other episodes too. Misunderstandings or someone else's fault, every one. No one ever took his side in a conflict, no matter how loud or firm his statement. He had no friends. It had never occurred to him that he was simply disliked because he was a coward and a bully.

He had married, although he was certain that people laughed behind his back and made jokes about why any woman would marry him. He did treat his wife well, within the limits imposed by his shiftlessness. That, of course, was primarily because separation and divorce among the Real People was the privilege of the woman. If she chose such action, she had merely to toss his possessions out the door. So, for his own protection, he treated her far better than people might imagine. Especially those few with whom he associated. They bore the brunt of his resentment toward everyone more successful than he, which was practically everyone.

But now this grand plan had occurred to him. He had overheard his wife talking to another woman about it—*the Raven Mocker*. . . . Somehow in his twisted, vindictive mind there grew the idea that this would be the ultimate revenge. He'd watch his enemies grow old and die, while he might live virtually forever. Along with this he somehow expected to acquire all the intelligence of each of his victims. Some would have acquired great wisdom simply by their longevity. Wisdom, to Whipper, was identical with prosperity. When he had acquired the status of the Raven Mocker, he could easily outwit the people who had wronged him all his life. He imagined himself laughing at their helplessness while he became rich and prosperous. Just how that was to occur he was not certain yet. But it was sure to come with wisdom.

The old woman . . . Ah, it had been easy to fool her, with his domineering voice and attitude. She probably thought him wealthy beyond belief, able to actually carry out his offer of wealth. Even if he could do such a thing, he would not, of course. The wealth would be for himself. As soon as she gave him the secret, she was dead. If she refused his offer, he'd kill her anyway, to keep her from accusing *him* at the Council tomorrow. He'd be no worse off than before. Maybe better. There might be something of value in that miserable hut. Then he'd set it on fire, to conceal his deeds.

These were his thoughts as he walked past her smoldering fire and toward the doorway. Over his shoulder he saw the tip of the rising moon. He paused, listening. There was a sound of deep, regular breathing . . . or was it only the wind? He lifted the doorskin and stepped inside. There was a catch in the pattern of the breathing now, and then it paused. Ah, yes, she was awake.

"Old woman," he said softly, "I have returned. Now let us talk. Are you ready to teach me the secret?"

There was a subtle rustling in the corner to his left. He turned to face that way. As he did so, he drew his knife. Something was wrong. . . . The old woman's bed was directly across the room from the doorway. She should be *there,* not to his left. Maybe she had moved. . . .

"Where are you?" he demanded, peering into the blackness. "We have trading to do!"

A very little starlight filtered in through the smoke hole in the roof. He thought he saw a movement. Maybe he simply heard or felt the presence there, this time on his right.

"Is there someone else here?" he demanded. "Answer me, old woman!"

In an attempt to see better he thought to let moonlight enter the doorway. He lifted the doorskin with his left hand, holding the knife in front of him in a defensive position. Now there were other sounds in the room. Rustling, thumping, footsteps. . . . There was still not enough light, and impatiently he tore the doorskin from its pegs over the opening and cast it to the floor. There was little to see—not even the bed he had expected to be there. Something touched the top of his head, and he struck out at it blindly. Oh . . . a bundle of dried plants. He knocked it aside impatiently.

"Old woman!" he practically yelled. "Show yourself!"

His demand was answered by more rustling and thumping, now to his left, then to his right, then behind him as he whirled, striking out in a panic. His knife encountered only empty space. He could have sworn he heard suppressed laughter, and he turned in that direction, swinging wildly with his knife. He lost his balance, his feet tangled in the wadded doorskin on the floor, hands outstretched to stop his fall. His knife dropped, and he tried to twist away from falling on it. It was happening so quickly. . . . There was only the space of a heartbeat before he felt that something had struck him in the soft place just below the V of his ribs. The blow knocked the wind from his lungs and he rolled over, grabbing at his midriff. To his horror his hands encountered the haft of a large knife . . . his own, jutting out of his belly.

The darkness deepened rapidly, and before he lost consciousness he thought again that he heard the sarcastic giggle.

He did not see or hear the two men who came running, pausing only to light a torch at the dying fire.

"What—what happened here?" asked Corn Plant.

Three Fingers shrugged.

"No one else came in, did they, Father?" asked the younger man.

"I saw no one," Three Fingers agreed.

"Could she use her power to do this?" asked Corn Plant.

Three Fingers was slow to answer but finally spoke, in awed tones.

"I think not," he said. "If she could, she *would* not, though. No, this is something else."

Halfway to Keowee, Snakewater stopped and dismounted to rest. Maybe she could walk a little while to ease her aching hips and legs. The mare began cropping grass beside the trail. The moon had risen now, and it was easier to see. She'd rest a little, and move on.

There was a slight rustle in a clump of bushes, and the mare jumped away in alarm, staring bug eyed at what seemed to be only empty space.

"What—" stammered Snakewater. "Who is it? *Lumpy?* What are you doing here? Go on home!"

There was silence for a little while, and then she spoke again.

"Really?" Tears were streaming down her cheeks now. "Going with me? Oh, thank you, Lumpy. . . ."

12

Back in Old Town the Council met the next day. The word was already out: Snakewater had gone. No one knew where, although the Peace Chief seemed to have more information, which would be shared.

There was also the killing to be discussed. The crowd gathered quickly as the word spread and the time approached. The town house was packed as Three Fingers rose and the crowd quieted. Much of the ritualized opening of the meeting was shortened considerably because of the shocking character of the situation.

"You all know," Three Fingers began, "that our one problem is solved. Snakewater came to me to discuss this. I was made to think that her heart is good. She had decided to leave, rather than create trouble here. So, she is gone. I do not know where."

This was true, of course. He did not know the exact destination of the traveling Real People. The situation did not require such information anyway.

"That is not good enough!" shouted Spotted Bird. "The witch woman killed my baby! She's a witch!"

A murmur welled up in the crowd. It was sympathetic in tone, yet it was plain that the majority present did not agree with such an interpretation.

"We would have discussed that," agreed Three Fingers, "but now it is not necessary."

"What about her other killing?" a voice from the rear called. "That of Whipper?"

The Peace Chief recognized the man as one of the ne'er-do-well associates of the deceased. He raised a hand to quell the rising murmur of the crowd. It was apparent that many thought that the death of the bully Whips His Dog was not a completely undesirable thing. Three Fingers felt pity for his widow, but she was young, attractive, and well respected. She would find a husband, and nearly any man would be better than the one she had just lost.

"Let me tell you what I know of this," Three Fingers told the assembly. "As I have said, Snakewater had informed me she was leaving, which she did about dark. But she also said that someone, she did not know who, had entered her house, and she expected him to return. Now, as Peace Chief, I did not like the sound of this. I asked my son, Corn Plant, to help me, and we concealed ourselves to watch the house. We knew, of course, that Snakewater was already gone. Her house was empty."

Now the room was quiet. Every ear was listening.

"Just about moonrise we saw a man—A *big* man—who came to the house and entered. We heard him talking, then he cried out. There was a scuffle, and then quiet. We took a torch and found Whipper, Whips His Dog, dead inside. The house was still empty, and he had been killed with his own knife. It is as I have told it. We came to the conclusion that Whipper had pulled down the door-skin—we *saw* him do that—and tripped over it, falling on the knife."

"No!" shouted Spotted Bird. "The witch woman came back and killed him."

There was actually a ripple of laughter.

"Do you think," asked Three Fingers, "that an old woman could take a knife away from as big a man as that, and then kill him with it?"

More laughter.

"She used her powers!" protested Spotted Bird.

Now there were hoots of derision.

"If she did that," observed Three Fingers, "she would not need the knife! Besides, to misuse her power would kill *her,* no?"

There was a murmur of agreement.

"Now," said Three Fingers, "I see no action that we could take *within* the town. The woman is gone anyway. Any decision about her now is not in the purview of the Peace Chief, but of the War Chief. Log Roller, what say you?"

The War Chief rose, shrugged, and spread his hands as if puzzled.

"What Three Fingers says is true," he agreed. "We have talked of this. The Peace Chief presides only over matters of the town. He has done that, and well. But I see no threat from *outside.* We do not need to defend the town. So I see no problem that should be discussed by the War Chief."

He sat down again.

There was a low ripple of conversation as the Peace Chief rose again. There seemed to be a letdown, a sense of disappointment almost. The crowd had gathered to hear and decide greatly important things, which now had been reduced to nothing. There was no problem to be discussed.

Three Fingers knew that the whole matter *would* be discussed, and at great length, after the Council dispersed. The women would talk about it. If it seemed that further action should be taken, he would be approached to do so, probably by his wife, or maybe by a delegation from one of the clans. But he thought not. After all his concern of the past few days, the situation had resolved itself well. He still had questions in his mind about the incident with Whipper in the house vacated by Snakewater. There were things he did not understand about that.

He remembered, though. . . . When he was younger, he had been talking to a wise old uncle who had taught him much.

"I don't understand," he had protested, about some apparently miraculous happening.

"If you still think you have to understand, boy," Gray Wolf had answered, "you are missing the point."

That admonition had served him well ever since.

Sometimes, he mused, *things turn out well, simply because they are meant to do so.*

And this was a good day. . . .

A day's travel to the north Snakewater was talking to the leader of the band of Real People who were moving west. There were three families, eleven people in all.

"I am called Snakewater," she introduced herself. "Paint Clan. . . . I am told that you are traveling west."

The group's leader was a man of perhaps forty. He had been pointed out to her by Keowee's Peace Chief when she went to pay her respects. His name, Kills Many. . . . No one seemed to know or to care, really, how he might have acquired such a name. Kills many . . . enemies? deer? squirrels? No matter—he was now called Kills Many because it was his name.

"That is true," he answered. "We are moving there. You are not from Keowee?"

He had noticed her horse, laden with packs.

"No, from Old Town. I was told of your party by a trader."

"Ah, yes . . . the Choctaw?"

"Yes, that's the one. He said you are a few days behind him."

"True. We had broken a wagon wheel. But how can we help you, Mother?"

Good, she thought. *A respectful young man.*

"I would join your party."

The man's mouth dropped open in amazement.

"But what . . . How . . . Why . . ." he stammered.

Snakewater had already decided that she would be willing to tell all. . . . She *must* do so, to be trusted. She took a deep breath and plunged ahead.

"I am a medicine woman. A conjuror. There are those in Old Town who do not trust me. Some have tried to kill me, and I have decided to leave. I can help your people."

The expression on the face of Kills Many was one of astonishment, but he quickly recovered.

"How do I know you can be trusted?" he asked guardedly.

"You don't. But you could ask the Peace Chief here at Keowee. You have met him. Or *their* medicine woman, Spotted Frog. Both of these know me."

Kills Many nodded tentatively. "But . . . *how* could you help us?"

"With my skills. My medicine. I am skilled with potions and salves as well as conjures."

"Hmm . . . that might be useful. But you might hold us back."

Snakewater bristled. "At any time I cannot keep up, you can leave me behind!"

"Yes, yes, Mother," he said quickly. "I meant no offense. But the trip may be hard. I was thinking of your comfort. Winter will be coming."

"It always does," she retorted. "Here, there, or somewhere else. Everyone will be someplace."

Kills Many chuckled. He liked the spunk of this old woman.

"I will ask those of whom you speak," he said. "The conjure woman, the Peace Chief. Maybe their War Chief too."

His mind was already made up. He had no doubt that he would receive exactly the answers that the old woman said. There was a complete forthrightness about her that he liked. He was certain that she was exactly what she appeared to be, a spunky old woman with the spirit gifts she had stated. His remark about the War Chief had been a gentle jibe at her aggressive nature. Well, he would ask anyway.

"You have supplies?" he asked, gesturing toward her horse with the bulging panniers.

"Enough," she stated flatly. "I'm pretty good with the blowgun too." She touched the mouthpiece of the weapon, as it protruded from one of the packs.

"I see. . . . Well, we are camping here today. We start on at daylight tomorrow. After going to water, that is. Meanwhile, I will ask about you."

"Good. You will find it as I said."

"I am sure of that."

The Peace Chief was a little vague.

"I don't know her well. I heard that there was some sort of trouble down at Old Town. You could talk to their Peace Chief."

"No, no. We need to move on. But this Snakewater . . . You know of her?"

"Of course. She was conjuring before I was born. Yes, that was it. . . . No one knows how old she is, and somebody accused her of being a Raven Mocker. You remember *that* story?"

"Yes, I think so. The Raven Mocker takes unused life-years of a dying young person?"

"That's the one. Do you believe it?"

"I don't know," said Kills Many cautiously. "But her reputation has been good?"

"Oh, yes. She's well respected. Or always has been. She wants to go with you?"

"That's what she has asked."

The Peace Chief nodded. "I think you would be fortunate to have her in your party."

"You would trust her, then?"

"Oh, yes. She could not use her powers for a bad purpose. It would kill *her,* no?"

"So I have heard. Oh, yes . . . Keowee has a conjure woman?"

"You can't have *her*!" said the Peace Chief.

"No, no," laughed Kills Many. "I only wanted to ask her about Snakewater."

The chief relaxed. "Oh. Of course. Frog . . . Spotted Frog. That is her house, near the big sycamore."

"*Wado!* Thank you, Uncle."

Spotted Frog was reluctant at first, but when she learned the purpose of Kills Many's visit, she became more friendly.

"Yes, she came to me with her problem. A bereaved family, rumors and stories . . . It was I who suggested that she move west."

"She can be trusted?"

"Snakewater? Of course! She will tell it as it is. And I tell you this: You will be fortunate to have her with your party."

That was the second time he had heard such a remark this morning, Kills Many realized. His heart was good for this.

Before the day was over, a traveler who had been to Old Town stopped at Keowee with an odd piece of news. A man who had entered an empty house in the dead of night for some unknown purpose had fallen on his own knife and was dead. There were few regrets, because he had been a scoundrel, it was said. The spirits must have a sense of humor. . . .

13

"Lumpy, did you have something to do with the death of that man in Old Town? Here, don't you disappear on me. . . . I know you're there. They said the man might have fallen on his own knife. . . . Where *are* you?"

Her tirade went unanswered. Snakewater stamped her foot impatiently and turned to unsaddle her horse. The party would not leave until tomorrow, and this was a chance for the mare to graze and for herself to rest. She had had no sleep. It had been a worrisome time for the past day and a half. She spread a blanket on the grass under a tree and lay down, eyes closed.

"Who were you talking to, Grandmother?" a child's voice asked.

Snakewater's eyes opened, startled. It was a girl of perhaps six summers, standing beside her blanket.

"Oh . . . nobody, child. Just the Little People."

"You talk to the Little People? Then you have *seen* them?"

"I did not say that, girl. I can talk to somebody in the dark without seeing them, no?"

"That is true," said the child. "But . . . it isn't dark yet. Besides, they would probably answer."

"And you heard no answer? Is that it? Maybe I didn't either," she said irritably. "But I can talk to Little People without seeing or hearing them, no?"

"Maybe you were talking to yourself?"

"No, I . . . Well, maybe so. Run along, now. I must get some sleep."

"Yes, my father said you will go with us tomorrow."

"Your father . . . ?"

"Yes, Kills Many. He said you will join us."

"That is true. Now, run along, child. What is your name?"

"Pigeon . . . I will let you rest, Grandmother. And I will watch closely for the Little People."

"All right. But if you see any, be sure not to tell anyone."

"Yes, I know that. But I could talk to them, no?"

"Of course. Now, go on! Let me rest."

Reluctantly Pigeon turned away, and Snakewater watched her go. "Lumpy," she said to empty space, "I hope you'll stay away from that one. She's too smart for us."

Maybe it was only the flutter of the leaves in the tree overhead that sounded like a giggle.

The little caravan traveled well. The others had already become accustomed to traveling together. There were three families, two approximately the same ages, all with children. Kills Many was the leader. Snakewater had already become acquainted with him, and with his daughter, Pigeon. She rather liked Pigeon, whose inquiring mind and quick understanding were refreshing. The child might become a nuisance, she thought, but was, for now, interesting. Pigeon's mother was a quiet, pleasant woman with a gentle smile and a comfortable inner satisfaction that Snakewater could see immediately. She was called Rain, and in her warm, calm attitude it was easy to visualize a gentle shower, so welcome in the heat of late summer. Snakewater liked her from the start. The woman was a well-fitted partner for Kills Many.

The couple had another child, a boy of about ten or eleven. That one seemed to be a small copy of his father, Kills Many. He was called Redbird.

Snakewater had had little chance to become acquainted with the other two families as yet. That would happen as they traveled. For now, it was enough to see that one had a wagon, like Kills Many. The man was called Smith, because of his vocation. His forge was carried in the back of the wagon. The Smith family had two children, both girls.

The third family was somewhat younger, had one boy of three or four, and pack horses instead of a wagon. Snakewater had the idea that they were relatives of Rain, wife of Kills Many. Maybe the women were all related, she thought. Rain had mentioned the Blue Cat Clan, which might indicate the matrilineal connection.

The wagon of the Smith family had broken a wheel, she learned, and caused the delay that had allowed her to join them. The wheel had been rebuilt by Smith, who seemed quite skilled in the use of tools. He had taken on many of the white man's ways, much to his advantage and to that of the party, as it turned out.

Snakewater declined an invitation to ride in the wagon of Kills Many. By evening of the first day of travel she regretted that decision. The bumping and shifting of the packs, bundles, and panniers was a constant challenge. There was no good position in the saddle, and the load kept sliding around. She decided that there must be a better way.

After they'd halted that first evening, as Snakewater was unloading her packs, Rain approached.

"Would it not be easier for you," the woman suggested, "to put some of your packs in the wagon? Since you do not wish to ride there yourself . . ."

Snakewater felt as if a great weight had lifted from her shoulders. She was trying her best not to show how difficult it was to move around. Her inner thighs ached, her buttocks felt as if she had been beaten, and cramps in the muscles of her calves seized her with every step. At least she was recovering some semblance of feeling in her feet. When she first stepped down it had felt like the stabbing of a hundred needles.

I must appear to be walking like—like an old person! she thought to herself. She chuckled quietly over that thought, then paused.

"What?" she said, apparently to nobody, "I am an old person. Stop it, now!"

That was only the first time that the others in the party noted that this new companion frequently talked to herself.

Within a few days the routine was well established. Snakewater found that the excruciating pain in the muscles of her thighs subsided after a day or two, and she began to enjoy the travel. After her body adjusted to the saddle, riding was much preferable to bouncing in the wagon. She had tried that, too, but only for a little while. The swaying gait of the mare was so comfortable that at times it almost lulled her to sleep.

Usually, though, she was not only awake but enchanted with new sights, sounds, and smells. She had never been far from Old Town, and her knowledge of different scenery was quite limited. It was a thrill to see a distant range of hills and to wonder what lay beyond. Even so, she now knew that those hills lay a full day's travel ahead. Maybe even two days.

She was also somewhat surprised that she felt better, younger by far. At first she had thought it was merely relief at her escape from the rumor, gossip, and actual threats to her life that had been oppressing her. Her newfound freedom had been exhilarating, and had replaced gloom with happiness and optimism. She soon realized, however, that it was more than that. She felt stronger, healthier. She could fill her lungs to their greatest capacity, head up and shoulders back, and it felt *good.* The travel was good, the *world* was good.

Days were warm and sunny, nights cool and crisp. Occasionally there was rain, and on those days they camped, kept a hot fire going, and they all huddled under the two wagons until they could move on.

It was during one of those times, when it seemed that the rain might turn to sleet or snow, that a thought struck her.

"Kills Many," she said, "how is it that we are traveling at this time of year? Winter is coming!"

He chuckled. "That is true. But it was not when we started. We had come a long way before you joined us."

"Yes . . . I know."

Then another idea struck her. She had not thought to ask before.

"I had not inquired," she said, a bit embarrassed, "but where are we going? Is there a destination, or are we just wandering?"

Kills Many threw his head back and roared with laughter.

"Maybe some of both," he said, after recovering his composure. "A specific place, no. Yet we are not just 'wandering.' There are towns . . . at least three or four, we have heard, in this place called Arkansas. Towns built by Cherokees like ourselves. Our own, Real People. They came from our own country."

"And how do we find them?" she asked.

"We know that they are beyond the Big River," he said. "The Mississippi. We must find a way to cross it, and then inquire among the locals as to where our people may be."

"You speak their tongue?" Snakewater asked.

"No, no. But there are ways. You know of the Trade Language?"

"Yes. I do not speak it, though. Do you?"

"Yes, but that is not it."

"There is *another* trade language?" she asked in amazement.

"No, no. There are hand signs. A trader told me of this. East of the Big River, Trade Language. West of it, hand signs."

"But where can you learn it?"

"The trader taught me. In a day or so one can learn enough to get by. Look, it is not difficult. See here: *you . . . me . . . eat . . . drink, speak . . .* Here is any question, all the same: *how, what, where, who . . .*"

He held up a crooked finger, moving it out from his mouth, then pointing to Snakewater. "*How are you called?* Here is *water . . .* a flowing motion of the fingers, like that of a stream. *Woman,* a motion like combing long hair. Well, you get the idea."

"Yes, of course. I had never heard of this, Kills Many."

"Nor had I. . . . I am eager to try it out."

"Would you teach me?"

"Of course. You have already started. Not too much at once. A little at a time is better."

At the beginning Snakewater had considered this journey an escape, her only course of action. She'd had no other choice. Now it was different. Not only was she feeling better than she had in years, she was actually enjoying the travel itself. And ahead it promised to become even better. What other surprises lay ahead, across the Big River?

14

Before they could approach the Big River, however, they must cross the mountains. Snakewater had little conception of the distance and time involved. She had been oriented to Old Town and the hut where she had grown up, just outside the town wall. Her recent trip to Keowee had opened her eyes to some extent, showing her the changes that were taking place. Still, there was no way that she could know how many whites were moving into the area, how many towns they were building.

"Of course! That is why we move west," explained Kills Many, when she had mentioned it. "You have been out of the mainstream, there at Old Town."

He seemed to enjoy talking with her, and the two people, of entirely different generations and traditions, struck up an enjoyable friendship. Snakewater was old enough to have been the grandmother of the young leader, but they seemed to understand each other, and it was good. She could ask him about the common things of which she had no knowledge, and know that he would not ridicule her ignorance. In turn Kills Many knew that he could benefit from her years of experience in dealing with things of the spirit.

Snakewater was still enjoying the newness of all the things that were happening. The new vistas of landscape as they crossed the mountains were wondrous to her. She actually felt years younger, with the fresh mountain air and the exercise that had been forced upon her. She had been aware of that for some time now and was reveling in it.

Then came the night when, for some unknown reason, she woke and lay there unable to sleep. She changed positions. . . . Then again. . . . She could not seem to recover the comfort that she usually felt in her blankets. Was she too cold? Or too warm, maybe. . . . She adjusted her covers, and still nothing seemed right. Maybe if she were to get up, empty her bladder, move around a little. . . .

She rose and attended to the call of nature. She noticed the chill of the night as she returned, and tossed a couple of sticks on the dying fire. Then she picked up a blanket and draped it around her shoulders, to sit by the fire a little while. It was not unpleasant, as she warmed, to be alone in her wakefulness, listening to the night sounds. It was too late in the season to hear crickets and other insects with night songs, but there were other noises. She heard the soft whicker of a raccoon down by the stream, and the call of a hunting owl. In the far distance, a sound that always sent chills up her spine, the scream of the great long-tailed cat, like that of a woman in agony. She moved a little closer to the fire.

Then, for no apparent reason, a thought struck her. She had been with Kills Many and his party for several days now, and her mood and her physical activity had been that of a much younger person. How had this happened, the rejuvenation? She gasped in surprise that she had not thought of it before, yet the sheer horror of such a thought repulsed her: *What if* . . . Could it be that her invigoration was not merely from exercise, but from some external source? She tried to remove her thoughts from the threat that now thrust itself upon her. What if this renewed energy was that which had been stolen from someone else at his death? There had been that death in Old Town on the very night she left. It had happened in her house, under circumstances that were very peculiar. She had suspected that the Little People were involved. At least *one.* She had found that possibility mildly amusing, but now . . .

Am I the Raven Mocker after all? she thought.

The man who had died by the knife in her house was said to have been a young man, with many years ahead of him. That same night her own world had changed completely. She felt now like a different person.

Maybe I am! Maybe these feelings of youthfulness are only from the stolen life-years of another, a younger person.

She did not return to sleep that night, and was tired and miserable as they traveled on.

It was not until their camp that evening that Kills Many approached her.

"Something troubles you?" he asked. "Do you not feel well?"

"No! I'm fine!" she almost snapped.

Then she relented. She had not been entirely truthful with the party's leader. . . .

"Forgive me," she asked. "I would talk with you."

"Come, then," he beckoned, and the two strolled a little way from the camp. Kills Many waited.

"There is something I have not told you," she began.

"Yes? Go on."

"Kills Many, I am made to think that I am a Raven Mocker. You know that story?"

"Of course. But how . . . ?"

"It is a long story. That is why I left Old Town. The man who was killed . . . The knife . . . You heard . . . The night I left?"

"Yes, but what does that have to do with you? You could not have killed him. You were on your way to Keowee."

"Maybe not directly, but I was responsible. And I took his life-years. I thought you should know. Now I will leave your party. I am sorry that I had not told you before."

"I knew," Kills Many said quietly, "—that you had been accused, that is. I did not believe this of you, and I still don't."

"But it must be!" she protested. "I feel much younger."

Kills Many laughed. "You travel well too. But maybe it is that you are more active now. You are tired at night when we stop, no? Like the rest of us?"

"Of course."

"Then there is nothing immortal about you. You are like the others. Besides, Mother, could you use your other spirit gifts without knowing you did so?"

"Maybe, sometimes."

Kills Many pondered a moment. "That was a bad question. Let me try again. . . . I do not know the ways of such a spirit thing, but I have been told that you could not use your power to do harm to someone."

"I would, maybe. But it would come back on me."

"Ah! That is what I was getting at. Your conjures are for good, not evil, no?"

"That is true."

"And you could not have used them to harm someone without knowing it?"

"I think not. . . ."

"And you did not know about the man in Old Town until the next day?"

She was silent, and Kills Many went on.

"So, you could have had no part in that?"

"I suppose not. . . ."

"Snakewater, your medicine is for good. Your power is from the One Above, maker of all things, no? I am made to think that you could not have both good and bad gifts of the spirit. But surely you could not without knowing it."

This made her feel somewhat better, but she would feel more confident if she had a chance to talk with someone like Spotted Frog—another conjuror. Still, the confidence of a man like Kills Many was a great help to her.

"Maybe so," she agreed, at least for now. But it was time to change the subject. "I wanted to ask of other things, Kills Many. How far is it to the Big River?"

He smiled. "You grow impatient. . . . We will know when we get there. But I have been told maybe fifty sleeps from where we started, east of your Old Town. Not that many if we travel well. A day or two of rain holds us back."

"Are there mountains all the way?"

The country through which they were traveling was much more rugged than that to which she was accustomed.

"No, no. These are called 'Cumberland.' We are starting down the western slopes. This whole area, here to the river, is being settled by whites. They have made it what they call a 'state.'. . . They bought some of it, just moved into other parts. It is called Tennessee."

"I have heard the name."

"Yes . . . We are told that the mountains slope down into a flatter part—a plain. It is warmer there, because it is lower."

"There are Cherokees there?"

"Some. Most, Chickasaws, in that part. But they are friendly."

"You intend to winter with them?"

He shrugged.

"Maybe. We will see how it happens. But I mentioned the warmer country? It goes to the Big River and beyond. There will soon be snow here, but not so much to the west."

"I see. . . . You plan to winter in the warmer country, beyond the mountains."

She felt considerably better having the confidence of Kills Many, leader of the little caravan. He reminded her, in many ways, of Three Fingers of Old Town.

It was easier, now, to settle into the routine of travel, stop for the night, travel on. They talked with farmers along the way, mostly Cherokees . . . "Real People" . . . Sometimes they bought vegetables or fresh meat. Once one of the men of their party, riding ahead, was able to kill a fat buck deer. They paused there for the rest of the day to dress out and care for the venison, and to enjoy a big meal of fresh meat, all that anyone could wish for.

Initially Kills Many had intended to spend the winter among the Real People in one of the towns in Arkansas. Then it became apparent that Arkansas was a great deal farther away than the travelers had imagined. To add to that a stretch of bad weather descended on the party, immobilizing them for many days. They camped, wet, cold, and uncomfortable, hoping that each dawn would bring a glimpse of the sun. Even on the best days it was only partly sunny. On the worst a mist of freezing rain built up a thick layer of ice on trees, grasses, even the canvas wagon covers. Beneath the icy crust on the ground was mud, deep and clinging, sucking wagon wheels down and holding them back. There was nothing to do but sit and wait, thawing and drying icy firewood before their fires so that it could be used next.

"Unusual weather," said a local man from whom they bought vegetables. "There will still be some good weather before winter. How far are you going?"

They were speaking in Cherokee. The farmer was fluent in several languages, including that of the white man, though he was Chickasaw himself.

"As far as we need," answered Kills Many. "We want to find Cherokees west of the river, in Arkansas. We have heard there are Cherokee towns there?"

"That is true."

"How far to the river?"

"Two, three sleeps."

"Maybe we could cross and winter with them?" Kills Many asked tentatively.

"Maybe. Depends on the weather. Pretty muddy now. A few dry days or a hard freeze, to travel on. But then you'd have ice in the river."

"Yes . . . would that become a problem?"

"Maybe not," said the Chickasaw. "The river is still open, I suppose."

"And how does one cross?" asked Kills Many. "The River must be wide at this place."

"Oh, yes!" chuckled the other. "But there is a boat, a big flat ferryboat, that will take you over. A white man runs it. . . . Cherokee wife . . ."

He paused and looked over the little caravan.

"Yes . . . Maybe two trips, for all your party. But should be no problem, as soon as the weather breaks."

15

Several days passed before it was possible to travel, with the alternate freezing and thawing. Then, two more before they arrived at the river. Snakewater knew that it must be big, but had had no idea of its actual breadth. It was a bit frightening, stirring the memory of old Cherokee tales of a water monster, said to resemble a giant leech. But those were only stories with which to entertain and frighten children. . . .

Or *were* they? She shuddered a little.

They moved on down the road past a cluster of houses, a smithy, and a structure that seemed to serve both as a store and a dwelling. At the water's edge there was a wooden platform, part of it jutting out into the river. A couple of small boats were tied there. The far end of that dock appeared to float, hinged to the solid portion, and tied to it was the raftlike ferry. The travelers had encountered ferries before. Sometimes there had been a rope stretched across a creek to prevent the platform from floating downstream. Here there was none. It was apparent that the river was far too wide to string a rope. There were several oarlocks along the sides of the flat ferry, with large oars resting between the pegs. There were also a number of heavy poles lying on the deck.

The ferryman was already looking over the travelers and their equipment, sizing them up.

"'*Siyo!*" he said when Kills Many approached him. "All want to cross, I reckon. Ye're all together?"

"Yes. . . . That's Arkansas over there?"

"Shore 'nuff . . . *Okay* . . . Two wagons, ten, eleven folks . . . Twelve horses or mules, couple crates o' chickens . . . No charge for the poultry, I reckon, but ye'll need two trips across for everything. Now, I'll cut ye a deal if some o' the men can use poles and oars. Current's pretty heavy out in the middle there."

"We can do that," said Kills Many.

They were talking in a mixture of English and Cherokee, initiated by the ferryman.

But Kills Many had a few questions.

"You use poles all the way across?"

"No, no," said the ferryman. "Too deep. No, we pole upstream a ways and then row across. There's a lot o' driftin' downstream afore we hit the other dock."

"What's to keep us from drifting on down the river? Out to sea?"

The boatman laughed. "Nothin', I reckon, except it's a long way to the sea. And it don't work that way. Floatin' trash, sticks and logs and such, drifts to the banks, except at flood time. Then it drifts to the middle. That's how ye tell if the river's still risin' or fallin'. You ain't from river country, I reckon."

"That is true," agreed Kills Many. "Not this kind. We just need to cross."

"Fixin' to settle over there?"

"Yes. . . We'll try to find Cherokees."

"Several towns of 'em over there," said the ferryman. "My wife's one o' the 'Real People'. . . . Reckon that makes me Cherokee, too, don't it?"

It would require at least half a day, the ferryman said, to load and cross with the entire party in two trips. It was already well past noon. . . .

Sun had left her daughter's house and started down the west side of the sky bowl.

"You don't want to land there just before dark," the boatman advised. "Camp here, and we'll cross in the morning."

So it was decided. They camped and watched the sunset beyond the far shore. Snakewater found herself eager to see what this new land would be like. At a distance it was hard to tell. There was a fringe of trees, but that was about all that could be identified at this distance. She watched the river a long time, listening to the sounds of the night creatures. She recognized the call of a hunting owl, the bark of a fox, and the soft whicker of a raccoon. Some things, she realized, remain the same.

The next morning one of the wagons was driven out onto the wharf and across to the ferry. There were rails on the sides of the raftlike vessel, and gates at the ends to enclose the wagon, team, and passengers. The agreed-upon fare was paid in the gold coins of the white man, which surprised Snakewater a bit. But it was convenient, she realized. More so than packing trade goods or bulky items of value. Yes, she concluded. Kills Many had planned their journey well.

Now she watched as the boatman instructed the inexperienced travelers in the use of the poles. They would stay as close as possible to the bank and push their way upstream "a ways," he said. Then turn and push out into the current, to use the oars as they crossed diagonally to a dock on the other side. The ferryman and his helper, a quiet young Chickasaw, would do most of the rowing and steering, though he invited the help of any who wanted to try a hand.

They pushed away and started the slow progress along the bank. The current was mild here, and once moving, the boat was propelled fairly easily. A few bow shots upstream they disappeared from view entirely, behind a bend in the riverbank.

Now Snakewater began to understand more about the principles involved in the use of this ferry. They would use the flow as it curled around the bend; it would be easier to row across to the spot on the other shore where the current struck the opposite bank. But the return trip . . . No, they would again pole a little farther upstream, to reach a point *above* the curl of the bend, and cross into the backwater. . . . It pleased her greatly that she had been able to reason this out. It would help, too, to lessen her dread of the mighty river and the creatures that might hide in its muddy waters.

It was well past noon before the crossing was accomplished. Days were noticeably shorter now, and the morning had been crisp.

"Well, good luck to ye!" the boatman wished them as he pushed off on the return trip. "Ye can see the town there—ask about where ye want to go. . . ."

A straggle of curious children gathered to watch them make camp. It was quickly apparent that there was much interest in the travelers. The "town" was hardly that, merely a cluster of assorted dwellings.

"I wonder," said Kills Many aloud, "if we should pay our respects to their chief."

"I wonder," said one of the women, "if they even *have* a chief."

The problem was solved when a delegation of three men approached, sauntering informally to where the women were starting cooking fires near the wagons.

"Osiyo!" said one of the strangers, with a courteous smile.

"*'Siyo,*" answered Kills Many. "You are Real People, then? Cherokee?"

"Most of us. I am Little Horse."

"And I, Kills Many. We are traveling, as you see. May we camp here?"

It was obvious that it was a campground, used by many, but it was only polite to ask.

"Of course. Welcome."

"You are the Peace Chief, Little Horse?"

The others chuckled.

"Not really. We are only a few families here. There is no need for organization. Where are you going?"

"We don't know. . . . Looking for a place. Our country is becoming overrun with white men."

"Ah, is it not so! Well, make your camp and let us gather at the fire later, to smoke and talk."

"It is good! *Wado* . . . thank you."

It was a very informal council, more like a social smoke. The travelers almost outnumbered the locals. But they were all Real People. There was much conversation and the joy of discovering mutual friends and acquaintances. They smoked and talked and ate and drank *kanohena,* the hominy drink. Traditionally served to guests, *kanohena* was almost a ritual welcome.

"It is good, sometimes, to follow the old ways," observed Kills Many.

"Is that your purpose in coming west?" asked Little Horse.

"No, no, not really. We do not object to new things."

Little Horse refilled the pipe with *tsola,* lit it, and handed it to Kills Many.

"I see," he said. "Like me you enjoy a good knife and a fire striker. . . . A blanket, a horse . . . White man's *things,* but not his *ways.*"

"Maybe," agreed Kills Many. "In fact, many of his ways are not bad, but there are so many of him!"

There was a chuckle around the circle.

"That is true," agreed Little Horse. "They are everywhere, no? We even have one, *Yona,* over there. He is our pet bear."

The chuckle rippled around the circle again. Yona the Bear was apparently well liked, not merely tolerated. The man looked like a burly, good-natured bear. A couple of small children in his lap gave credence to that idea. Their appearance and their reddish hair suggested that these were Yona's own offspring.

"I am teasing him," Little Horse went on. "Yona is my sister's husband. He is a white man but knows our ways. He is almost a Real Person."

There was general laughter, and then a moment of silence.

"You spoke earlier," Little Horse said, "that your destination is unsure. Tell us more. Maybe we can suggest."

"Yes," answered Kills Many. "We had heard that there were Cherokee towns beyond the reach of the white man, west of the Big River. We had thought to find them, and to settle there. Someone said to cross the river and then inquire. So . . . well, here we are!"

The good-natured chuckle rippled around the circle again. The goal of the travelers had been reached. They had crossed the river, after many days of travel.

"It is good!" said Little Horse. "But as we have said, this is not entirely beyond the white man's reach. He seems to go where he wants. No matter. Some of them are good, some not. About the towns, though, the Cherokee towns . . . Yes, there are several, starting with ours here. Another, a day's travel to the west. They are mostly strung along this road westward."

"How far?" asked Kills Many.

"Ah, I do not even know, my friend. The road goes on, I am told, many sleeps west. Maybe to the edge of the sky dome. We have heard of wide plains, and even mountains, bigger than those you came through."

"We don't want to go that far," said Kills Many. "For now, what we need most is a place to winter."

The other nodded. "That would be my choice. Time grows short. So consider. . . . Stay here a few days, hunt a little, lay in some supplies. Maybe send a scout or two to the nearest towns, to see if they will meet your needs. You need only a wintering place for now."

"That is true. What we need next, though, is to know where we will plant next season's crops."

"Good. You have seed, I suppose. So . . . a few days here will let you begin to make plans, and we will enjoy your company."

16

Back in Old Town a visitor inquired and was directed to the home of the Peace Chief. After the initial greeting he came quickly to the purpose of his visit.

"I am called No Tail Wolf," he began. "From Keowee. I come to ask about the death of my brother, Whipper—Whips His Dog."

"Yes," mused Three Fingers. "An unfortunate thing."

"I have heard only stories of stories," the visitor said, his voice filled with emotion. "I was away on an extended hunt when the word came. I want to know what happened."

"It is hard to say," said Three Fingers cautiously. "I investigated, of course. The house was empty. No trace of anyone there. Your brother was killed by his own knife. His feet were tangled in the doorskin, which had fallen down. So it appeared that he had tripped over it and landed on his knife."

"There must be more to this," said No Tail Wolf irritably. "Whose house is this? Why was there no one there?"

"Oh . . . it had belonged to an old woman, but—"

"I have heard that," the visitor interrupted. "I would learn more about this old woman. She had died?"

Three Fingers studied the other for a moment. Anger seethed in the man's face. The Peace Chief saw that he was seeking not only information, but revenge for the loss of his brother. This man clearly did not believe the story of an accidental fall.

"No, not dead," said Three Fingers, instantly regretting that he had done so. But too late now. . . . "I do not know where she went," he said truthfully. "Her house was empty, abandoned, when this happened."

No Tail Wolf was skeptical.

"An old woman does not simply move out and leave," he insisted. "Who is this woman?"

There was no point in withholding information that the visitor could obtain from anyone.

"Her name was Snakewater," said Three Fingers. "A conjure woman. She had been here a long time."

"Why did she leave?"

The Peace Chief spread his hands, palms up in question.

"Who knows?" he shrugged.

"*Someone* does!" said No Tail Wolf angrily. "I will find out."

"Do you want to see the house?" asked Three Fingers.

"Yes!"

"Good! I will show you myself."

The two men walked through the town, out through the entry passage, and approached the hut.

"*Outside* the town?" asked the visitor. "I saw this place, but . . ."

"Yes, she preferred to be alone," said Three Fingers.

They peered inside, and the visitor entered, kicking aside the doorskin.

"There is nothing here!" he said.

"It is as I said," Three Fingers reminded him. "Snakewater had moved out."

The visitor was thoughtful for a moment.

"Who discovered my brother?" he asked suddenly.

"I did myself. My son and I. We heard someone cry out and ran here. . . . We lighted a torch, and found your brother there."

"A torch?"

"Yes . . . there was a fire outside, over here. It had died to coals.

"Wait, now. . . . The woman had moved out, but there was a *fire* in front of her door?" No Tail Wolf asked suspiciously.

"It seems so," said Three Fingers cautiously. "A fire had been laid to burn slowly, and she had departed after dark. We did not know where she was."

He was trying his best to be truthful yet give no more information than necessary.

"Then she disappeared the same night? The night my brother was killed."

"It must be so. But you have said 'disappeared.' Not like that. . . . There was no magic about it. She *left*. Moved somewhere else."

"How do you know this?"

The conversation was becoming uncomfortable now.

"She had told me that she intended to do so," said Three Fingers.

"So . . . you *knew*. I am made to think you know more, too, old man."

Such a rude accusation, especially directed to an elder, was completely inappropriate for one of the Real People. Three Fingers tried to maintain his composure, wondering how one family could have produced two such unpleasant people as Whips His Dog and No Tail Wolf. And there might even be more. What sort of a mother had whelped such sons? And had they no uncle to educate them?

"No Tail Wolf," the Peace Chief said solemnly, "you are a guest in our town. I will not tolerate accusations such as this. The town met in Council over this, and the matter was settled."

"Not to my satisfaction!" blurted the visitor.

"Would you prefer that I turn the matter over to our War Chief?" asked Three Fingers. "You are from *outside* the town. Maybe this falls under his authority."

"No," said No Tail Wolf, maybe a little too quickly. "There is no need. I will ask around."

Three Fingers was not happy with this approach. There were many, of course, who would verify the meeting of the Council and its result. What he feared was that the vengeance-seeking brother would chance to ask one of those who had started or had spread the story of the Raven Mocker. But what could be done now?

"Go ahead," invited Three Fingers. "It is good to do so. But before you leave Old Town, would you come back and tell me what you have learned? Maybe I can help you."

The visitor appeared surprised, but that expression was quickly replaced with one of suspicion.

"We will see what I am able to learn," said No Tail Wolf tightly.

He wandered around the town, pausing to question someone occasionally.

"Do you know where I can find a woman called Snakewater?"

This query brought forth the same answer each time. The conjure woman was gone. Most people spoke well of her, some said that she would be missed. Her departure had indeed occurred on the very night that the death of Whips His Dog was discovered.

He considered going to pay his respects to his widowed sister-in-law. Maybe he could console her for the loss of her husband. That was an intriguing idea. . . . For a moment he fantasized how she might dissolve into his arms, soft and warm and totally yielding. It was an attractive thought, but not very close to reality. In the real world his brother's wife detested No Tail Wolf. Maybe he could bully her into cooperating, or even take her forcibly if need be. He abandoned the whole idea, realizing that she might have moved back into her mother's house anyway. Even if not, this town was unfamiliar to him. He did not know where the power and influence lay. Besides, he doubted that his brother had enjoyed great popularity. Few would mourn the death of Whips His Dog, unless he had changed greatly since the brothers had last seen each other.

No, he would avoid contact with the young widow, ask a few more questions, and then return to Keowee. He had picked up a hint here and there that Snakewater had talked at length with a traveling trader. Maybe she had followed him or some other traveler. . . . *Wait!*

Had there not been a party traveling through Keowee at about that time? Just before he returned from the hunt . . .

He would ask a few more people. . . .

Even then he was astonished at the response from the next woman he queried about Snakewater.

"Yes, I know her!" the woman hissed. "She killed my baby to steal her life-years."

"*What?*"

"Yes! She is a Raven Mocker."

"But what has this to do with—?"

He stopped short. He had not revealed much about his purpose in asking about the woman, to anyone except Three Fingers. Even in his blunt and bullying approach there was a certain clever caution.

"Raven Mocker?" he asked innocently. "I do not understand."

"You remember the story of the Raven Mocker, don't you?" demanded the woman. "Takes the unused years of a person who dies young? Even kills to obtain these life-years, to live forever."

"But Snakewater," he said innocently, "—where has she gone? Can the Raven Mocker disappear?"

"I don't know. Don't care, really. But this one ran from Old Town rather than face the town Council."

"Ah, yes, I heard something of that." No Tail Wolf was pleased with his own cleverness now. "Something was said of a death in her house too. . . ."

"Yes! She killed him. They said he fell on his own knife. *Huh!* She used her *powers* to kill him and take his years too."

The woman was almost shrieking now. He hesitated to prolong the conversation lest he draw too much attention, but he wanted to ask one more question.

"Where do you suppose she might have gone?"

"*West!* Isn't everybody going west to avoid the white man? Now, leave me alone!"

The woman turned and stalked away.

No Tail Wolf paused to ponder his new information. Maybe he should inquire a bit more at Keowee. He recalled the party of travelers who had passed through the town shortly before his return.

He retrieved his horse and started back to Keowee as fast as the animal could lope. Soon, though, he realized that this was impractical. He would pace himself as well as his mount, to accomplish what he must.

At a more leisured pace he took a little time to think. There was really not much reason to inquire further at Keowee. He was convinced now that the old woman *had* joined that party. Two or three wagons, someone had said. . . . There was only one road westward out of Keowee. He would take that route and inquire at the next town. Yes, that would be better. He was not well liked in Keowee anyway. Probably strangers in another town would give him more information.

"Yes, they came through here. Two wagons, another family with pack animals . . ."

"Tell me," said No Tail Wolf, "was there an old woman with them? I am trying to find my mother."

The woman smiled sympathetically. A loving son, trying to find his mother. . . . "Why, yes, there was. A tall woman, old but spry. She was riding a gray mare."

"Yes, that is the one." He chuckled. "In her second childhood, no? I must catch up to them, to protect her from herself."

He remounted and hurried on.

The woman with whom he had been talking looked after him, smiling.

"What a nice young man," she said to her husband. "So concerned about his mother."

17

Kills Many and his party had decided to winter at West Landing, as the little settlement was being called. Some of the men would make short trips on westward as the weather permitted to look for a place to settle and plant next year's crops.

Of first importance, however, was the construction of shelters for the winter. Time was short, and nights were cold. Twice there had been a light dusting of snow, and once a chilling rain that froze in icicles on trees and grasses and on the manes and tails of the horses. On days when the sun shone it was quite comfortable, but these days seemed to become fewer, and definitely shorter. Sun seemed to become weaker and slower to rise, crawling across the inside of the sky dome with difficulty. She was not able to take the road directly overhead, even, but a pitiful arc farther to the south than her summer path.

All of this was expected, of course, but in the permanency of Old Town there had been little preparation beyond the storing of a food supply. Here, dwellings for the winter were not only needed, but would be essential.

With the help and advice of Little Horse and his people of the settlement, it was accomplished: small dwellings, temporary in nature, one for each family. Snakewater was included by invitation in the winter shelter of the family of Kills Many. She had lived alone for many years, since the death of her namesake and mentor. She had long since convinced herself that she liked it that way. Now she found that her attitude was changing somewhat. She had enjoyed the wisdom of young Kills Many, as well as his assistance and understanding. She liked his pretty young wife, Blossom, and especially their daughter, Pigeon. It was not often that Snakewater regretted her solitary life and the absence of a marriage and family. She had never felt that she was missing much, but now she could see clearly that she had been. The sheer joy and exuberance of the little girl, Pigeon, was contagious. It was hardly possible to be glum with this bright and enthusiastic child around. *Maybe,* thought Snakewater, *I have the best of both ways.*

"Grandmother," demanded Pigeon, "tell us a story."

There were several other children of assorted ages around the evening fire. This ritual had not been planned. It had simply happened as they traveled. Pigeon was a curious child, always asking questions, and as a matter of convenience Snakewater answered as many as she could.

"Why is Possum's tail bare, Grandmother?"

"Ah, child, that goes back a long way, to the time that all the people and animals spoke the same tongue."

"Were you there, Grandmother?"

"No, no, child, of course not. Be still, Lumpy! It is not funny."

"What?" asked Pigeon. "Who are you talking to?"

"No one, child. Just the Little People."

"Tell us about them!"

"No, no. You asked about Possum's tail. That goes back to when Man needed fire, for light and to warm him and to cook his food. The animals wanted to help Man too. Or maybe they just wanted fire for themselves. I don't know. But several went to try to bring back fire to the island where they lived."

"What is an island, Grandmother?"

"That is a piece of solid ground with water all around. That is how the world started, with mud from the bottom."

"Who brought it up?"

"You ask too many questions, child. Let me finish about Possum. Now, the fire was on another island, in a pit in the ground. Several birds and animals tried to bring it. Mostly birds at first. Crow and Raven tried it, and were covered with black soot from the smoke. Then Buzzard, who got closer and blistered his head and neck. The same thing happened to Turkey. Some of the animals tried then. Possum was one of the first. He had a fine bushy tail, of soft fur. He thought to curl his tail around the fire and hurry back, with the flames shooting out behind instead of burning him. But it did not work out. He lost not only the fire, but his beautiful tail too. Now it is only dry and scaly and scorched."

"Who did bring fire, then?"

"Oh! It was Spider. She made a little basket of clay and carried it on her head, to keep the fire from burning her. She could walk across the water to the fire island, and she spun a thread to find her way back."

There was a gasp of surprise and appreciation from the little group of children.

"Tell us another!"

So it was that the conjure woman who had seldom talked, except to herself, became a teller of stories. Her skill improved with practice, and she began to remember stories from her own childhood. She had almost forgotten the times when she herself was a child, and would sit on her own mother's lap for stories. Now, with the recalling of each story, she began to remember more.

It was, she thought, almost like a pleasant shower in a dry season. First a few fat drops, falling on dry foliage and grasses, bringing forth the delightful smell of a new rain . . . At first only a moistening of the ground, but then, as the big drops continue, there are little puddles. These begin to run together and to flow in the easiest paths the water can find, making rivulets toward the nearest ditch, gully, or stream. It seemed so with the stories. A few pleasurable evenings as they traveled led to more, which stirred the cobwebby recesses of her memory, awakening stories she had forgotten. They were new stories to the children, and new, almost, to herself. It had been many years since she had found such enjoyment in anything.

Among the favorite stories to both herself and the children were stories of Rabbit. Sometimes wise, sometimes foolish, always amusing, Rabbit could bring a smile to childish faces. And a warming to the heart of Snakewater as she related the stories of Rabbit's adventures.

"Tell us about Rabbit!" was a frequent request.

Sometimes she feared that she would run out of Rabbit stories, but then she would remember another. Maybe the memories were a bit vague, yet usually she could recall enough of the story line to add her own details.

Rabbit is the trickster to the Real People. He is a joker, a mischief maker, lovable although sometimes selfish. His adventures provide a learning experience for the young, and a chuckle for the adults who are able to look back on their own adventures. In the same telling of the Rabbit's stories there is authenticity, because other creatures are portrayed with their distinct characteristics as well. Snakewater soon realized that she was appreciating the stories much more than she had as a child. And when a storyteller enjoys her own story, it is all to the good.

Rabbit was once caught by Wildcat, who was about to kill him to eat.

"Wait!" said Rabbit, thinking quickly. "Wouldn't you rather have venison? Let's go catch a deer and eat together."

"*You* eat *deer*?" asked Wildcat.

"Of course. I catch deer all the time," boasted Rabbit. "I know where they feed, along the river."

Rabbit led the way to the river, where many deer ate the lush growth along its banks. Rabbit climbed a tree and dropped down on the back of a large buck, which fled across the stream. Rabbit fell off in the fastest part of the current and swam to the other side, away from Wildcat. So he got away again. Wildcat killed a small deer for his own dinner.

Another time Rabbit was approached by Wolf, who is a notoriously fast runner. Wolf suggested a race.

"But you are so fast," protested Rabbit modestly. "You can probably beat me. Could I choose someone to represent me?"

Wolf was delighted and flattered, knowing that he and Rabbit were probably the fastest in the woods. He quickly consented. The course was agreed upon, a trail over the hills and through the forest. There would be seven markers along the course of the race.

But before the appointed day, Rabbit enlisted the assistance of his friend Turtle. One turtle looks pretty much like another, and Turtle selected six of his friends to help with a joke.

The race started, with a crowd of the other animals yelling and cheering them on. Turtle was left far behind. But as Wolf neared the first marker, there was a cheer, and he saw a turtle in the path ahead. By the time he reached that point, though, the turtle had concealed himself in the dry leaves. Thinking that he must have passed him, Wolf ran on.

At the next marker the same thing happened, and at the next and the next, Wolf was exhausted and sweating, and reached the finish line just in time to see Turtle crawling slowly across it. It is not good to feel too proud.

On the back trail of the travelers a man on an exhausted horse stopped for the night at a small town in Tennessee. He had many questions about travelers ahead. In particular, he told those at the trading post, he was concerned about his mother, who had run away with some travelers heading for Arkansas. There were two wagons and some pack horses. . . .

"Yes, I remember them," said the trader. "They asked about how far to the river, and how does one get across. An old woman with them."

"That would be the party," said No Tail Wolf. "When were they here?"

"Oh, some time ago. Maybe ten days. . . . A little longer."

"And about the river?"

"Two days. There's a ferry—a Scotchman with a Cherokee wife. He could tell you. About those travelers, that is."

"Good. Well, I'll be on my way."

The trader and his wife watched the man climb back on his horse and jab a spur into the animal's flank to jolt it into motion.

"There's an odd one," said the trader.

"I wish you hadn't told him so much, Zeb," said the woman.

"What do you mean?"

"Oh . . . I don't know, really. There's just something about him. He's not completely honest."

"One o' your feelings?" he asked, half amused, half serious.

"Maybe. . . ."

"Look, honey, I know you see and feel things that I don't. Your Choctaw people say it's a gift, don't they?"

"More like a curse sometimes," she mused. "Zeb, that man is dangerous."

"You're probably right. But what can I do? People ask directions, I tell 'em. It goes with what we do here."

"Yes . . . I know."

"You want me to go after him?" Tell him somethin' different?"

"No, no. Of course not. It's just . . ."

"Damn, woman! Now, I wish you hadn't told me. You think he means harm to somebody? That old woman?"

"Maybe . . . I don't think she's his mother. I remember her. I'd guess she's a doctor woman. They were Cherokee, weren't they?"

"Seems like it."

"Well . . . I hope her power is strong. . . ."

18

"Yes, they came this way," said the ferryman. "Maybe ten days ago. Seems they're plannin' to winter with the settlement over there. West Landin', they call it."

"Good! Take me over, then," ordered No Tail Wolf.

"No! It's too late in the day to cross," the ferryman insisted. "Stay the night. . . . Ye can sleep in the shed there. I'll take ye in the mornin'!"

"Take me in the small boat, then. I'll leave my horse here."

"No, I said. I'm not crossin' the river with night comin' on! Sleep in the shed if ye want. We'll see about crossin' in the mornin', like I said."

He entered the house and yanked the door shut behind him, pulling the latch string in for the night.

"What is it?" asked his wife.

"Damn fool," he muttered. "Tried to talk me into takin' the ferry across alone, an' comin' back in the dark with no help."

The woman shook her head in disbelief, as she continued her work at the fireplace.

"They just don't understand the river and its ways," the ferryman fumed. "Then he wanted me to take him across in the small boat! Leave his horse here. He sure wants to cross in a hurry. . . ."

His wife looked up from the fire and their eyes met, and held for a moment. Then realization dawned.

"Damn!" he said softly, as he turned and headed for the door.

As soon as No Tail Wolf had seen the latch string slide out of sight through the rude plank door, he moved quickly. Down the slope he trotted, to the dock where the ferry and the small boats were tied. Darkness was falling, but he could still see what he wanted. He hesitated only a moment, glancing from a small boat to the canoe tied alongside. He was more familiar with a canoe. . . . Yes, there were the paddles, lying in the bottom. Quickly he untied the mooring rope and stepped in carefully, keeping his weight in the center. He shoved off with the other foot, balancing skillfully, holding to the sides as he sat down. There . . . Now the craft would be more stable. He picked up the longer of the two paddles and dipped it into the water with a long stroke that pushed it well into the river.

"Come back here!" yelled the ferryman, as he came running down the slope to the dock. "You thievin' bastard!"

He stopped, realizing the futility of further effort. The canoe was a bow shot away now, heading slightly upstream into the current. A fairly skilled canoe man, he judged. Might even make it across, if the evening twilight held. . . . Shame to lose the canoe, but he still had the man's horse and saddle, which were worth more than the canoe. Not a bad trade. He glanced across the water toward the location of Little Horse's settlement. A light showed there, a pinpoint of brightness against the darkening western sky, and the even darker shore. It was like watching the stars appear one by one as the evening sky deepens in tone. Well, the man could use the light as a guide, maybe. . . .

No Tail Wolf paid no attention to the yelling ferryman on the wharf. The canoe handled well and was responsive to the paddle. The excitement of the chase stirred his blood. He hadn't decided yet just how to carry out his vengeance. He was sure the old witch-woman was there, in that little settlement. He had talked with the ferryman long enough to glean that information, before the man became so unreasonable. The travelers, it seemed, had decided to winter at this tiny Cherokee settlement. Good! But his plan was to arrive there quickly and unexpectedly. That would prevent the old woman from performing some spell or curse on him. It would be over before she even realized what was happening. When she came out to go to water in the morning, maybe. He touched the knife at his waist. He'd have the deed done and be gone before the others even realized what had happened. He'd hide the canoe out of sight while he scouted the camp. . . .

Well, one thing at a time. The lights of the settlement could be seen more plainly now as twilight deepened. Yes, things were going well.

He was nearly halfway across now, he judged, although it was hard to tell. Both shores seemed far away. The western bank, merely a dark line of trees against the purple of the darkening sky, did not seem to be getting much closer. His arms were tiring. . . . Strong and muscular as they were, they were not accustomed to the use of a canoe paddle. The action uses different muscles, he realized.

A dark shape swept past him in front of the canoe's bow. He was startled, and a moment of fear grasped at him. Wait . . . only a log. He steadied, but then began to realize something he had not thought of before. Flotsam in the middle of the river . . . He was not sure of the significance, but one log meant that there could be more.

A dark, shapeless blot bore down on him and a moment of panic clutched at his heart. Dim thoughts of tales about the water monster stirred in the dim corners of his memory. Then he realized that this was only a raft of small sticks and debris, flimsy material that separated and scattered under the stroke of his paddle. He grunted with satisfaction and resumed his paddling.

But there were other shapes in the water now. Sticks, logs, a large dead fish, easily seen by its clammy whiteness. Another carcass, a bloated deer or maybe a cow. There was an eerie feeling about dead things in the water. He shoved at the floating carcass with his paddle, and it rotated, dipped and rose again, and moved on downriver.

He glanced around quickly, reorienting himself after the rotation of the canoe from his thrust of the paddle. He aligned the bow toward the distant lights again and, with aching arms, kept paddling.

More debris . . . He shoved off from a big dead tree whose limbs protruded high out of the water. For a moment there the limbs had looked like reaching arms above him and his frail shell, reaching *down* to shove him under as the tree rolled. He tried to drive such thoughts out of his head.

Now the canoe rocked softly, as if by an unseen hand. It must have struck some object in the water, he thought, yet he had felt no impact. Odd . . . Something soft, probably another carcass. There were dark shapes in the water all around him now, drifting, twisting, turning, sometimes even seeming to move in *opposite* directions. At the same time he had the feeling that the canoe, along with other floating objects, was gaining momentum in the current, moving downstream. There was a momentary feeling of helplessness, but he shrugged it off and thrust his paddle into the water to correct his course. It became tangled, and he pulled to free it from the clinging debris. For a moment it seemed that someone or some *thing* actually held the paddle and was pulling it away from him. He yanked it free, struggling against the terror that rose in his throat.

Nonsense! All he had to do was remain calm, push free of this tangled mass of flood debris from upstream, and continue to the other shore. He pushed against a log, which rolled slowly. There was a large burl on the trunk, with swirled and gnarled irregularities, reminding him for a moment of a grotesque human face. It rolled under again, but the image had unnerved him badly, confusing him further.

He might have recovered his composure, except that now the rocking of the canoe began again, more severe this time. Once, as a child, he had been in a canoe that was rocked and upset by older boys. It had frightened him badly, but he was a strong swimmer. The experience had not bothered him greatly—until now. . . .

"Stop it!" he screamed.

The rocking ceased, and he felt foolish as the echo of his scream rebounded from the distant shore. He grasped his paddle firmly again, and thrust it into the water to propel the canoe out of the tangle.

But now, again, there seemed to be movement in the water. Shifting, churning, rolling, in different directions, like a family of otters at play. The canoe rocked, and this time he *almost* saw a handlike object rise quietly over the side of the canoe to grasp it and create the rolling motion. He struck out with the paddle using all his strength and it shattered, leaving the broken shaft in his hand. Tossing it aside, he half rose to stumble forward and pick up the other paddle. Without it he would be helpless.

The canoe overbalanced and rolled, throwing him into the debris-filled water. He struggled against the clinging tangle of sticks and vines and small branches. He became panicky as the tangle seemed to reach out and grasp at him, holding, pulling, sucking him down. He was sure that he felt a hand or a paw or some grasping tentacle close around his ankle, drawing him toward the murky depths. He screamed again, but the sound was stifled in midscream as the water closed over his nose and open mouth. The water was cold and dark and he felt consciousness fading away. The grasp around his ankle was still there, even more firmly fastened now. He held his breath as long as he could, but his reflexes demanded that he try to fill his lungs. He gasped involuntarily, drawing in nothing but muddy river water as his world slipped away. . . .

Snakewater had been restless all evening, and now lay awake in her blankets. She listened to the light snores of Kills Many and his wife, Blossom, and the contented breathing of little Pigeon.

She did not understand quite why she should be restless. Their preparations for winter were going well, and all seemed right with the world. Things had progressed well ever since she had left Old Town and joined the travelers.

Maybe it was something she had eaten. . . . But, no, her stomach seemed fine. It must be her spirit that was troubled, though she could not imagine why.

She finally drifted off to sleep, and woke sometime later. There seemed to be no change, except that the fire had burned down. The soft snores and regular breathing of the others had not changed. Maybe if she went to empty her bladder . . .

She groped around in the dark and found the sticks, kept near the fire for such purpose. She tossed a stick on the glowing coals, and waited until the resulting flame lighted the lodge. Then she slipped outside, drawing her blanket around her shoulders.

The dim starlight allowed her to see her way, around behind the fringe of bushes. She stumbled along sleepily, and suddenly stopped and gasped at an unexpected movement of some kind. A rabbit? Not a skunk, she hoped.

"What . . . ?" she questioned, peering into the shadowy woods. "Lumpy, is that you? Don't scare me like that. What are you . . . ? Get back, Lumpy! It's cold out here, and you're soaking wet. Go on in by the fire. . . ."

19

The winter passed, somewhat milder than those to which the travelers were accustomed. Some of the men made exploratory trips to the west and found other settlements of the Real People, as Little Horse had said. Most were glad to see the newcomers, and gave helpful information about what could be expected from the weather as the growing season approached.

The season out here was somewhat longer, it was said, beginning earlier and running later before the first frost. The climate was good for all the traditional crops of the Real People. Corn, beans, pumpkins, potatoes, all would grow well here.

"The seasons travel as before," one man told them. "South to north in the spring, back again in the autumn. When spring comes, it moves about as fast as we would."

"What do you mean?" asked a puzzled newcomer.

"Well, look at it this way. . . . There is a time for each plant to flower, no? Dogwood, redbud, plum thicket . . . each has its time. Now, when the first dogwood are blooming here, they have already done so to the south, but not yet to the north. If we were to travel north when the first blooms begin, each day we would see the first blooms of dogwood in a new place."

"Ah! I see. And this happens a little earlier here than where we came from? We would plant corn earlier?"

"A little bit, maybe. The same signs are still good."

"The ground-sitting?" asked Kills Many with a smile.

"Yes, that one is good. When the old men who are fishing sit on the ground instead of standing, the earth is warm enough to plant corn."

"Is there land here where we could plant?"

"Of course. Some is taken, but there is more."

"How about farther west?"

"Probably. Too far west you would encounter Osage people, who do not welcome us."

"They are farmers?"

"Yes . . . Hunters too. Some of them are bold fighters, and they resent newcomers. The turkey gobbles sometimes."

Kills Many smiled. The traditional war cry of the Real People was the gobble of the turkey cock.

"You have fought with them?"

"Not here . . . Farther west."

"Maybe it would be good to avoid that."

"Probably. You could settle here."

"We will think on it," promised Kills Many. "We will have to decide before the planting of the corn."

"Before that, if you plant potatoes."

"True . . . Probably not, though. Potatoes, I mean, until we're settled. Next year, maybe."

In most of the places they visited they were invited to settle. The loyalty of the Real People insured that no Cherokee would starve while others still had food. It would be difficult to decide, and a council was called to discuss the question. This gathering was considerably different from the town meetings that were the custom, but some of the formalities were observed out of habit. Pipes were smoked, and various opinions expressed in turn. There was no general consensus.

"May I speak?" asked Little Horse finally.

"Of course," said Kills Many, who was presiding as leader of the travelers.

"*Wado* . . . Thank you. You have looked at several places, and have been treated well, no?"

"That is true."

"Good. But, why not stay here? It has been proven that we get along well, has it not?"

There was a general chuckle. It had been a season of pleasant contact with others of the Real People. It had been plain that the children of the two groups had become friends. Little Horse and his people had been more than helpful, but it had been assumed . . .

Well, why not? There was a bit of discussion, mostly favorable, but with an amused surprise that it had not been mentioned before.

"I am made to think," said Kills Many finally, "that this is a good thing. Yet it is a choice so important that we should sleep on it. Let us meet tomorrow."

When they met again, there was little doubt. They would stay and settle here at West Landing.

Now began the real planning, and the real work. With assistance from the settlers the newcomers chose and marked areas where they would plant. There were trees to be cut and brush cleared, but the logs and poles that resulted would be used for the construction of houses.

Snakewater found herself in a time of indecision. Her thinking, unlike the plans of the settlers, had not progressed much beyond escape from the pressures of Old Town, with its misunderstanding and hatred. Among these people she had found friendship such as she had never experienced before, and even a feeling of *family.* But now, with everyone else making plans and preparations for their new lives at West Landing, what would be her part? She felt left out.

"What shall I do, Lumpy?" she asked aloud to an apparently empty space. "Yes, I know you can't help me with things like that. You don't have to be sarcastic, you know. . . . What? Oh, yes . . . *Wado.* That *is* a good one!"

She stooped and with her digging stick exposed the root of the medicinal plant she sought. From long habit there were things that she must carry out seasonally. This particular forb was heralded by its first growth in early spring. It was time to gather a supply.

She moved along, carrying on her one-sided conversation. At least it would appear so to any casual observer.

"Yes, things grow well here. The earth is mellow. . . . Yes, I see that one. . . . Thank you."

There had been little occasion to use her healing skills and conjures this season. There were not enough people involved in her world that winter. A few coughs, sore throats, but no major troubles. There were no young people of courting age, so no demand for love potions or spells to bring on infatuation. But she could not continue to depend on the charity of others, giving nothing in return. When the others moved into new dwellings, what would she do? In a way she dreaded the time when she would have to decide.

Perhaps Kills Many, with his keen perception of people, saw this in her. For whatever reason he drew her aside one afternoon.

"Mother," he said, "we must talk of something."

He had first called her "Mother" as a term of respect, then as a gentle joke. To young Pigeon she was "Grandmother," and to any casual observer she might have been just that. To all intents and purposes she was the female elder in the house of Kills Many.

"Of course," she said. "What is it?"

Her tone was cheerful, but her heart was heavy. What would Kills Many, to whom she felt close family ties, wish to discuss? Should she forestall any unpleasantness by offering to move out?

"You know," Kills Many said with some hesitation, "that we will soon move into a new house."

Ah! Here it comes, she thought.

"Yes, I—" she began, but he gestured her to silence.

"Be still and listen a moment. You know that you will always be welcome in our family—"

"But I—"

"Let me go on! I know that you have long lived alone. If you like, you could have the smaller house. We would help you improve it."

She was silent for a moment, and he misunderstood her emotion. She could not have spoken just then.

"Or," he hurried on, "we can help you build a better one."

Snakewater took a deep breath. "It is not that," she was finally able to say. "But wouldn't you . . . I had supposed you would salvage logs and poles for the new house from that one."

"No, no." He laughed. "We might have. . . . We might yet. But this is your choice, Mother. With us, or in your own house. Do you want to think on it? Sleep on it, maybe?"

There was a tear in the corner of her eye.

"You have been good to me, Kills Many. You are like a son . . . at least, I suppose so. I have never had a son, so how would I know?"

She laughed at herself and continued. "I don't need to sleep on it," she said. "I probably need the space to myself, for the plants and roots and all that I use. And I may need to conjure a spell. That would be easier in my own place. Now, the house we just shared for the winter is probably better than the one I had in Old Town. So, yes! I accept. Thank you, my almost-son!"

It seemed that spring came quickly and that there was too much going on. Building, clearing, planting, all nearly at once. Snakewater tried to help as she could, especially with the planting. Encouragement, the creation, almost, of new life, seemed to her an appropriate pursuit. She had had some experience with a small garden plot maintained by her namesake mentor, but tending it had not been a favorite pastime of hers. Nevertheless this was different: she *had* taken on a new life.

With the renewal, however, came a responsibility. She was still a guest among these people. The community was not large enough to afford a medicine person, a conjuror such as herself. Therefore her contribution must come in other ways. The telling of the stories, which amounted to instruction of the young, was one. Her assistance with the planting, another.

Occasionally she had prepared a potion or salve, or conjured a "medicine" for someone. But it was becoming clear to her that her function in this new town must be different from anything in her previous life. This was troubling to her. The skill with plants and roots and conjures and spells was her gift, and it was good. Now, it was not to be used enough to maintain its power. *If you don't use the gift, you lose it,* her old mentor had warned. She feared this could very easily happen to her. There was not enough use here to keep the power of her medicine alive.

There was the possibility, of course, that the little community would grow. It had done so with the arrival of the party of Kills Many. With the coming of spring there might be other travelers, and some might settle here. The town *could* grow and become self-sufficient, like Keowee. But *when*? Could she wait to see?

The other alternative for her seemed to be to attach herself to another party moving west. There had been none yet, and might *not* be. But it was something to consider.

Over all of this consideration there was a restlessness within her. Possibly it was simply the age-old urge to migrate that comes with the spring. What human is there who does not thrill to the call of the wild geese high overhead, honking their way northward to unknown places? There is always a curiosity to see what lies just beyond the next hill.

It must be assumed that this factor, too, lay within the breast of Snakewater as she planted corn and beans and pumpkins. She straightened occasionally to rest her back, and to watch the long lines of snowy white geese honk their way northward. She really had no yen to seek a colder climate, but one to the *west* might prove interesting.

20

The newly planted crops were not even showing green yet when the first travelers passed through West Landing en route to somewhere. There were all types imaginable: Trappers, heading for new country beyond the Mississippi . . . They would spend the summer searching for an area in which to harvest furs next winter. . . . Settlers, families searching for a place that would be their own . . . Occasionally, a loner who looked behind him frequently and darted furtive glances at any movement in the edges of his vision . . . And, sometimes, an individual whose spirit could be *felt* as it reached out in question: What does lie out there? Snakewater found that she could easily spot that one. She knew that he felt the same restless migration urge that puzzled her as she watched the geese high overhead.

There were, of course, occasional parties of the Real People, moving away from the encroachment of the whites. It was always good to see them. Some stayed an extra day or two, to inquire and explore before moving on. At first Snakewater was hesitant to have any contact with them. They might have come from Old Town, and she could have that unpleasantness to deal with again. Gradually, however, her dread began to fade. Children of the travelers always enjoyed her stories, and she continued to improve with practice.

She was remembering sayings and proverbs, too, from her own childhood, and used some of them in talking to Pigeon and the other children. It had never occurred to her until now, what importance lay in some of the old sayings. It was an education, the teaching of a way of life. . . .

You can dance just as well in the rear as in the front rank. . . .

Don't expect anything too much, especially if it is misfortune, or it will surely come. . . .

Too much fun and happiness are always followed by sorrow and trouble. . . .

A big warrior does not always drive center with his arrows. Even a small warrior can drive center. . . .

Don't tell another all you know. Then he will be as wise as you are. . . .

Stories of animals, birds, and plants were always popular. Rabbit, the trickster, was a great favorite. Snakewater began to remember tales she had forgotten. . . . How the Moon came to be . . .

Two towns were having a contest. *Aneja,* "little brother of war," was the ancient ball game played using sticks with a cup-shaped pocket of woven thongs at the end. The ball must never be touched with the hands, or *any* part of the body. But in the heat of competition one player seized the ball. He threw it so hard toward the goal that it stuck up against the inside of the sky dome. There it stays to this day, sliding along, following the sun.

The Real People soon noticed that at times the moon is much slimmer. It was assumed that this was associated with the shame over infraction of the rules. After that it became the custom that the game of *aneja* could only be played at the time of the full moon. This would avoid further embarrassment, and would help to remind the players of the importance of fairness in the contest.

Despite her enjoyment of these distractions Snakewater grew more restless. The corn was up now, usually seven tiny plants in each hill, from the ritual seven grains planted. They would not be thinned, only weeded and tended, and watered if necessary. Beans, almost equal in importance to the corn, were doing well also. She wondered idly why there were not the tales of beans associated with the Creation story, as there were with corn.

But that was not as important to her as the puzzling restlessness that continued to haunt her. She realized that she was changing as a person, but was not at all certain what was happening to her.

"I don't understand what I'm supposed to do, Lumpy," she complained one day to apparently empty space. "What is happening to me?"

She stooped to pick an especially nice plant of the type she sought, and put it in her basket.

"What? Oh, yes . . . I know you can't help me. But you don't have to tease me about it. Sometimes you are a real pain, Lumpy. I—"

She broke off in midsentence as someone else approached.

"Hello, Grandmother," said Pigeon. "I heard you talking."

Her eyes were full of mischief.

"The Little People?"

"Ah, child! Do you see any Little People?"

Pigeon smiled as if the two shared a great secret.

"Ah, Grandmother . . . Suppose I did? I could not say so. So, probably not. But maybe someday, no?"

The two laughed together.

Snakewater was almost certain that this special child would be offered, in some way, gifts of the spirit. Not too soon, she hoped. It would be better if the girl could enjoy her childhood before assuming all the responsibility that goes with the spirit gift.

"I am looking for special plants today," she explained to the child. "This is a good time of the year, before the grasses are too tall. And some are scarce. I can't pick every one. I must find and reject six before I pick the seventh."

"But why, Grandmother?"

"So they won't be lost, child! If we picked them all, there would be none to grow next year, and their medicine would be lost forever."

"But . . . you could not pick every one in the world, Grandmother!"

"Maybe not—but we must make sure. If every old conjure woman, or doctor man, leaves six of the seven they must find, there will always be six in the world to begin the next season."

"Who makes the rules?"

"I don't know, child," said Snakewater, a little more irritably than she felt. "The One Above, maybe, since Creation. Who makes you ask so many questions?" she teased.

Pigeon giggled. "I don't know. They just come into my head."

"Of course. And that is good. But you don't have to know all things. Some are not meant to be understood, only enjoyed. But it's all right to ask. That's how you learn."

"Is there anyone who knows *everything*?"

"Of course not! But there are those who *think* they do. They are to be avoided."

"Why, Grandmother?"

"Because they are dangerous, child! Think about it. One who thinks he knows everything is . . . Well, look: If he did, he would be as wise as God, no? And of course that could not be. That person is very stupid to think so, and stupid people are the most dangerous. The smartest people are those who have learned to gracefully say, 'I don't know.' Or even better, remain silent. . . . Ah, child! How did you get me started on this? You are a nuisance!"

But her smile and expression plainly said that Snakewater was enjoying every moment. Pigeon giggled again.

"Then I will never ask another question, Grandmother."

"No! I did not say that!" scolded the old woman in mock anger. "You must *always* ask questions. Only sometimes, not so often, and maybe not out loud! Questions are not always welcomed by those who think they know all."

"But why not? If they know all, they should be glad to answer."

"Ah, but that is the point! In their own mind they have doubts and fears like the rest of us, but cannot admit it, because to do so would prove they do *not* know all."

"Who is the wisest person of all?" asked Pigeon.

"Who knows?" answered Snakewater. "I once thought it was the old woman who taught me, and whose name I bear now. She told me much about these things. I am made to think that it is *because* she knew how much she did *not* know that she was the wisest. So let that be a lesson. Besides, many things are not meant to be understood. It is better so. Enjoy what is given to us, question sometimes, but be ready to learn when the time for it comes."

The corn was knee high when the ferry brought a party of travelers who disembarked like the others at West Landing. As usual the children trooped down to meet them. There were two wagons, with extended families, some on foot or riding horses. They drove a small herd of pigs, pushed along with sticks by the older boys.

As children do, the newcomers and the children from West Landing met and mingled almost instantly, and it was good. Unlike adults, even children who do not know each other's language are able to do this. But in this case the travelers were also Cherokee, the Real People. The mingling of children and adults alike was like a homecoming.

Snakewater always kept her distance from newcomers, partly from long habit, but also for another reason, nearly forgotten. It was a real surprise, then, when it happened. Pigeon came running to her.

"Grandmother!" she called, breathless from running. "Guess what! These people are from Keowee! Isn't that good? That's where we found you!"

A cold clutch of fear and dread grasped at the heart of Snakewater. Not good, really . . . These travelers were from far too close to Old Town and all the problems it had meant to her.

21

Snakewater managed to stay out of sight as much as possible while the visitors were at West Landing.

"Grandmother, come and tell us stories," pleaded Pigeon.

"No, child . . . Grandmother is sick. Go away, now."

"But there are children with this party. They will like to hear about Rabbit."

"No. Not now. Run along."

Snakewater had not been outside for two days except after dark, and then very carefully. The travelers from Keowee might not recognize her, but she felt that she could not take the chance. If they did, it would rekindle the dormant fires of the unpleasantness back in Old Town. At best the travelers would be curious. At worst, accusing and argumentative. It was much easier and less risky simply to stay out of sight until the visitors moved on.

So far they showed no signs of doing that. They were enjoying the company of the Real People of West Landing. A couple of the women were clan sisters—Bird Clan. In their present situation this carried very little importance, but there was a good feeling of family and home, encountering a friend unexpectedly in a far country. This alone was reason to stay another day or two. . . .

On the third day Kills Many approached and knocked at the door of Snakewater's hut.

"Mother . . . it is Kills Many. May I enter? I would talk with you."

"Of course!" she answered cheerfully. "Come on in."

He stooped to enter and squatted against the wall.

"Are you all right?" he asked. "We were concerned about you. Pigeon said you were sick."

"No, no. An excuse. The visitors are from Keowee, too close to home. I thought it better to stay out of sight."

He nodded, understanding.

"I see. They have said nothing, but you are probably right. Why take the chance? They will move on soon. Do you need anything?"

"No. I do get out at night, and early morning. How long will they stay?"

"Who knows? They are enjoying the company of the Real People. Somebody has a clan relationship. . . . Mostly just a pause in the hard travel, I think. I could ask about Old Town, if you like."

"No, no. As the saying goes, Don't poke a sleeping skunk," she said.

Kills Many smiled. "It is good."

"This does make me wonder, though. Will it always be so?"

"What do you mean?"

"Well, you know my story, my almost-son. Will I have to worry about every party of travelers that comes along? Wonder if they are likely to accuse me of murder?"

He started to laugh and then realized how serious she was.

"I don't know," he said finally. "I had not thought of this. Did you have an idea? Something else you want to do?"

She sighed deeply. "I don't know. I had thought of joining some group of other travelers. Maybe Real People from some other area. Or even Chickasaws or Muskogee or somebody. Close to our people, but who would not have heard about the trouble at Old Town."

Kills Many nodded thoughtfully. "I had not even considered this problem," he admitted. "Surely such a thing should be forgotten. But people are strange, no? Some stranger than others."

"Kills Many," she said after a few moments of silence, "have you heard of mountains to the far west?"

"Of course. There are many stories. Open grassland, many days' travel to cross . . . As many buffalo as there are stars in the sky . . . Mountains beyond . . . Why?"

"Oh, nothing . . . I only wondered what they look like. Somebody said they are taller, with snow on the tops, even in summer."

"I don't know. Different from ours back home, I suppose. But why . . . Snakewater! Are you thinking of trying to go there yourself?"

"Oh, no," she said quickly. "Well, not really. But maybe . . . There wouldn't likely be anyone from Old Town there. I might think about it. . . ."

It was three more days before the party from Keowee moved on, and a great relief for Snakewater. She could now move about freely. But the interval had given her time to think. More and more she considered the idea that had formed itself almost spontaneously as she talked with Kills Many. She was still surprised by it, and even more so that she would take it seriously. How and why would such a thing come into her mind? Things do not occur without reason. . . . Or *do* they? No, she thought . . . this must be part of the understanding thing. It is not necessary to understand it *all,* just that it happens. And something had definitely happened to her. This odd urge to move on had not left her with the departure of the migrating geese this time. If anything it was now growing even stronger. There must be a purpose that she had not yet reasoned out.

But if it was meant to be, the means for it to occur would also be provided. So, she decided, she must be patient. But that was hard.

"Lumpy, can you help me?" she asked. "You are good at helping find things. . . . *What?* Just herbs and roots and medicines? Not answers? *Huh!* Big help *you* are! Well, you don't have to *laugh* about it!"

"What's the matter, Grandmother? You look angry. Were you talking to someone? Ah, I know! The Little People!"

Pigeon, just approaching the hut, clapped her hands in delight.

"Silly child!" Snakewater scolded, still disgruntled. "Do you see any Little People around here?"

"Why, of course not, Grandmother," said the little girl, a twinkle in her eye. "But if I *did,* of course I could not tell, could I?"

Both laughed at the repeated ritual.

"That is true," admitted Snakewater, her temper moderating. "What are you doing today? Surely there are better things than talking to an old woman."

"We wondered," said Pigeon seriously, "about some more stories. We've had none while the travelers were here from Keowee."

"I know, child. I've been sick. But I'm better now. Yes, of course we can have stories. This evening? Some stories are better after dark, you know."

The corn was nearly as tall as young Pigeon when the trader and his wife happened by and crossed the river on the ferry.

"Ah! Your town has grown since last season!" he joked with Little Horse. "Maybe I'll stay an extra day before moving on west. Do some trading?"

"Maybe so," agreed Horse. "You're heading west again?"

"Yes . . . Interesting places out there. Trading is good. They have no source of metal things—knives, fire strikers, things like that. The women like mirrors, needles, beads . . ."

"Well, stay a little! Tell us more," said Little Horse. "Any of the Real People out there?"

"Cherokees? Some, of course. Not many in the plains. Just a few in the nearest mountains beyond. Why?"

"Just curious. Some of our people wondered. Some have passed through here, going west. Not many, though. Just thought I'd ask."

Snakewater, who overheard, wondered . . . Maybe, if the trader would stay a day or two, she could manage to visit with his wife a little while.

The trader's wife was friendly and congenial, and it was no trouble to start a conversation with her. The woman was fluent in the use of the language of the Real People, and of several others, as it turned out. It was important to be able to communicate in their occupation as traders.

"I am Snakewater, of the Cherokees. How are you called?"

"Rain Cloud, Seminole," answered the other woman. She was short and robust.

Snakewater nodded. "You have traveled with your husband a long time? You speak my tongue well."

"Yes, a long time. Since we married, almost."

"You have children?"

"Yes, two. Both grown, a boy and a girl. You?"

"No. I have never married."

"Ah . . . you do not like men?"

"Oh, yes. Just not enough to marry one."

Both women chuckled.

"I am a conjuror," explained Snakewater. "I was raised by an old conjure woman, who was unmarried. I think now that maybe the boys were afraid of me. Or more likely, afraid of *her*."

Both laughed again.

"Of course," Snakewater continued, "I *was* somewhat different. Tall, skinny, not very attractive."

"You thought *that*?" asked Rain Cloud in surprise. "Ah, we think strangely about ourselves. I had been wishing for height such as yours!"

Snakewater was beginning to like this woman.

"How far west have you been?" she asked. "I have heard of mountains there."

"That is true. We have traded among the people there. We have heard of another great salty sea beyond that, but haven't been that far. I suppose Fox will want to try that next!"

"That is your husband's name?"

"Yes . . . Most just call him Trader, though. It is easier and tells of what he does."

"I see."

They continued their woman talk, which was far more productive than Snakewater could have imagined. Each had certain characteristics as well as experience that the other admired or wished for.

"Some of the people here are your relatives?" asked Rain Cloud.

"No, no. I did not even know them until last season. They were traveling west and I wished to, also, so I joined them."

Cloud laughed. "It is good! And you settled here only last season, then?"

"Yes . . . Little Horse and his people were here already. Kills Many, leader of our band of travelers, liked the place and the people, and here we are."

"I see. . . . But do I suspect that you might have wanted to go farther west?"

"No . . . not really. Not then, anyway. Maybe . . ."

She was confused by the rapidity with which Rain Cloud perceived her true feelings.

"I understand," said Cloud. "This is fine, but there may be somewhere else as good? Perhaps *better*?"

"Well . . . yes. That is pretty close. I never used to wonder much about other places, but since I joined the party of Kills Many, I have seen many things. Now I begin to think: Will new wonders never cease?"

Rain Cloud nodded solemnly. "Probably not. I have enjoyed our years on the trading roads."

"What of your children?" asked Snakewater. "You took them along?"

"Oh, yes. Most of the time. The boy was born one summer when we were among the Cheyennes. When they were older, they sometimes stayed with my brother's family. That was good. I missed them, but they came back better for it."

"How so?"

Rain Cloud smiled wistfully.

"Well, there comes a time when one's parents seem very stupid, no?"

Snakewater's memory reached back to her own unhappy childhood.

"I—I don't know. My mother died and my father remarried. . . . New clan . . ."

"Ah! I did not know. My heart is heavy for you, Snakewater."

"It was long ago. But I understand what you mean about parents."

"Yes . . . Well, the Absarokas—'Crows,' the white man calls them—Crows have a custom that we thought good. They trade children."

"What?"

"Just for a season." Rain Cloud laughed. "When the two branches of the nation meet for their big council, relatives exchange children. A family of the Mountain Crows might take with them a youngster of a brother or sister among the River Crows, and the other way around. At the council the next year they take their own back. The young people have learned much during that year, have seen new country. Besides, they find that during that year both sets of parents have gained much wisdom."

Snakewater nodded. She had never managed to reestablish a good relationship with her father, but through the years she had at least come to *respect* him. She wished now . . . But that was all behind her, long ago.

"I can see how that could help," she agreed.

22

"You seem to know many tongues," Snakewater said to her new friend the next day, "but you could not know them all. You use the hand-sign talk I have heard of here in the west?"

"Yes, we use that quite often," answered Rain Cloud. "Do you know other languages, Snakewater?"

"No. Only a little of the hand-sign talk. I have learned it as we traveled last season."

"It is good! You can use it if you go on west."

For the next day Rain Cloud was busy helping her husband with trading. Snakewater spoke in passing, but did not want to bother while the trading was in progress. That evening, however, Rain Cloud knocked at her door. The visitor came immediately to the point.

"I am made to think," she said, "that you should go with us."

"What? I could not do that!"

"I dreamed of this last night," said Cloud. "It is meant to be."

"But—but I did not dream of it!" protested Snakewater. "This is too sudden."

"I know," said Rain Cloud, chuckling, "and you should sleep on it. We will be here another night. Let us know before we leave tomorrow."

Cloud turned and walked quickly away toward where her husband was setting out his trading goods for the day's business.

Snakewater experienced a moment of panic. She must think about this. Already she had nearly convinced herself that West Landing was too vulnerable a place for her to stay. Nearly all the travelers crossing the big river here would have come through the area of Keowee and Old Town. Sooner or later there would be a confrontation, and the unpleasantness would begin all over again.

Added to that was this strange, restless urge to travel that had come on so strong this season. It must be that she was meant to move on.

But . . . now, with people she had hardly met? She was accustomed to a certain amount of deliberation—well, until the last year. . . .

"Lumpy, what should I . . . ? Oh, I know you can't . . . Damn it, stop laughing. It isn't funny!"

She needed to talk to someone. Maybe Kills Many. He was wise beyond his years. . . .

". . . and I am made to think I should consider this. What do you think, my almost-son?"

Kills Many pondered a moment. This was a reversal of roles. Among the Real People a young man would normally seek the counsel of an older woman. His mother, usually. Possibly his wife. He hardly knew how to answer.

"You have had no dream?"

"No. The trader's wife invited me. *She* had the dream."

He nodded thoughtfully.

"Well," he said at last, "you and I have talked of this. West Landing will always bring people from your area. Some will remember you with kindness, but some hate you—unjustly, of course, but you can't change them. Maybe this is meant to be. They leave tomorrow?"

"Yes. Rain Cloud said that I should seek a vision before deciding."

"Is there a potion you could use?"

"Maybe. A dream vision happens or it doesn't, and it cannot be controlled. But there are things to help it happen, if it is meant to happen."

"And you have tonight. . . ."

"Yes." She smiled. "It seems simple, once it is spoken, no? I need to be ready for the dream, and I will know in the morning. Thank you, Kills Many."

The young man chuckled. "I did nothing!"

"Oh, yes," she said. "You told me what was in my head."

She retired early, after a cup of tea brewed from selected herbs. For a long time sleep would not come. She tossed and turned in her blankets, and then lay there trying to decide whether she should get up to empty her bladder. Finally she did that, and returned to her restless attempts at slumber. Maybe she should have another cup of the soothing tea. . . . But to do that she would have to build up the fire, and that would bring her farther from sleep. Finally she did fall asleep, those thoughts still undecided.

She was running, over open country. It was a land of broad skies and far horizons, with rolling hills in low ridges covered with bright grasses. The color near her was the green of early spring, and the distance of hills a day's travel away were of a bluish cast. Beyond that the blue of distance painted each ridge a few shades darker and more blue than the one before. In the far distance the last range of hills was so blue that she could not tell where the earth ended and the sky dome began.

A few cottonwood trees were scattered over the rolling plain, and she approached one as she ran. She was amazed at its size and paused to look at it. The tree was a magnificent specimen, which surprised her some. It had not looked very impressive, but at close range it was possibly the biggest tree she had ever seen. It had been dwarfed by the wide horizon. She ran on, not tiring at all.

This was the sort of dream in which one knows that it is a dream, seeing it both as observer and participant. Snakewater knew that she could waken if she wished. She might also waken spontaneously but she hoped not. This strange world was far too enjoyable.

She ran up a steep slope, not even tiring, and found herself on the flat summit. She stopped to drink in the beauty of the scene. The prairie was dotted with small bands of buffalo and elk, and somewhere near her a meadowlark sang. A hawk soared overhead, and she waved to it, watching the perfect circles that it drew against the bright blue of the sky. Maybe . . . She took a short run and rose into the air, soaring on the warm rising currents with arms outstretched. Her heart leaped with the excitement of the experience.

In the distance a flock of snowy geese traced their long lines northward in perfect formation. Their traveling song sounded like the barking of a great number of small dogs, and she smiled to herself.

There was a motion to her left, caught in the corner of her eye, and she turned to look. A pair of geese from the distant flock drew in alongside her as she flew, their black wing tips a stark contrast to the snowy white of their plumage. One of them looked directly into her face, eye to eye, and spoke.

"Come, fly with us!"

"But . . . I . . ."

"Come, it is meant to be!"

"I . . . Where?"

"Wherever your quest takes you. . . ."

"But you go north. . . . I am drawn westward."

"Then, go!"

The gander flew, in a long sweeping curve away from her line of flight, and his mate followed. Snakewater was alone again, looking downward. The rolling plain stretched below her, and she could see below her a village of conical tents. Hundreds of horses grazed in the prairie nearby. Beyond that the plain stretched on toward a brilliant sunset . . . *west.* She could see on the horizon a thin irregular strip of dark blue that might be . . . mountains?

In her concentration and amazement at the majesty of what lay before her, she forgot, somehow, that she must keep flying. But how . . . Panic seized her. *I can't fly! I'm not supposed to fly!*

Like a crippled bird, struck in midair by a well-aimed arrow, she began to tumble. Down, down . . . The prairie rushed up at her, and she screamed. . . .

Then she was awake, sweating in her blankets. It was still night. She wondered if she had actually screamed aloud, and whether anyone had heard.

She rose, pulled back the door curtain, and looked outside through the clear, cool night. The position of the stars told her that morning was near. In fact, she could at least imagine a graying in the eastern sky across the river that would soon mellow into dawn. The town was quiet. . . . *Good!* Apparently her scream had not wakened anyone. Maybe the scream had happened only in her dream, not in this world at all. No matter now.

She filled her pipe and lit it with a glowing stick from the ashes of her fire. Then she took a deep breath and sat down on the log bench beside her door. The dream, or vision . . . much the same, she thought. What was its meaning? There was not much time to try to interpret it. Some things were clear. She had been shown some of the future, great vistas that she would probably see. The call was plain, the urge to follow the geese. But her intuition was probably right: not to the north, but to the west. That agreed with what she had felt for some time.

The two geese, traveling like the flock, but not *with* them. They had asked her to follow them, but *their* destination was different too. Follow partway? Yes, that must be it. The gander had all but explained it. Follow us, but wherever your quest takes you. She nodded in satisfaction.

There was one more thing, a very troublesome part of the dream: the impression of falling. She pondered that a little while. What was its meaning? Everyone has had that dream, of course. She had experienced it before. Clearly it had not been a warning of an actual fall. At least, not yet. It was more like a warning of danger. A vague warning . . . *of course!* There would always be dangers in new and unknown places, would there not?

So, in essence, the meaning of the vision that had been given her was simple. She was called to travel westward on a quest of some sort. Her guides, the geese—travelers like the rest of the flock, but different. The trader and his wife? Possibly, but maybe they were just geese, the guides in her dream. Or maybe both. No matter. Time would tell. . . . The fall, a warning to be careful.

Yes, that must be it. There was a great sense of satisfaction. But also much to be done this morning. The sky was really turning yellow-gray in the east now. She rose and prepared to go to water.

By the time the sun rose above the distant line of trees on the far bank of the big river, she had begun preparations to leave. She must talk with Kills Many.

She found him as he returned from the ritual bath.

"I would talk with you, almost-son."

"Yes, what is it, Mother?"

"I—I am made to think that it is meant for me to go west."

He nodded. "This does not surprise me, Mother. I have seen it coming. It is good, though you will be missed. You go with the trader?"

"Well . . . yes."

Kills Many already knew.

"You must take your horse."

"Oh, no," she protested.

"Yes, Snakewater. I have no use for her. She is yours!"

"But, I—"

"Don't worry about it. It was meant this way."

"I must go and tell the trader's wife. She asked me yesterday, and I had a dream last night."

He nodded. "As I said, Mother. It is meant to be."

"Kills Many," she said hesitantly, "there is something I must ask you."

"Yes—what is it?"

"Well . . . your name, my almost-son. It seems not to fit you. How is it that . . . ?"

He was laughing, now.

"Grasshoppers!" he said.

"Grasshoppers?"

"Yes. It was a bad year for grasshoppers in the cornfield. I was of maybe ten summers. My feet were big. They still are. I could stomp on many grasshoppers."

Snakewater was laughing now. "It is good!" she said.

23

In many ways leaving West Landing was more difficult for Snakewater than leaving her lifelong home at Old Town. That had been easy. At Old Town she had few friends, and even those were not close. Everything connected with Old Town had become unpleasant, if not downright dangerous. It had been a relief to escape it, along with the dangers and the unpleasant memories. There was no sadness. Her only real, emotional tie with her youth had been her old mentor, and many winters had passed since the old conjure woman had crossed over. She had left her home, her skills, and even her name to the younger woman, and it had been hard.

But by the time Snakewater left Old Town, there were none of those memories left. The unpleasant ones had come crowding in. Even her home, once a place of refuge, had become a threat. It had become a dangerous place, and it was good to be gone from there.

What a contrast now. She had been here only a season, but she had friends here. There had been no one in her life, since the death of Snakewater the elder, to whom she had been close. Now she realized with some surprise how difficult it would be to leave Kills Many and his family. They had joked about it, she and the young man. She had called him "almost-son." He had become the son she had never had, and could never have now. That possibility was long behind her. Yet, for a season, she had been able to experience the emotions, the feelings, and the joy of having a family. It had been good. But the ever-present danger of her past had become, in a way, a danger to them, her adopted family.

Pigeon . . . Ah, what a joy! Looking back, she saw that the child had done much for her. A season ago Snakewater would never have imagined that she could become a storyteller. Now she was actually in demand as one. Could Pigeon ever realize how much influence she had wielded in Snakewater's transformation? The old woman smiled to herself. Quite possibly—she had always felt that Pigeon seemed to have all the wisdom of an older adult, packed into a small body. She must take some time with the little girl, to explain her impending departure.

"Pigeon," she began haltingly, "I must tell you something."

"What is it, Grandmother? A secret?"

The child's eyes danced with excitement.

"No, no . . ."

This was more difficult than she could have imagined. . . .

"No, not a secret. Everyone will know. I wanted to tell you first, to explain."

She took a deep breath.

"Are you troubled, Grandmother?" asked the girl sympathetically.

"No . . . well, yes, a little. I am troubled that I must leave here."

"When will you come back?"

"I—I don't know. Maybe never."

A look of alarm swept across the small face.

"You are to cross over?"

"No, no, child, not that. But I will be far away. I am going with the trader and his wife."

"But *they* will come back!"

"Yes, that is true. . . ." She had not even thought of that. "But I will probably not."

The large dark eyes filled with tears.

"You are angry with me, Grandmother?"

Snakewater put an arm around the girl and drew her close.

"Of course not, child. This has nothing to do with you. I have had a dream, a night vision, that calls me to go."

Pigeon brushed away tears. "I don't want you to go." She cuddled more closely.

"Pigeon, I . . . Ah, we must do things sometimes that are hard, no?"

Now there were tears in *her* eyes too.

Pigeon sniffed and wiped the back of her hand across her nose.

"And your dream tells you to go?"

"Yes. Dreams are important."

"I know. . . ."

Of course you do, child, thought Snakewater. *You understand all things.*

"I will miss you, of course," said Pigeon, more calmly now. "My heart is heavy. But *maybe* you will come back?"

"Maybe so." Snakewater smiled.

"But"—Pigeon's face fell again—"I will miss you both."

"Both?"

"Yes, you and Lumpy. He will probably go with you."

"Lumpy?"

As far as she could remember, Snakewater had never mentioned the name. This was very disconcerting, maybe even a bit dangerous.

"What do you know of someone called 'Lumpy'?"

Mischief sparkled again in the dark eyes.

"Why, nothing, really, Grandmother," she teased. "What could I mean?"

Now Snakewater was truly confused. Had Pigeon overheard her talking to the Little Person by name? Possibly . . . or . . . could it be that Pigeon, too, was in contact with the Little People? Not unheard of. She tried to remember a similar conversation with her own mentor, when she first thought she saw a lumpy-looking shadow in the corner. At about Pigeon's age? But it was a conversation that must not go on.

"You make no sense at all, child. I don't know what you're talking about," she scolded.

Pigeon giggled. "Of course not, Grandmother. But I will never tell."

Tell what? Snakewater longed to ask. But she could not do so. The answer to that question would itself break the taboo. Pigeon had led this conversation very skillfully, and in a way, Snakewater was pleased and even proud.

"I know you won't, Pigeon."

An understanding passed wordlessly between them, and it was good. *This child,* thought Snakewater, *has truly received the gift.*

"When will you leave, Grandmother?"

"I don't know, Pigeon. When it's time, I guess."

The departure was delayed as Snakewater made her hurried preparations to accompany the traders. Time, except for the changing of the seasons, was of little serious importance. A little more trading, a social smoke, the readying of Snakewater's mare, the packing of Snakewater's few possessions, all helped to consume most of the day. Tomorrow would be soon enough.

There were two pack animals, in addition to those ridden by the trader and his wife. Snakewater's packs and bundles were easily added to the load of the pack horse.

The other pack animal was a strange looking creature, unfamiliar to Snakewater. It had the long ears of a donkey but the body and legs of a horse. It had startled everyone from time to time with its loud braying call. Snakewater was a little uneasy about it.

"This is a big donkey?" she asked.

"No," laughed Rain Cloud. "It is called a mule. Its sire was a donkey, from which it gets its ears and its voice. Its body and legs, from its mother, a mare. It is very strong and, in some ways, wiser than a horse. It will not overeat like a horse and can go longer without water."

"Where did it come from?"

"Fox traded for it. Before that, I don't know."

"It has worked well," added Fox. "Its long ears and loud voice attract attention."

"And this is good?" asked Snakewater, somewhat puzzled.

"Oh, yes, for a trader. Anything that will gather a crowd. I had thought," he added as he and Cloud expertly looped the hitch on the pack mule's load, "that maybe a wagon would be easier. Maybe we will try that next year."

"Kills Many travels with a wagon," offered Snakewater. "I came here with them last season."

"Yes, I know," said Fox. "I have talked with him. But some of the trails farther west may not be suited to wagons. We will see, this season. Then, maybe next year . . . For now, our pack horses can go anywhere a person can walk upright. Maybe they are better than a wagon, no? We will see."

The mule did travel well, even with a bigger load than the horses. They camped that night without any settlement near. At least none that they knew of. Their start had been a little later than they'd expected. The time to leave had not arrived, so it had become a short day's travel.

Their campsite had obviously been used before, as had most of the stopping places on the ancient trails. Any traveler, stopping for the night, needed the same amenities: water, a level place to sleep, and grass or browse for the animals. Some camping spots became famous in their own right, for an especially good spring, or a magnificent view, or for geographic features that provided safety. Many of these spots later became towns and cities, for the same reasons.

But, for this evening, it was a pleasant place to camp. The horses and the mule, freed of packs and saddles, rolled luxuriously on the ground, and rose to shake themselves free of any debris before beginning to browse.

They quickly established their camp and built a fire. It was not so much for warmth, or even for cooking, but to establish a presence, a permission to camp here. *Here I propose to camp* is the statement that a fire makes. It is a ritual, a contact with any spirits who might dwell here.

Fox opened his pack and tossed a pinch of tobacco on the growing flames as a ritual to honor those same unknown spirits and to ask their help and protection. Snakewater was glad to see this. Those who spend much time in contact with other cultures sometimes forget their own. It was good to see that Fox had not departed from the simple amenities that any traveler should observe. She was sure that the spirits, too, must appreciate such recognition.

There was a twinge of loneliness for a moment as the shadows lengthened. This startled her when she actually thought about it. She had been a lone person by choice for most of her life. It had been only in the last year that she had actually enjoyed the company of other people. Back at Old Town her relationship with Log Roller and Three Fingers, the town chiefs, had been understanding, but mostly business. She had respected and admired both but had not considered either a close friend.

Her closest relationship was that with Kills Many, her almost-son, and that was good. And little Pigeon . . . ah, she had never missed the joy of motherhood until now.

Looking back over the year just past, she found to her surprise that she now almost enjoyed being with people. Except for her old mentor, these friends among whom she had been living were closer to her than any others she had ever known. And all in a single year? She must be changing herself, because surely there must have been *some* people in Old Town worth knowing.

These lonely thoughts whispered through her head as she watched the trader and his wife walk down along the stream, hand in hand. She had felt a shadow of doubt about going off to unknown places with unknown people. But had she not had a dream-vision? And the trader *was* known to Little Horse and his band. Even so, it was a great lift to her spirit to see the couple in this setting, relating to each other with such affection. A slightly bittersweet lift, maybe, since she herself had no one. She sighed, then turned suddenly toward a patch of shadow across the fire.

"*What?* Oh, yes, Lumpy. Yes, I *do.* And I appreciate it. Don't tease me about it."

She was feeling much better, however, by the time twilight deepened and Fox and Rain Cloud returned. Both carried sticks for fuel, and they seemed content with the world.

In such a setting and in such company, who could feel otherwise?

24

The country through which they traveled was rough. Not in the sense of crags and bluffs, though there were many of those along the rivers. This land was a series of hills and ridges, steep yet rounded, and mostly heavily timbered. In some respects it reminded her of the mountainous regions near Old Town.

Fortunately, there were trails or roads, begun centuries before by the hooves of deer and the padded feet of the bear. Even smaller creatures made use of the ancient trails—quail, turkeys, and the foxes, bobcats, and other predators who hunt them—and, Man. Moccasined feet had traveled these paths for countless generations, as man utilized the primitive instincts of his fellow creatures, seeking the easiest way to travel from one place to another. Still more recently the tread of horses' hooves had marked the ancient paths.

In some places there were massive blocks of stone littering the trail, making it necessary for them to thread their way among the fallen slabs from the shelving hillside above.

"I am made to think," said Fox, "that the white man's wagon would not do well here."

The women laughed.

"Maybe," said Rain Cloud, "that is why there are few *yonegs* here. Those who do come are trappers, and they walk or ride horses, as we do."

They stopped to trade at towns along the trails. A day without travel was good for both the travelers and their animals.

"A horse spends much time in eating," Fox explained. "About half the time. But when we travel all day, it is hard for him to get enough to stay fat. Now your mare, there, is an easy keeper. But even she has lost some flesh. Cloud's gelding loses quickly, and so does the pack horse. Rabbit, there, is always fat."

Rabbit was the pet name that the trader used for the mule.

"He calls him that because of his ears," Rain Cloud had explained.

Her husband chuckled. "Well, that and the look on his face," he said.

Snakewater looked. Yes . . . It was not that a mule looks like a rabbit, but that this *individual* animal did. The facial structure, the downturned nose, and the big, suspicious eyes . . . yes, it was easy to see the startled, half-frightened look of a rabbit in the mule's face.

"I like him," Fox said. "He draws attention when he cries out, and a trader needs attention. I was told that a mule is stubborn, but I am made to think this: If Rabbit does not want to do something, there is a reason. A pack is slipping, the trail is unsafe—he sees things that we cannot."

"Things of the spirit?" asked Snakewater.

"Maybe that too," answered Fox, "but I was thinking of his skill on the road."

Snakewater was learning to pack the animals, an entirely new experience for her. There was a rhythm, a sequence for looping the lashing across the packsaddle and the bundles, carefully balanced on each side. It required two persons to accomplish the best job, with short, one-word communication at the proper moment.

"Take slack. . . ."

"Hit!"

Both packers gave the appropriate response, and the four-cornered hitch tightened. Fox was pleased to have another packer. It was not long until any two of the three travelers could quickly load and pack. This eased the tasks of setting up and breaking camp considerably.

"We should have found you before," Cloud told Snakewater. "It is good. But did Fox warn you? Rabbit has a bad habit. There is a place on his flank. I'll show you. . . . Right there."

She gently touched the soft flank just in front of and below the hipbone. The mule jumped and squealed, first hunching his back and tucking his muscular hips under him, then lashing out.

Snakewater had seen horses kick. They often do, in play or in a scuffle for superiority in the herd. Never had she seen anything like this. Both heels struck out, straight behind, as sure as the strike of the rattlesnake and almost as swiftly. Just as swiftly it was over. Rabbit stood quietly, almost sleepily, head drooping lazily with eyes half closed.

"So," laughed Fox, "don't touch him there!"

As they stopped to trade, Snakewater quickly learned some of the traders' secrets. On one occasion Fox was in the final stages. The potential customer had apparently reached what he considered his limit. His array of the items offered lay on the blanket in front of him. In front of Fox, an almost new rifle. It seemed that the bargaining was about to collapse.

"You will offer nothing more? This is a fine gun," lamented Fox, disappointed.

"But it is not new," complained the other. "I do not know if it shoots well."

Just then Rain Cloud passed by, and paused a moment.

"You are trading your favorite rifle for *that*?" She gestured at the assortment of furs on the blanket between the men. "Huh! Your favorite rifle!"

She marched away indignantly.

The customer hesitated only a moment, then gave a deep sigh. He reached into a pack behind him and drew out a beautiful mink pelt, nicely tanned, which he added to the display.

"This is my last offer," he said.

Fox appeared to ponder for a moment, but that was only for appearances.

"Well," he said finally, "if that is your limit . . ."

He lifted the gun almost reverently and handed it across, just a hint of doubt in his expression. One would have thought the weapon a family heirloom. In reality Fox had traded for it only a few days before at another town. He had cleaned and greased it, and added some brass tacks to the stock as decorations.

Snakewater, always observant, watched such proceedings with interest. Human nature, though sometimes unpredictable, is often quite transparent. And in the realm of trade a very slight shift of mood is everything. It becomes a matter of showmanship.

A few days after the episode with the rifle, Snakewater noticed a potential trade that had nearly come to a stalemate. The customer was quite indecisive about some shiny ornaments, and she thought that Fox was becoming impatient. Fox would never show that, of course, but it was slowing the rhythm of the trading.

"Fox," she said abruptly, "I was made to think that your wife wanted to keep those trinkets."

Instantly the item became more desirable. Fox looked irritated, but that, too, was an act. The trade was quickly completed.

"Snakewater, you would make a good trader!" he told her later. "That was well done."

Her other function, that of storytelling, she had not particularly seen as allied to that of the trader. It had been something of a shock to her to find that children were attracted to her. Pigeon had been the reason, initially. But she had found herself associating with the children of West Landing, and *enjoying* them. They, too, enjoyed her. It had been a new experience. All of her life children had feared her and would even run and hide when she approached. Now she admitted sadly to herself, it had been partly her doing. She could throw a furtive look that would make the most determined child quake in his moccasins.

Now, thanks to Pigeon, Snakewater's approach to a child was no longer with a glowering stare, but a friendly smile. She was not quite certain how and when that transformation had taken place, or how and why. But something was happening to her.

"Lumpy, did you have anything to do with that? Don't laugh at me! *Ah!* Go on, then. Disappear, just to show you can."

Irritably she turned to something else. It was futile to waste emotions on the Little People. She recalled, though, that they are said to have a sense of humor. Would that not be a great joke, to watch a grumpy and disagreeable old hag become an attraction to children? Even Snakewater could see the humor involved. She could not share this theory, of course, because Fox and Rain Cloud had not known her before. They would not understand an account of such a transformation. In truth, she did not understand it herself. She only knew that she was becoming a different person.

When they came to a town, children often ran to meet the strangers out of curiosity, usually accompanied by a number of barking dogs announcing their arrival. The children were sometimes shy at first, peering from behind a tree or bush with wide, wondering eyes. Gradually they would become more courageous, venturing into the open and following the travelers toward the central part of the town. No matter what the tribe or nation, usually there was some sort of open area that served as a meeting place. Even white men had a tendency to plan their towns that way, Snakewater noticed. Maybe it was not a matter of planning, though. Towns, she thought, probably just have a tendency to happen, Little Horse's settlement of West Landing being a prime example. That town was Cherokee, but they had passed the towns of several other tribes, and usually stopped to trade. Where there are people, there is the opportunity to trade, Fox reasoned, so why not try? He was cautious about people whose traditions he did not know, and about all white men.

"Some are good," he admitted. "I don't mind trading with them. But there are bad ears in every cornfield, you know. The same with people—red, black, or white. Sometimes a bad crop."

Even with this open-minded approach Snakewater noticed that Fox did not tarry in the white man's towns any longer than necessary. In a town or camp of the Real People he was relaxed and in no hurry. He might even stay an extra day to relax, visit, smoke, and inquire about the road ahead. It was much the same with Choctaw or Muskogee, of which they encountered a few. Others, of unknown background, could often be evaluated in the course of a day of trading. They were usually predictable, which could seldom be said of whites. If the feeling of trust was not there, it was better to move on, no matter what the nationality of the town. This was new territory, with many unknowns, but they were making good contacts that might be profitable for years.

It had become rapidly apparent that the gathering children in a new town were attracted to the new personality of Snakewater. They related to her quickly, and were soon talking with her in a mixture of tongues or in hand signs. She was becoming proficient with sign talk, and usually used signs in addition to the oral narration of her stories. It took very little effort to attract a crowd of listeners for a story fire, both children and adults. The children were always eager to spread the word.

"You like stories?" Snakewater would ask the curious children. "Then come to our fire tonight. Hear some of my stories. Bring your friends, your mother and father!"

Quite often the story fire would be at the town's gathering place, with local storytellers participating as well.

And the gathering of a crowd for any purpose always encouraged a good attendance for the next day's trading.

"It is good!" Fox told her, laughing. "I don't know how we could have traded all these seasons without you. You draw a better crowd than Rabbit!"

25

They traveled westward, through the spring and early summer, stopping to trade as they went. They spent some time in the towns of the Real People, but also among strangers. Missouri, Osage, Wichita . . . people with vastly different customs from their own. They encountered a few white men, mostly French, living among these natives. Usually they had Indian wives and families, and had completely adopted the customs of those with whom they lived.

Trading was good, and Fox kept pushing on westward. They were now depending almost completely on hand signs to communicate. They were learning some of the languages they encountered, but the process was slow and cumbersome compared to the ease of the hand talk that Snakewater used even for telling her stories, which still delighted young and old alike. Among the favorites of all the listeners they met were the tales of Rabbit, the mischievous trickster of the Real People. Rabbit always brought smiles to her listeners' faces. He was agile, quick, and amusing, yet at the same time lazy, indolent, just a bit deceptive . . . *like most of us,* Snakewater reflected, chuckling to herself. We enjoy Rabbit because we see ourselves in his schemes and in his predicaments. Many of his problems are of his own doing, yet we admire his cleverness in devising his escapes.

Maybe, she thought, *the young enjoy Rabbit because of his silliness, and the old because of his wisdom.*

One time Rabbit and Possum decided that they needed wives. They went to a big stomp dance at the town house, where there were many girls. Rabbit danced with all the girls and was very popular, because his attract-medicine is very powerful. He could have his choice of any of the girls there.

Possum, though, has very poor attract-medicine. His nose is too long and his legs too short. His tail is bare and scaly (how he lost his beautiful furry tail is another story). His teeth are ugly and they show when he smiles.

No one would dance with him, and he was so embarrassed that he pretended to faint, and fell down on the floor. He still does this in emergencies, because he isn't much of a fighter either.

The country was changing now. It was midsummer. They were seeing long stretches of treeless grassland, interspersed with dense patches of scrubby oak thickets. Along the streams heavy timber still grew—oak, sycamore, and cottonwood—as well as several kinds of nuts—hickory, pecan, walnut, and a shrubby hazelnut that bore a heavy crop this year.

Snakewater wondered about that. There was a saying that a heavy nut crop means a bad winter ahead. She had often wondered whether it merely means a good summer *now*. Maybe both. A good summer is often followed by a hard winter. The squirrels were beginning to be active—another sign—but were they gathering nuts simply because there *were* more nuts? This line of reasoning brought her back to her starting point. No matter. She would wait until the hickories and pecans ripened. She'd see if their crops were as heavy as those of the hazelnuts, and how the squirrels might respond.

It was necessary, anyway, to prepare every year for the most severe winter that could be imagined. Truly bad winters were rare, but could happen any year. To guess wrongly on such a matter could be fatal.

That was in the future, however. For now she enjoyed the experience of new country, and of an occasional hunt for squirrels with her blowgun. These were different squirrels from those at home around Old Town. There were some that were similar, gray in color and fleet of foot, but most in this area were larger, nearly twice as heavy, and red, like a fox. They were also fat from feasting on hazelnuts, and provided a welcome change in the diet of the three travelers.

Snakewater was enjoying all this newness, but she was also experiencing a strange feeling. It was true especially when she would glimpse a large area of grassland ahead as they topped a hill.

I have seen this before! she would think.

It was not an uncomfortable feeling—rather the opposite. *I am home.* But how could that be true? She had never seen anything like this grassland. She tried to push such feelings aside but with little success.

Then there came a day when Fox, a little way ahead of the others, topped a hill and motioned for the women to join him.

Before them lay an endless rolling prairie, still dotted with scrub oak but more open as they looked westward. Scattered bands of buffalo and elk grazed the tall grasses. Here and there gray wolves circled patiently, waiting for a straggler, an individual too weak or sick to keep up with the moving herds.

Straight in front of them, at a distance of less than half a day's travel, was a village of conical skin tents. There were perhaps thirty of them, randomly scattered. To the south was a stream marked by willows and cottonwoods, darker green than the prairie grasses. In the bend of that stream and beyond, hundreds of horses grazed, loosely herded by young men on horseback.

Snakewater gasped aloud.

"What is it?" asked Rain Cloud, concerned. "Is something wrong?"

"What? Oh . . . I . . . No, not wrong. *Right,* maybe," Snakewater said softly, hardly above a whisper. "Cloud, this is my dream—the one that led me to join you and Fox. But . . ."

Bewildered, she looked up into the bright blue of the summer sky. High overhead a pair of red-tailed hawks circles.

I saw this, she thought with a thrill of excitement. *I saw it, but from up there!*

And, as if in answer, one of the hawks screamed its shrill hunting call. Her heart beat faster, and she smiled.

"Yes . . . thank you, my brother," she whispered.

A pair of well-armed young men rode out to greet them.

Fox halted his little procession and they waited for the approach of the scouts.

"These are called 'wolves,'" said Fox quietly.

"Wolves? But why?" asked Snakewater.

"They circle the camp, or the traveling column as they move, as wolves circle a buffalo herd. For a different purpose, of course." He smiled. "These 'wolves' are for protection, not to prey on stragglers. I think it is a joke, in their tongue."

"You speak their tongue?"

"No, no. I do not know who these might be. But they will use hand signs."

As if to prove the point the young "wolves" drew rein a few paces from where Fox sat on his horse, his right hand lifted, palm forward. The empty hand, holding no weapon, served as both a greeting and a reassurance, *I come in peace.*

The more forward of the young men, who would apparently do the communicating, sat unmoving for a few moments. This for the purpose of maintaining control of the situation. He could keep the newcomers slightly in doubt, a trifle off balance, guessing about their reception. This "wolf" had handled such a situation before.

What do you want? he indicated with the sign for a question. It was quickly followed by another question. *How are you called?* (Or, *Who are you?*)

We are traders, signed Fox. *I am called "Fox," but "Trader" comes easier. This, my wife*—he indicated Cloud *the other, my mother.*

Snakewater was not sure that she welcomed such a designation, but understood its use. There was no purpose in trying to explain the relationship any further.

You have trade goods? asked the young man, gesturing toward the pack animals. Then he seemed to notice the mule for the first time.

"Aiee!" he said aloud. Then in hand signs: *What is that?*

It was apparent that they had not seen a mule before. As if in answer Rabbit, impatient at the delay in stopping for the night, raised his head in a long, loud protesting bellow. The horses of the scouts jumped away in terror, that of the spokesman bucking for a few steps. He quickly regained control and glanced around angrily.

He will do no harm, Fox signed quickly. *It is his way of speaking.*

The other man still appeared suspicious but was calming somewhat. Now he showed interest in the fact that the mule was calmly grazing.

It is much like a horse? he signed.

Yes, replied Fox. *I was about to tell you. My horse died, and we caught this large rabbit to carry packs. . . .*

Suspicion still stiffened the expression on the face of the scout. Then he suddenly seemed to realize that it was a joke. He smiled.

A very loud rabbit! he signed, a sarcastic look on his face. *Come on . . . I will take you to our chief.*

"How do they have a meeting with no town house?" asked Snakewater.

"Outside, when the weather is good," Fox explained. "But there is room for many in one of the big lodges. The leaders meet in the house of the chieftain. We will go there now."

As it happened, they had no chance to enter the lodge of the chief. As they entered the camp, Rabbit once more announced his presence, scattering children and dogs like quail. People popped out of lodges, some with weapons ready. Their escort called something to the crowd, and the expressions of fear or concern began to change. For a few moments there was puzzlement, gradually changing to humor as the people began to realize that there was no danger. The young scout called out again, and there was general laughter.

I told them, he signed, *that the trader has a large singing rabbit to attract a crowd.*

"I am made to think," said Fox to the two women, "that trading here should be good."

They were escorted to the lodge of the band's chieftain, who was a handsome man of middle age.

"Ah-koh!" said the man aloud.

"Ah-koh," answered Fox. Then, in hand signs, *We do not speak your tongue, Uncle, but we come to trade. I am called Fox, or Trader.*

So I have heard, signed the chief, with a sweeping gesture at the crowd that now followed the trader's party.

I have some gifts, said Fox in hand signs. He reached into his small pack and took out a knife and a couple of small mirrors. *How many wives have you?* He gestured with the mirrors.

Only two.

An attractive young woman looked out the door of the lodge and ducked back inside.

My daughter, explained the chief.

She deserves a mirror, too, Fox stated, bringing out another.

It is good, signed the chief, obviously pleased. *Camp with us, trader! I am called Far Thunder.*

"I am made to think," said Fox to the women, "that we will like these people."

26

These people, the travelers learned, called themselves the People, as did most others, in their own tongues. Just as the Cherokees consider themselves the Real People, so do most groups consider themselves *the* People. It was no different here.

They learned also that this was the Southern band of a far-flung nation. Their neighbors sometimes called them the "Elk-dog People," and the hand sign for this nation was that of a horse. They had been among the first in the Southern Plains to acquire the horse, many generations ago, it was said.

There were several other bands, some as far west as the mountains, and others to the north and east, as far as "twenty sleeps" away. All of these bands met annually for the Sun Dance, to celebrate the return of the sun, the grass, and the buffalo. These were hunters, nomads who could move when and where they decided with their skin tents.

It was hard for Snakewater to imagine a people who grew no crops, since the Real People had been farmers almost since creation.

Fox had been in contact with such people before and helped her to understand.

"But . . . where do they buy corn, pumpkins, beans?" Snakewater asked in confusion.

"They trade," explained Fox. "They use all parts of the buffalo. Skins for their lodges and for clothing, or tanned with the fur on for robes. Meat, dried or made into pemmican. Even the bones and horns are used, for tools and weapons. What they don't need for themselves, they trade to the growers in exchange for corn and beans.

"Growers?"

"Yes—Kaw, Wichita, Omaha. Those who farm."

"But they hunt too."

"Of course. Like the Cherokee. But for these the hunt is the main—no, the *only* thing. Well, they trap some furs in the winter. But you can see how important the buffalo become to people such as these."

Snakewater could not have explained it. It was completely illogical, but since they first came over the rise and saw the endless grassland stretched before them, she had felt at home. She had felt such contentment only a few times before. *No, only once,* she thought, when she had seen this strange country of far horizons as part of her night vision. There had been an excitement, a thrill, but at the same time a calm reassurance. Somehow she knew that for these people, it was the same. They were one with this land, a part of it. She wished to learn more about them.

That opportunity arose quickly as evening came and people drifted together for a story fire. It was not a planned or announced event, just something that it was assumed would happen. Snakewater had become familiar with this process as they traveled, and as her role of storyteller grew.

One question never failed to arise when they camped with strangers: How did *your* people come into the world? Each would tell the story as handed down among his or her own people. Sometimes there were striking similarities, sometimes an even more astonishing variety. Most of the people she had encountered since crossing the Big River had originated from inside the earth, she noticed. Usually through a hole, sometimes in a sacred place, but, in all cases, through an entrance into the outer world that was no longer open. Some specific event had closed the hole long ago. Sometimes they had come up through the waters of a lake or pond, the exact location now lost.

She always started with her own, the story of the Real People. By contrast with the origin stories of others, theirs related how the Real People started at the top of the inverted bowl of the Sky Dome, looking down at endless waters below. It was crowded on the top of the dome, with all the animals and plants and the Real People. They wondered what was below the water. Beaver volunteered to go and see, but he failed. Then Loon, the diving water bird, and he, too, was unsuccessful. Finally the little Water Beetle, whom the Cherokees call "beaver's grandchild," dived very deep and brought up a little dab of mud, which he spread on the water. Then another, and another, until an island grew and became Earth.

The One Above, Maker of all things, saw that this was good and helped the people by fastening a cord to each corner of the Earth, suspending it from the sky dome so that it would not sink back into the water. But it was still wet and boggy, so the people asked Buzzard to fly over it and fan it dry with his great wings. When he became tired, Buzzard's wingtips sometimes struck the drying mud, and this is why we have mountains and valleys. Is it not so?

Snakewater finished her signing, among exclamations of astonishment, and an old man, obviously the storyteller of Far Thunder's band, cleared his throat. Every eye turned toward him, indicating that he was greatly respected among his people. He spoke both aloud in his own tongue, and in hand signs for the travelers.

Theirs was a good story, he admitted. He had a few questions. . . .

"What happens when the cords grow brittle and old—those that hold the earth from sinking?"

There was a murmur of interest, with a little concern.

"When the world grows old and worn out," Snakewater explained, "all the people will die. The cords will break and the Earth sinks into the ocean again. But that is a long while away."

"That is to be hoped!" said the old storyteller, a twinkle in his eye. "Now, here is our story. Our people were inside the earth, and it was dark and cold. Then a man saw a light and climbed toward it. He was helped by a sound from above, a *thump-thump-thump.* There was a round tunnel with the light at the end, and he crawled through into the sunlight. This was First Man, and his wife, First Woman, followed him. Then they saw what was making the thumping sound. They had crawled through a hollow cottonwood log. An old man sat astride the log, holding a drumstick. And, now, each time he thumped the log, another person crawled out into the light. These are our people."

The storyteller paused, and there was an air of expectancy. There must be more to the story. *What happened next?* Snakewater wanted to ask. But it was Fox whose curiosity could not be contained.

Are they still coming through? he signed.

Ah, no, the storyteller answered. *It was unfortunate. After a while a fat woman became stuck in the log. No more could come through. That is why we have always been a small nation!*

There was a roar of laughter. It became apparent that this was a private joke among these people. Everybody except a stranger would know about Fat Woman. It would be a joke on the stranger, who could usually be counted on to ask, as Fox had done.

Fox laughed good-naturedly with the crowd, realizing that he had been the butt of the joke.

Snakewater was quite amused and a little bit startled at her enjoyment of it. Never, in her old lifetime, had she enjoyed such things. Her mentor had been a sour old woman, she now realized. There had not been much pleasure or enjoyment in her own life until she had made the break away from Old Town. Maybe a sense of humor was a part of the new person she had become. . . .

Snakewater found that she related well to these people of the prairie. There had been a time when she would have considered them backward and uncivilized, compared to the Real People. Now, with more experience, having had contact with several separate cultures, each different from the other, she had some basis for comparison. Far from being a primitive band of savages, these people had a highly complicated civilization. Not *lesser* than her own, but *different.* In some ways, as intricate as that of the Real People.

Their skill with horses was astonishing to watch, and well it might be. Their entire lives were built around the hunting of the buffalo, and the horse was necessary for that purpose. It made her wonder how they had managed *before* the white man brought the horse.

Their skin tents, which Snakewater had always considered a primitive makeshift, now astonished her. She had heard of this contraption all of her life, and had even seen small examples used by some people as seasonal shelters while traveling. But it was not at all what she had imagined. Some of the lodges in Far Thunder's camp were made from thirty or more buffalo skins sewn together. As many as fifteen or twenty people could easily be seated in many of the structures.

In addition there were complicated rules and customs for putting up or taking down the lodges. It was almost a ritual. She was to learn much of this later, but for now certain things were easily apparent. All the doorways faced eastward. . . . Why? *It must be so.* Not only custom and tradition, but a *requirement.* Well, she would learn more of that later too.

Meanwhile she found that as she liked these people, apparently Fox did too. Trading was good, and Fox showed no signs of impatience to move on, as he sometimes did among other people. The hospitality was warm and generous, and the exchange of stories was pleasant. Their sense of humor was enjoyable and quick.

Linked closely to all of this was a feeling that these people were a part of the grassland. Its far horizons and its spirit had impressed her powerfully, both in her dream vision and when she first saw it in reality. She had thought that such an impression might fade, but it had not. It was still as thrilling and exciting as her first view when they topped the rise. The prairie was always changing too. The changing light produced new colors and patterns of shadow constantly, from the time she rose to go to water until darkness fell, and even beyond. She had never seen stars so many and so bright.

On their fourth night in the camp the moon rose nearly full. The story fire lasted until late, but after the gathering broke up Snake-water was still reluctant to retire. There was an excitement in the air, a feeling that if she sought her blankets now, she might miss some-thing. Maybe the best part of the night, when some marvelous event might occur that would open to her all the mysteries of creation. She could not risk it. She walked in the moonlight, down along the stream and then up to the crest of a low rise overlooking the scatter of lodges below.

There were night sounds. . . . Insects, night birds, the whicker of a raccoon in the trees downstream . . . A distant coyote, and the hollow call of a hunting owl. The whole scene should have been new and unfamiliar to her, yet it all seemed to fit into place, as if she had experienced it before. Possibly many times before. It was a strange yet comforting feeling. She sat on a limestone ledge that projected out of the slope, still warm from the sun. She drank in the feeling, calming, yet at the same time exciting.

Then she spoke aloud, to a spot beside her that to anyone else would have appeared empty.

"Yes, Lumpy . . . Of course I feel it," she said softly.

27

She hoped that Fox would decide to stay a little longer with these people. Already she was feeling a strange kinship.

Fox seemed in no hurry to leave. He and Rain Cloud, too, seemed to be enjoying this stay, though not with the same strange attraction that Snakewater felt.

"Maybe another day or two," Fox would say.

But the trading was still good, and the weather continued to be favorable. There was nothing urgent to cause Fox to become restless, and Snakewater was glad.

Nothing had been said about wintering. She had originally thought to look at some of the towns of the Real People with the idea of settling there, but none had really appealed to her. This, too, puzzled her. Maybe it would be best to go back to West Landing with Fox and Rain Cloud. She knew people there, and she was respected both for her skills as a conjuror and for her storytelling.

But that might be risky. Someone would turn up who remembered the circumstances under which she had left Old Town. Besides, Fox had not yet mentioned whether he intended to return that way. Or, she now thought suddenly, whether he intended to return at all.

Could he be planning to winter here, with these people? Then yet another thought struck her. They had no idea when this nomadic band of Far Thunder's people might decide to move, and *where.* Where would they winter? Snakewater was not accustomed even to think about such things, but now she began to realize that she needed to ask some questions. Hers was a rather precarious situation, with no family or close kin. She was respected as a storyteller, but for some time she had not had an opportunity to practice her conjure skills or exercise her healing powers. Her bundles of herbs and roots lay in her packs, neglected.

The incident that began to resolve her problems was as strange as all the other events that had affected her life since she'd left Old Town. She sometimes felt that she had no control at all, and was somehow being drawn in directions that seemed to make no sense.

She was sitting by the fire in their temporary camp when it happened. She and Cloud had erected a small lean-to of willow branches to furnish a bit of afternoon shade. Both Fox and Cloud were elsewhere at the moment, and Snakewater was relaxing in the comfort of the arbor.

From where she sat, she could see much of the camp. Most families had untied the bottom edges of their lodge covers and rolled up the skins like lifted skirts to let the cooling breezes of the prairie drift through. This provided shade and comfort, and the lodge covers could be quickly rolled down in case of an approaching storm. She was impressed with the versatility of these dwellings, though she still had doubts about how they would fare in winter.

She saw Far Thunder rise from the willow backrest in front of his lodge. He made his way among the scattered dwellings, around cooking fires, playing children, and sleeping dogs. She wondered idly where he was going. Suddenly her eyes seemed to be playing tricks on her. The chieftain had been obscured from her sight for a moment while he passed behind one of the lodges. When he emerged on the other side, her eyes blurred somehow, and Far Thunder seemed to be in two parts. His upper body continued along his course. His legs and hips did also, moving normally, but *a step behind his torso!* She gasped and rubbed her eyes. . . . A trick of vision, an illusion . . . No, it was so. . . .

Then the two images came together again, smoothly and uneventfully, and Far Thunder walked as before, apparently whole and hearty. Her heart raced. . . . There was meaning here, a serious situation, but she was caught off guard and confused. Somewhere in her past this had happened before, in exactly that way. Was she reliving this whole scene? No, that could not be. When she had seen it before—in a dream? No, it had been real, but the setting different. Not a village of skin lodges, but in a town . . . *Old Town!* Yes . . . Many years ago It was coming back swiftly now, in bits and pieces.

She had been hardly more than a child, or in her early teens, and she was living with the old conjure woman already. That had been one of the events that led her mentor to begin to share her medicine skills.

A man had walked past their hut with this same dissociated image, and the girl (she was called Corn Flower then) had gasped in astonishment. There had been a moment of silence and then the old woman spoke:

"You *saw* that too?"

The girl nodded, confused.

"Yes . . . I . . ."

"Ah! As I suspected. You do have the gift, then. Very well, I will teach you."

She could not remember much more except that the old woman had, at about that time, begun to instruct her in many things. They had already discussed the Little People.

But, yes, it was coming back, now. The man (was it not Whips Along?) had been torn apart by a problem. Maybe it was a thing of the spirit, or maybe something physical. She could not remember. Possibly both, for one influences the other until they are one, anyway. And there were specific remedies. That part she remembered well.

A special smoke for the pain involved, if necessary, a conjure ceremony, and a healing potion of herbs. She thought she had the proper components.

Now, how to approach the problem? Normally people would approach *her* for such purposes. Here she was a guest in the camp of which Far Thunder was the leader. Would he be offended if she approached him?

She spent a restless night in doubt as to how, when, and *whether* to act. Surely there must be some tradition and manner of treatment for such things among these people. There was the old holy man, White Buffalo, but his medicine seemed far removed from hers. She gathered that the name had been handed down with the office for many generations. The people seemed to regard the old man with great respect. His medicine must be very powerful.

But it was *different.* The power of White Buffalo's medicine had to do with the buffalo, the knowledge of the movements of the great herds, and their annual return . . . with the grass, and the sun and the buffalo, around which their lives revolved.

Possibly they had healers among them. Probably so. She could inquire.

There was no one, she was told in hand signs.

Is there something you need?

No, no, not for myself. I do a little medicine, she signed quickly.

We once had an owl prophet, answered the woman whom she had asked. *He is with the Eastern band now. A good move. He was foolish, which will make him at home with them.* The woman laughed.

Such a remark was puzzling to Snakewater. The conversation, in hand signs, was difficult enough to follow. There must be some sort of inside joke about the Eastern band and foolishness. She could ask about that later.

But for now she was concerned. This was a serious situation. Serious enough, in fact, that she was certain something must be done. If there was no one else, then it must be meant as her responsibility.

With determination she made her way to the lodge of Far Thunder and shook the deer-hoof rattle beside the door.

"Who is it?" came the answer from inside, in the tongue of those inside. At least that was assumed to be the response.

"Snakewater," she answered. "I would speak with Far Thunder."

There was little chance that those inside would understand the words, but surely her meaning would be clear. She had identified herself and had asked to see the chief by name.

A woman looked out, nodded in acknowledgment of Snakewater's presence, and withdrew. A few words were exchanged, and then Far Thunder himself stooped to exit the lodge. He straightened to full height and faced her.

What is it? he signed.

His face looked tired and drawn, and his color was poor, his skin grayish in tone rather than the ruddy gold that marked the countenance of most people here.

Snakewater took a deep breath. This would be difficult at best, but in hand signs . . . ?

I am made to think, she signed slowly, *that you are troubled. You need my help.*

It appeared that Far Thunder was ready to laugh, but then his face softened.

What do you know of this? You are a medicine woman?

I do a little medicine, she answered. *I can help, maybe.*

There was a long pause, as the chief pondered. Then he signed again.

You are Cherokee, no?

She nodded.

We must talk better, he signed. *There is a man . . .*

He turned and called something inside the lodge, and a young man emerged with a puzzled look on his face. Far Thunder gave him quick instructions, and the boy trotted away.

Wait a little, signed Thunder.

It was only a short while before the boy returned with a man of about thirty, who wore a puzzled or curious look on his face. He spoke to Far Thunder, and a brief conversation ensued. The man nodded understanding and then turned to Snakewater.

"I am Chases the Dog," he introduced himself in Cherokee. "I wintered with your people once, in the mountains." He pointed west.

Snakewater nodded. She was aware that there was a small colony of the Real People far to the west. The accent of this man was a trifle different from her own. His speech was also a bit halting from disuse, it seemed.

"Far Thunder says that you would speak with him, and you need an interpreter. You are a medicine woman? A conjuror?"

"I do a little medicine," she answered quickly. "And, yes, he needs my help. His person comes apart."

Dog Chaser relayed this information, and the chief nodded, still suspiciously. The two men conversed briefly.

"How do you know this?" asked the interpreter.

"I have seen it," she answered, looking straight into the chief's drawn face. "I can help."

There was another conversation, which seemed almost endless to her. Finally Chases the Dog turned to her again.

"What would you do?"

"He must tell me a little more of how he feels. It might require a conjure . . . a potion. . . ."

More talk. Then the interpreter turned to her again.

"Thunder wants to know . . . can you stop the pain in his head?"

She turned to the chief, looked him full in the face, and answered in hand signs.

I don't know. But I can help it.

It is good, answered Far Thunder. *Do it.*

He turned and spoke to the interpreter, who relayed the more complete message.

"He asks when, where, and what do you need?"

"Tell him it will take some time, several days, maybe longer. I have the herbs I need."

The chief nodded as this information was relayed.

Let it be so, he signed.

About the only necessary item she didn't have was a few bits of wood from a tree struck by lightning. She had noticed a craggy old cottonwood on a rise a few bow shots outside the camp. She walked up that way and found that her guess was correct. A cottonwood in the open always draws lightning. Yes—there . . .

Down one side of the massive trunk was a slash, a hand's breath in width and running upward to the tallest branches. It had stripped the bark and blasted chunks of wood away from the heart of the tree. Most of the fallen branches that usually lie around an old cottonwood had been carried off for fuel. But she managed to pry out a few sizable slivers from the scarred stripe itself. They would be sufficient, she thought.

As she returned to the camp, she was met by Rain Cloud.

"Where have you been? I was looking for you. Fox wants to leave early tomorrow. We must be ready."

28

"Cloud . . . I can't go."

"What?"

"I can't go. I am needed here."

"I don't understand. . . ."

"Neither do I, but it is meant to be. Come, I must tell Fox."

Fox was sympathetic. He nodded as she explained.

". . . and I am made to think that this was meant for me to do."

"Yes . . . we must do what calls us," he agreed. "My heart is heavy, Snakewater, but I understand. You will winter here, then?"

She had not even had a thought for that far ahead.

"I don't know, Fox. What will happen will happen."

"We may come this way next season. We will ask about you."

"These people may be elsewhere next season, Fox," protested Cloud. "They move often."

"No matter," said Snakewater. "I will be somewhere. I cannot plan next year yet!"

Such reassurance was largely for herself. Snakewater had begun to think that she had some part in the direction of her life, but now it seemed otherwise. This was somewhat disconcerting. But things happen. . . .

"I will help you pack," she told Fox.

That very evening she began the treatment for Far Thunder. To avoid any distraction this first ritual would be carried out well away from the camp. Dog Chaser was called upon to explain to Thunder and his family what was to be done and what was expected. Thunder's principal wife was present to observe.

This part is to help the pain, Snakewater signed. *The rest comes later.*

She kindled a small fire, offered a pinch of tobacco to any spirits who might be lingering in the area, and offered a ritual prayer in her own tongue. Her fire, made of small twigs and a few larger sticks, quickly burned down to coals. She raked them together, and carefully began to add a few splinters and shards of the wood from the lightning-blasted cottonwood tree. She had soaked these in water, because they must not burn too fast. Their smoke was more desirable than their light or heat.

She had positioned the fire and the reclining Thunder so that he would be near and slightly downwind from the smoke. It was a still evening, however, and the soft south breeze unreliable. She drew out a fan, made from the wing of a hawk, and gently wafted the healing smoke in his direction. Not too much . . . just a hint, to help remove the pain in the patient's head so that the healing could begin. Far Thunder coughed once, and she quickly used her fan to thin the denseness of the smoke. *Ah!* Now it was moving properly, drifting gently and thinly past his face. The songs of the night creatures provided a calming background for Snakewater's ritual prayer.

The fire broke into a blaze, and she sprinkled it with water. The lightning-blasted shards must not be consumed too quickly. Still, she needed to heat some water. . . . Maybe she should have had two fires. . . . No, there would be enough heat. . . . She added fuel to one side and allowed it to blaze up, setting her small pan of water on a couple of stones over that source of heat.

When the water began to simmer, she removed the pan and sprinkled some rubbed herbs into it, setting it aside to cool. She continued to waft the smoke from the other side of the fire toward Far Thunder's face.

It was completely dark now, and she saw the blood-red arc of the moon's rim start to creep up under the eastern edge of the sky dome. It was only a little past full, and she wondered if that would affect her ceremony. She was not certain, but she decided that it would probably not interfere and might even help. Far Thunder's face appeared peaceful in the growing light of the rising moon.

She roused him to drink a little tea, and helped him to lie back again on the pallet of robes and blankets. She covered him with one of the blankets against the chill of the prairie night.

Thunder's wife spoke a few words in her own tongue, very softly, and Dog Chaser interpreted.

"She says his face is peaceful. . . . His head pain is gone, and he sleeps!"

Snakewater nodded. "Tell her that this is the beginning. He must drink the tea each day. . . . If the pain returns, we can do the smoke again."

Dog Chaser nodded and conveyed the information to Thunder's wife, Swan, who nodded understanding.

"Let us allow him to sleep," Snakewater whispered, accompanying her words with hand signs. The wife nodded.

It is good, she signed, as the chief began to snore softly.

Snakewater had been glad to learn that among these prairie people there was a custom much like the "going to water" of the Real People. While not so ritualized, it was a well-established practice. When morning came, a quick dip in the stream was the accepted norm if at all practical. This was good and should be of help in the process of Far Thunder's healing. She was not certain how the ceremonies and practices of her people would apply to members of another culture. But surely no harm could come as long as there was no violation of *their* customs. Her ceremony had seemed to work well for Far Thunder.

When they rose in the morning, she suggested in hand signs that Thunder go to water, and he nodded. Dog Chaser had returned to his own lodge for the night, and the two women had spent most of the time watching the sleeping Far Thunder. Snakewater had tended her fire, adding a few sticks and some of her precious lightning-blasted wood to keep the healing smoke alive. Thunder's wife had drowsed from time to time as he slept.

But now it was daylight. Snakewater went to bid good-bye to the traders and to assure them that she would be all right.

"Our trails will cross again," she promised. "For now, Far Thunder has asked me to stay in his lodge."

"He is better, then?" asked Cloud.

"Yes, the head pain . . . There is more to do, but it will take time. May your journey be a good one!"

She watched them out of sight, and waved as Fox turned to swing an arm overhead in a farewell gesture as they crossed the low ridge outside the camp.

"I will miss them, Lumpy."

The next few days were spent in preparing the potions of herbs that were intended to help with Far Thunder's problems. There were times when Snakewater felt it ridiculous to have stayed behind. She could have prepared the herbs and left them for him to use. She quickly rejected the thought, though. Her presence was necessary, in a sense, to make the conjure work. She must be able to observe her results, to adjust the potions as needed. Besides, it was not merely a matter of physically providing the medicinal herbs. A major part of the power of her position was her own interaction in the ceremony and the resulting healing process.

She was uneasy, never having undertaken such a task as this. Not only was there a question in her mind as to whether her medicine would be effective in this, another culture far removed from her own. Would the spells and conjures work? She even had doubts about whether her own *doubt* might weaken the power given her. Added to all this, the inability to communicate . . .

That was worst of all. In making medicine for any of the Real People, she had always had the luxury of being able to explain as much as she needed. Now, unless Chases the Dog was present, she had only signs. Even so, it seemed to be working. Far Thunder was looking better each day. She must be doing something right.

A few days later she climbed the rise behind the camp, to the area near the old cottonwood tree. It would be a good plan to have a few shards of the lightning-blasted wood in case Far Thunder's headaches returned.

She gathered what fragments she needed, placed them in her bag, and sat down to ponder a little while. It was hard for her, who had lived alone for many years, to move into an active and noisy household, the lodge of Far Thunder. The most frustrating thing was her inability to communicate, she thought. No, maybe not . . . even worse was the fact that she had no idea how long this situation would last, or what she would do after that.

She roused from her distant thoughts. . . .

"What? Oh, yes, Lumpy . . . very crowded. But you don't have to try to *talk* to them, as I do. That's true, I chose to do so—what else could I do?"

She paused a little while and seemed to resign herself. Then she spoke again.

"Yes, I know. I must learn their tongue. . . . Yes, as quickly as I can. . . . Damn you, Lumpy, don't tease me. I"m too old for this!"

The lodge of Far Thunder was a busy place at best. She had met Swan, his First Wife, the night of the pain-smoke ceremony. The Second Wife, Walks Alone, was the mother of several of the children who seemed to be always underfoot. There were seven youngsters in all, ranging from a handsome young man of perhaps twelve summers to a small baby, who obviously belonged to Thunder's *Third* Wife, since she suckled him. All of these children looked much alike, and all answered to the instruction of any of the women.

It was some time before Snakewater learned most of the facts about these relationships. Walks Alone, the Second Wife, was a sister to First Wife. The husband of Walks Alone had been killed in a skirmish with white men on the old southwest road. It had been a misunderstanding, according to information learned later, but Red Moccasin was just as dead. His widow, after a season of "walking alone," had moved into the lodge of her sister and had become Second Wife to Far Thunder. The oldest girl in Thunder's lodge was a child of Walks Alone by her first marriage. She had been adopted by Far Thunder.

Third Wife, a younger woman, had wandered into their camp, lost and half starved, and with incomplete memories of who she was or where she had come from. There was evidence that she had been abused, Snakewater was told. She had apparently escaped her captors and survived on her own until she walked into the camp of Far Thunder. The women had taken her in, and after her recovery she had become Third Wife.

All of this Snakewater learned over time. She was familiar with the general principles of households like this, but such a situation had seldom occurred among the Real People in modern times, even at Old Town.

But in a situation where there are more women than men, what better answer could there be? Although Thunder's lodge sometimes seemed like bedlam to the solitary Snakewater, its occupants appeared healthy and reasonably happy. Thunder was improving. What more could a family want?

29

As Far Thunder's condition improved, he began to appear restless. It seemed that his illness had progressed so slowly that no one had noticed it. Especially himself. Now Snakewater was just beginning to see what a dynamic leader Thunder could be.

She was learning their language. It was sometimes a frustrating effort, but she realized her tendency to become impatient with *any* situation. She *was* learning, and continued to do so. She understood more than she could speak, of course. This led her to hear a conversation between two of Thunder's wives one afternoon while he was enjoying a smoke in front of a friend's lodge some distance away.

"He will want to move soon," said Walks Alone to the others.

"Yes," agreed Swan. "I can see him become impatient."

"He does that," agreed Wife Number Two. "But the camp *is* becoming dirty."

With scores of people and even more dogs a camp such as this could, over a short period of time, become quite odorous. A campsite was chosen for its setting, and with great care. Requirements must include grass for the several hundred horses, as well as water for both people and animals. The location and purpose of this water was perhaps the most important factor. The source of drinking water must be upstream from all else. Below that, an area for washing cooking pots and pans, clothing, and other personal items. Still farther downstream the horse herd could water.

There was an area loosely designated for the emptying of bladders and bowels, somewhat segregated by gender. There was little formality in these matters. Dogs, of course, were even less formal in the way they relieved themselves. In hot weather a camp of these buffalo hunters could become quite fragrant. A move was indicated when any of several conditions occurred: grass for the horses was depleted, water supply threatened to dry up, hunting was poor, or the odor and the flies began to offend the sensibilities of the leaders.

Snakewater was quickly learning the ways of a people completely unfamiliar to her. The discussion of the wives served partly to instruct, partly to verify her own observation.

She also began to see more clearly her own status as a guest in the lodge of Far Thunder. It would not be appropriate for a woman other than a wife to be living in the lodge of a man. *Except*, of course, for her age. This conferred on her a different status. One of the first words she learned in the language of these prairie people proved to be *Grandmother*. This was her title and her status among the people of Far Thunder's camp. She was Grandmother, she who had never been a mother, and she found this amusing.

She found, too, that she retained her position as a storyteller, even as she regained respect as a healer. Word of the recovery of Far Thunder had spread quickly through the camp. There was much shaking of heads as people realized, after the fact, that their leader had not been at his best for some time. Now he had been restored to them, and the tone of the camp had changed. Before, the mood had been steady, even good. But now, with the anticipation of a coming move, there was an air of excitement, partly attributable to the change in their leader, Far Thunder. For this, credit was given to Snakewater, the Grandmother who now dwelt in his lodge. It now appeared that she was not only a storyteller, pleasing young and old alike, but a skilled healer. Increasingly, people began to seek her advice for minor illnesses and injuries. There were requests for potions and spells, and it seemed that she had found her place. She found, too, that she enjoyed having the children around her in Thunder's lodge. One little girl reminded her of Pigeon, back in West Landing. She did wonder sometimes how Pigeon was doing. But all in all life was good.

The move would take place three days from now, at daybreak, it was announced. There was a flurry of activity. Everyone had something to do, or repair, or accomplish, before the journey was attempted.

"Where will we go?" asked Snakewater, somewhat confused by all this activity.

"Who knows?" answered Swan. "We will know when we arrive."

"South," suggested the Second Wife.

"Oh, yes!" agreed Swan. "Probably winter camp, though it's a bit early. Maybe one more move."

It was the Moon of Ripening for the prairie people, September by the calendar of the white man. The word passed quickly that they would head south and west, toward an area where they had wintered before—an area where scrub oaks met tallgrass prairie. The oaks, keeping their leaves through the moons of snow, would furnish some shelter from the freezing blasts of winter. They would pause en route to hunt as opportunity offered. They could camp for a few days, or a few weeks if needed, to process the bounty of a successful buffalo hunt. It was expected that they would encounter herds on the move.

There seemed to be no order or chain of command for the day of the move. At daylight the big lodges began to come down. People called to each other, children ran, dogs barked, horses whinnied. . . . The whole scene reminded Snakewater of an anthill when someone had swept a branch across it, destroying its integrity. There seemed to be no general purpose, and chaos reigned. If any goal was distinguishable, it must be to become one of the first families in line.

Very quickly horses were brought. The lodgepoles that had formed the frames of the tepees now became part of the transport system. Fastened in pairs and placed across the horse's withers, they formed a drag upon which a platform could be tied, made of shorter poles. Baggage, possessions, small children, and sometimes the elderly or infirm would ride on the platform of this *travois.* A horse dragging a travois could also be ridden by a woman, who could in that way supervise the movement of her household goods.

"Will you wish to ride a travois, Grandmother?" asked one of the wives.

"Of course not," Snakewater said tersely, sounding more irritated than she actually intended. If bumping in a wagon was uncomfortable, how much worse one of the pole-drags must be to aging bones!

"I will ride my horse," she answered more gently. "But could my packs be placed on one of the travois?"

"Of course, Grandmother," said Far Thunder, amused at the interchange, "and one of the young men will bring your horse when they bring ours. A gray mare, no?"

"Yes. My saddle is here. Thank you."

Families began to form a loose column for travel. The first to be prepared were already out in the prairie a couple of bow shots away, waiting for others to fall in behind them. Snakewater marveled at the quick efficiency with which the women could spread and fold the big lodge covers. Most were canvas. *Times change, even here,* she reflected. The canvas lodge covers were lighter and easier to fold, and represented progress.

The sun was still not far above the eastern horizon when the column began to move. Out in front rode a pair of scouts, well ahead of Far Thunder and a couple of subchiefs. Other "wolves" rode parallel to the flanks of the column, sometimes even out of sight, constantly on the alert for danger or for game, or both.

Far in the rear straggled the back of the column. There are those who from habit or general inadequacy for any situation always gravitate to that position, eating the dust of the more competent members of society. Some even appear happy in this position, since it avoids a certain amount of responsibility.

On the downwind side from the column, parallel to it and slightly behind, traveled the horse herd, pushed along by a number of young men. They were not old enough to be classed as warriors, but were proud to be entrusted with this responsibility. For some it would be their first as members approaching adulthood.

By midmorning the caravan had settled in to steady, efficient travel.

As the sun began to sink toward the western horizon, a scout rode back to inform the leaders that a campsite was ahead. Water, grass, fuel in the form of dried buffalo dung.

"Any buffalo?" inquired Far Thunder.

"No. Only dung," the scout answered.

"No matter. We will find the herds later."

The scout nodded and rode off.

By the time shadows lengthened, they had reached the proposed night camp. It was a pleasant setting, with a hilltop well suited for observation by one or two sentries.

In a short while the individual campfires of the various family groups began to blossom. The weather was good, so the lodges would not be erected. Some constructed meager shelters of branches from the scrubby willows along the creek, but most chose to sleep under the open sky. Everyone was tired from the day's travel, and after darkness fell, the camp quieted quickly. Snakewater remained awake for a long time, listening to the somewhat unfamiliar night sounds. She never could have imagined herself in this setting, yet she felt a thrill of excitement at the thought of unknown vistas.

As last, tired and a bit stiff from the long day on horseback, she fell asleep to the song of distant coyotes.

It was about midmorning when a scout from the left of the column rode in to confer with the chiefs. It took only a moment to make the decision. The column would halt. Several warriors rode back along the column to spread the word.

"Close up the spaces . . . stay close together. . . ."

Toward the back of the column, "Come on, catch up. There may be danger!"

"What is it?"

"Another column of travelers—strangers. . . . Close up the gaps!"

Now, a flurry of excitement, as the column tightened. The other scouts came loping in to rejoin the main body.

"What happens now?" asked Snakewater in alarm.

Swan shrugged, concerned but not frantic. "We'll see. . . ."

30

The men quickly armed themselves and began to take defensive positions between the column, now halted, and the as yet unseen enemy. The horse herders pushed the herd closer to the column, and several warriors hurried to protect the animals from potential theft.

All of this was completely foreign to Snakewater. The Real People had not been at open warfare with anyone in her entire lifetime. There were some neighbors with whom they were allies, and others who were considered untrustworthy, but she had never seen this sort of preparation for combat.

"Will they attack us?" she asked Swan, not so much in fear as in amazement.

"No, no," Swan assured her. "This is probably a band of Cheyennes, or maybe Kiowas, traveling to winter camp, like we are. They don't want trouble any more than we do. Both groups have women and children with them, and a herd of loose horses. They have too much at stake to risk fighting. We aren't at war with anyone."

"So, what will happen?"

"Oh . . . the leaders will meet and talk. Brag a little . . . If these are friends, maybe exchange small gifts . . . Talk about the weather and the hunting . . . Where we intend to camp for the winter."

"And if they're *not* friends?" Snakewater asked anxiously.

"About the same, but more carefully. We have no real enemies just now. Sometimes we avoid Comanches, but they would be farther south and west. We don't like Osages, but these wouldn't be Osage."

"Why not, Swan?"

"They don't move as we do, lodges and all. We might meet one of their hunting parties, but we would have more warriors. Nothing would happen."

"You said we'd tell them where we intend to winter. . . . You mean, even if they're Comanche or Osage?"

"Of course. *Especially* if we don't trust each other."

"I don't understand."

"It saves a lot of trouble," Swan said. "Look!" She swept an arm to indicate the column and the horse herd. "We can't hide all this. They could find us if they mean us harm. It makes it simpler. Besides, it tells them what we intend, so there's no misunderstanding. Even if they're friends, we don't want to winter too close together. Both must have grazing and browse for the horses, a little space to hunt. . . . Oh, look! Here they come."

Far Thunder and three of the other men had moved their horses out in front of the column to greet a similar greeting party from the other group. They sat and waited. It was better, it seemed, to sit still and force the others to approach. This gave a technical advantage in the coming discourse. Around the shoulder of the hill could now be seen the other column, much like their own. Both had been traveling southward, and their courses had happened to coincide.

Snakewater moved her horse to a point where she could see better, and a young warrior cautioned her to stay back. She nodded understanding.

The newcomers drew their horses to a stop about a bow shot away and waited. Two could play the game of *you* come to *me.* Far Thunder and his companions moved forward at a walk. It was logical, Snakewater supposed, not to approach the family of a stranger too closely. That in itself might be considered offensive.

Now Thunder raised his hand in the palm-forward signal *I come in peace,* and his counterpart in the other group did the same.

Then followed a series of hand signs that were difficult to follow at this distance. Some, however, were obvious to her.

"Arapaho?" she asked. "Trader People?"

Swan appeared surprised. "Yes . . . But you are Cherokee. . . . Oh! You have been with the traders."

"Yes."

"This is good!" Swan went on. "Arapahos are good neighbors. They get along with everybody."

There was a general murmur of recognition and approval as the word passed quickly back along the column: *Arapaho. It is good. . . .*

At the meeting point of the two parties the discussion was now frank and open. They spoke in Arapaho, which was a familiar tongue to Far Thunder.

"You move toward winter camp too?" he asked.

"Yes. We had thought to camp on the Arkansas River, maybe."

Far Thunder nodded. "There is plenty of space. Has your hunting been good?"

"Good enough. We had hoped to see buffalo. A little more meat would be welcome," said the Arapaho.

"For us too. Always, a little more is better than not enough."

Both men chuckled.

"I would suggest a hunt together," said Thunder, "except that there is nothing to hunt."

The other man nodded. "Maybe another time. But . . . have we not met before?"

"Maybe . . . I am called Far Thunder. You are . . . ?"

"Yellow Horse. Yes, I am certain . . . maybe ten seasons back. On the Washita, was it not?"

"I am made to think so. It is good. Shall we camp together tonight?"

"Why not? A day or two, maybe. Race some horses, maybe trade a few?" suggested the Arapaho.

"Let it be so," agreed Thunder. "But keep the horse herds from mixing, no?"

"Of course." Yellow Horse laughed. "*Aiee!* That would take many days to sort out! We will camp beyond the stream there, and keep our horses west of our camp. The young men can herd them."

"Ours also . . . to the east of our camp, away from yours."

So it was decided. Most of the men of these horseback cultures loved a contest of any sort. If there were horses involved, so much the better. If it could also lead to an opportunity to gamble on the results, and to trade horses, life was truly good. By sunset both bands had established their camps, and family campfires blossomed orange as purple shadows crept across the rolling plain and poured into the gullies and streambeds.

A gathering place had been chosen partway between the two groups, for a story fire and informal council. There was no deliberation or decision to be made. Most formalities were omitted, except for the expected social smoke among the circle of chiefs and subchiefs of both groups. The young men of the two bands would be boasting and challenging their counterparts to the contests that would be taking place tomorrow. The older and more experienced of both would smile and observe and enjoy memories of such contests in the exuberance of their own youth.

And it was good.

The Arapaho told of their tribal structure, and their close affiliation with the Cheyenne, whose organization was even more complicated. They had joined a band of Cheyennes for the spring hunt, which had been highly successful. They were hoping for a fall hunt, which would help the winter larder.

Snakewater's recognized skill as a storyteller came into good use here, even with the language differences. Everyone present was familiar with hand signs, and she was rapidly gaining confidence in their use.

The Arapaho were entranced with the Creation stories of the Real People, so different from their own and those of the other prairie people. Most First People came from *inside* the earth in their stories of the past, not from *above* it.

The stories lasted far into the night, and in other groups old men gambled with the plum stones or the stick game, while young men boasted about their horses and promised match races for the next day. There were tentative offers to trade horses, but not sight unseen.

"Let us consider trades *after* we see them run" was a common agreement.

The women, also, gathered in their own small groups to talk, boasting or complaining about their respective men, as occasion demanded. The younger women, giggling and flirtatious, discussed the possible romantic merits of the young men of the other party. It was possible that a few trysts might take place in the next day or two. . . .

The beginning of the new day saw the start of races and contests. Running races matched horse against horse, with heavy side betting. These began almost as soon as daylight permitted, and grew in tension and importance through the day. The crowd of observers grew also, with cheering sections as the gamblers urged on the contestants on whom they wagered. Much goods and property changed hands.

Aside from this, much horse trading was constantly in progress.

There were conversations, sometimes in hand signs, which were perfectly understood but would have made no sense to anyone but a member of these buffalo hunting cultures.

"He runs well. Does he favor right or left?"

"He runs to the right, mostly."

"Too bad. I use the lance. But my brother, there, uses the bow. Talk to him!"

A horse, in pursuit of a running buffalo or, in later times, a steer, approaches the animal eagerly, running alongside. Then the rider executes his part—shooting, lancing, roping, or wrestling. Some horses prefer to approach from the right, some from the left. A right-handed bowman would find it next to impossible to shoot to his own right. But a lancer, with the spear in his right hand and the shaft under his arm, must be to the *left* of the quarry, and strike to his own right. Thus the selection of a horse for hunting buffalo depends much on the method to be employed by the hunter.

By noon several targets of skins stuffed with hay had been set up for practice and trial of horses intended for sale or trade. The hunter would mount and take a run to try the horse's approach to the target, shooting an arrow or thrusting the lance as he passed. It was not long before someone painted a target spot on one of the skin targets. In another short while it had become a contest of skill, competing for accuracy as well as speed. Soon spectators were betting on *that.*

All in all it was a good day. Many horses changed hands, some in trade and some lost and won in wagers.

New friendships were formed, and possibly a few grudges over lost races or lost wagers, but it was all in a tradition of marvelous games played by horsemen from the time they first rode astride in the dim and ancient past.

31

As if it had been planned, the scouts reported next morning that buffalo were approaching from the north. A plan was quickly organized by a selected cadre of leaders from both bands, who would direct the hunt. No one was to strike off on his own, until after the main hunt. At that point a long hunt should not be necessary.

"They all have lances or bows," Snakewater remarked to Swan. "Your people do not have guns?"

"Of course!" laughed Swan. "But it is too hard to load on horseback, and you can't dismount to do it in the chase. They leave the guns in camp."

The plan was formulated, and hunters began to move into position. The scouts were watching the herd carefully, as it slowly grazed up the grassy valley. They could see, beyond the leading edge of the slowly moving leaders, the entire prairie blackened with buffalo. There was no other edge to the seething mass. It undulated with the rolling slopes and valleys of the prairie until it was lost in the mists of distance at the horizon.

The area selected for the hunt was a circular bowl perhaps a mile in diameter with the stream circling around one side. Hunters would take hidden positions in the timber and in small gullies that opened into the main meadow. They would try to cut off the first few hundred animals and force them to circle in the bowl-shaped area. The riders would attempt to keep them circling, while they pressed the herd from the flanks, shooting and lancing as they ran.

The plan worked almost perfectly, as such complicated schemes sometimes will. The first of the buffalo made their way into the meadow shortly before noon, undisturbed and calmly grazing. As they spread out to look for better grass, the hunters waited, alert for the expected signal, still hidden in the brush and trees in the bend of the stream. A few more, not yet . . . maybe another hundred . . . *now!*

Far Thunder and his riders charged out of the trees whooping and yelling, separating the buffalo in the meadow from the main herd. They managed to turn the leaders, which had wheeled to retreat and found their way blocked. They wheeled again and suddenly the whole mass of this smaller herd had begun to circle to their left, away from the trees that might conceal more riders. They were hotly pursued now.

As they passed each small gully through which they might have fled, other riders would rush out, turning back any that attempted escape. Quickly the milling herd was turned in upon itself, and the hunt began. Buffalo started to fall, pierced by lances and arrows, and a pall of dust began to form above the rumbling herd.

Snakewater and the other women watched from the ridge, able to see more from there than would have been possible in the thick of the hunt. Individual animals broke free from time to time, to head for open prairie. Mostly these were allowed to escape. No rider left his position in the narrowing circle to pursue a single buffalo. That would allow a breach through which many more animals might pour.

They circled, whooping, yelling, shooting, lancing. . . . More buffalo were stumbling, falling to lie kicking in the rising dust cloud as the harvest continued. The earth seemed to tremble with the impact of hundreds of galloping hooves.

Now the excitement of the activity in the meadow moved back toward the multitude in the open prairie. Animals that had escaped the gather fled in terror, and the contagion spread as they ran among the others. In less time than it takes to tell, there was a change in the mood of the hundreds of thousands of slowly grazing animals. It began with a wave of restlessness that in the space of a few heartbeats became fear and then panic. The great herd began to run.

For Snakewater, who had never before seen even a few hundred buffalo at the same time, there was a moment of terror. The sound of galloping hooves in the meadow below became a trembling of the earth itself. The sound, like distant thunder, became a rumble and then a roar, as the dark blanket began to undulate in waves, into the distance. Dust began to rise like fog to overspread the distant hills, obscuring the dark blanket.

What have they done? Snakewater thought in alarm. It was easy to wonder whether the earth itself would be shaken apart by the tremor.

The other women, although showing some concern, did not seem to feel the anxiety that swept over Snakewater.

"Is this not dangerous?" she asked.

"Not much," said Swan. "They will probably go around us to the west."

"But why? How do you know this?"

"The prairie is more open there. To the east are more trees—forests. Straight ahead, where we are, they have found trouble. They are made to think that safety is in the open. So . . . they will pass us on the west."

"But . . . how do *they* know? That the open country is *west*?"

Swan shrugged. "It is their way. Maybe their grandmothers came that way."

"Our biggest problem," observed Walks Alone with a wry chuckle, "is that they will foul the water."

Snakewater had not even thought of that. A million bison, trampling across the landscape, pausing to drink at every stream, river, and spring . . . They must, of course, urinate and defecate, and the total volume . . . Ah, this *could* be a problem!

"There is a river to the north that we call 'Dung River,'" Swan added. "It is fouled nearly every season."

"What can be done?" asked Snakewater. If this was an annual problem, there must be a cure.

"Don't drink much," giggled Walks Alone. "Not from open water. Clear springs are safe. We dig seep springs sometimes."

Here the language barrier became a problem. The concept of a shallow hand-dug water source was completely foreign to Snakewater, and did not lend itself well to hand signs.

"You will see," said Swan. "But, look—the hunters are finishing!"

The milling buffalo in the meadow had managed to break their circling pattern in a dash for the prairie, through the line of horsemen that was closing around them.

"Let them go!" called Far Thunder. "We have enough."

A few riders, unsatisfied with their own performance, pursued the retreating animals for a short distance. Another buffalo or two fell kicking, but the hunt was over. Any further kill would be too far from the rest of the harvest to be practical.

The butchering parties trooped over the ridge as the dust began to settle and a general evaluation of the results of the hunt could begin. Nearly a hundred buffalo lay strewn across the meadow. A few were still showing signs of life, and the hunters moved among them, administering a merciful final blow or spear thrust. And of course, even a mortally wounded animal could be dangerous.

The hunt had been effective, but not without cost. The horse of Black Wolf of the Arapahos had been gored by a huge bull and tossed high. It now lay gasping, its bowels gushing out in a series of white loops in the dirt. Sadly Wolf borrowed a stone ax to end its suffering. He had escaped with only minor scrapes and bruises.

One of Far Thunder's young men had not been so fortunate. Little Eagle's horse had stepped into a gopher hole, throwing the rider to the ground. Eagle now sat in the grass cradling a shattered right arm with his left hand, still dazed by the fall. The doomed horse stood nearby, head down, a foreleg dangling at an improbable angle. Friends and family hurried to assist, while other people tended to other wounds of horses and men.

Several performed a ritual apology, addressing the deceased buffalo:

"I am sorry to kill you, my brother, but on your flesh my life depends, as your life depends on the grasses of the prairie. . . ."

Snakewater had never experienced such a scene as this. She was amazed at the incredible bravery of the young men, and at the magnitude of the hunt, both in effort and in results.

"Grandmother," Far Thunder called, "can you help Little Eagle, there? His arm . . ."

"Of course!"

She hurried over to where a couple of young men were helping the injured Eagle to his feet.

"Bring him over there," she ordered. "Does someone have a blanket?"

Someone hurried to spread a bed on soft grass, away from the activity that was now beginning in the meadow. Quickly she evaluated the young hunter's injuries. *No sharp splinters of bone protruding through the skin . . . good! A clean break, a hand's span above the elbow. Again, good.*

She was more concerned about the bump above his right ear, half the size of a man's fist. It might account for his confusion. But he must be watched carefully. Now, how to proceed?

A young woman hurried over and dropped to her knees beside the injured man.

"His wife?" Snakewater asked one of the other men.

"Yes—only a short time."

"Can you get up?" the wife was asking.

"He should lie still," Snakewater told her. "I can help him. I need some things from my packs."

"A travois?" suggested one of the young men. "We can take him back to camp."

"Of course!" said Snakewater. "It is good."

She had been thinking in terms of bringing her medicine *here,* but this would be better.

"Bring the travois," she went on. "I will stay here with him."

She was already thinking of what treatments might help. For the pain, some of the smoke that had been so effective for Far Thunder. A potion of herbs . . . Maybe a poultice to the bump on the head . . .

Eagle lay back, eyes closed, pale in color.

"Is he all right, Grandmother?" asked the young wife anxiously.

Snakewater smiled and patted the woman's shoulder.

"He is young and strong, no? That helps. You are a help, too, just by being here."

Now, she thought to herself, *the arm . . .*

"I need a thong," she told the young woman. "We will hang the wrist from around his neck, so. . . ." She gestured.

The woman nodded, and cut strips from the fringes of her own dress, knotting them together to form a thong of appropriate length.

Eagle's friends returned with a horse and poles to provide transport for the injured man. They lifted him carefully and placed him on the platform. He opened his eyes. . . . *Pupils equal in size,* Snakewater noted. All signs remained good. Now she must watch him carefully, begin her medicines and her conjures, prevent his becoming too active. The pretty young wife could be a great help.

"Come, walk with me," she told the girl, as the horse and travois started the slow and anxious journey back toward the camp.

32

The injured Little Eagle was doing well. He had suffered considerably, Snakewater thought, but without complaint. The injured arm, dangling from its thong, must have been very uncomfortable from the bouncing of the travois. Eagle tried walking, and that eased the jolting pain of the arm but brought on a thumping headache.

Snakewater tried to explain as best she could with the language barrier. There were two problems: the injured head and the injured arm. What was good for one was bad for the other. Sitting or lying still was best for the head injury, as any physical activity caused the heart to pound and the head to throb. But lying on the travois and submitting to the grinding bounce of the swinging arm . . . *Aiee!*

She considered attempting to bind the arm with a splint but decided against it. The lower portion of the broken upper arm was too short. She must depend on the weight of the arm itself to align the bone. Eagle must sleep in a sitting position on his willow backrest.

By the end of that first day he was pale and drawn and Snakewater was quite concerned, especially for the head injury. He insisted on trying to get up, and would stagger and fall if someone did not assist him. His anxious wife was a great help. A pretty young thing, she seemed also to have a wisdom beyond her years.

"You must stay with him," Snakewater told her. "He is quiet when you are near."

"I should help with the butchering," the girl protested.

"Anyone can do that," Snakewater advised, "but only you can keep him quiet. Your place is here."

The two of them watched over him through the afternoon. Snakewater administered her smoke treatment and applied a cooling compress to the lump above the ear. The bone seemed to be fairly well aligned, as nearly as she could tell with the swelling that was taking place. The evening held a promise of crisp cool autumn, and she thought that would be good.

When morning came, Eagle, though tired and weak, seemed no worse. The lump on his head had even diminished somewhat. Snakewater looked carefully at his eyes. Yes, there was no difference in the size of the pupils. . . . Good.

"Oh! He is awake!" said the wife, returning to their fire just as he woke. "Eagle . . . how do you feel, my love?"

He blinked at her in confusion. "What—who are *you*?" he mumbled sleepily.

Panic seemed to grip the young woman.

"Eagle . . . Please . . . I am Dove . . . your *wife*!"

"Oh." He sighed weakly. "I have a *wife*?"

Snakewater was quite alarmed by this turn of events. One who has no memory may be severely damaged. His mind may return, it may not.

"Eagle . . ." she began. Then she noticed a gleam of mischief in his eye. He was teasing. His eyes closed.

The girl had dissolved into tears, head bowed. Snakewater touched her shoulder to get her attention. *He is joking,* she said in hand signs.

"I will help you find another husband," Snakewater offered aloud. "This one is no longer useful."

Dove was startled but quickly understood.

"Too bad," she said. "This one seemed to have some good things about him."

Eagle's eyes popped open wide. "Wait!" he said. "I . . . Ah, I remember now! You *are* my wife. What is your name? Limping Frog?"

"Stop it, stupid one!" she insisted. Her tears now were tears of joy.

He circled her with his good arm, and Snakewater smiled. He would be all right. But there was an empty spot in her own heart. This was the sort of relationship that she had never sought and now could never have.

While Little Eagle's treatment was initiated, the tasks of skinning and butchering the kills were already taking place. As Snakewater was able to observe more of this process, she was astonished at its efficiency. Family units worked together and with neighbors in the heavy part of the work. Often the men assisted, perhaps bringing a horse to turn a carcass.

The skinning itself was a highly skilled procedure. The hide was split up the belly and the legs skinned out. Then the skin was separated from flesh and bone as far as possible across the back and spread, flesh side up, on the ground. Next, with a horse or several people pulling on the legs, the carcass was rolled onto the fresh skin, so that the other side, too, could be separated and spread. All of this took place in a remarkably short time.

Meanwhile a couple of women would have started the butchering. Intestines were removed and set aside while the meat was separated into manageable pieces and placed on the fresh skin to be transported to camp for further processing.

There would be feasting tonight, to utilize the cuts not readily dried or smoked, such as hump ribs. Well browned hump ribs, tender and moist with the best fat of the animal, would be the reward for the day's work.

In the ensuing days Snakewater watched as the tons of flesh became strips of dried and smoked provisions for winter. Since they would be here for at least a few days, most families erected their lodges for shelter and comfort.

The dried meat, now called "jerky" by white men on the frontier, could be stored for some time with no further preparation—chewed as they traveled, or used in cooking stews with vegetables or to flavor soups.

Another common use was in the preparation of pemmican. The jerky was pounded fine and mixed with melted suet and whatever berries and nuts might be available. This mixture was stored in casings made of the intestines of the buffalo. These had been emptied, stripped of their lining, and washed. Pemmican, a major winter staple, was much like the sausages of the white man in appearance and use when so stored. It could also be handled as a soft meal.

Virtually every part of the buffalo was used, Snakewater noted. Horns and bone became utensils, tools, and ornaments. The skins would be converted to lodge covers, *parfleche* packs and containers, and the better-furred skins to robes. She helped as she could, learning as she did so. Still, it was plain that the family of Far Thunder considered that her talents lay in other directions. She was the Grandmother, teller of stories and healer, maker of potions and conjures.

In a few days there was nothing left in the meadow but bones. Tradition and a covenant since Creation awarded to Coyote all that remained from the butchering of a kill. This, Coyote sometimes shared with Buzzard, who could see a kill from many miles, and bring his friends and family. All ate well at this kill, and the bones were polished clean and well gnawed. Each night the chortling song of the coyotes lulled the camp to sleep, and once Snakewater thought she heard the distant cry of the big gray wolf who follows the herds.

This was a world entirely foreign to her. She had lived all her life in a town, following the customs of the Real People, and even some ways of the whites. She suspected that, if the truth were known, the ways of these people of the prairie, though vastly different, were probably as complicated as her own.

She walked outside the camp to look at the night sky and listen to the songs of the night creatures. She had found a need to be alone for a little while from time to time. A lifetime of habit cannot be completely ignored.

"Yes, Lumpy," she spoke softly to the night, "it is different. But . . . I like it."

Nights were cooler now. As soon as the sun died, one quickly sought a robe or a blanket or a fireside. The butchering and preparation of winter supplies had gone well, and Far Thunder's band parted from the Arapahoes to continue into winter quarters. With the successful hunt to cement their friendship, the two groups hoped to meet again.

They traveled to the south for a few more days and camped in a place known to the prairie people. They often wintered here, Thunder said. It was customary, however, not to do so more often than every three or four years. This, to allow willow and cottonwood, on which the horses could browse, to regrow.

The families scattered among the thickets of scrub oak to select their camping sites. This would be home for several moons. These oaks were unlike any that Snakewater had ever seen. The tallest of the trees were little more than twice the height of a man. They grew in dense clumps and patches, with the lower branches reaching clear to the ground. It was easy to see that this could be an effective windbreak. She had also been told that, like some other oaks, these would keep their leaves for most of the winter. She still rather dreaded the prospect of winter in a tent, but these people had lived in this manner for many lifetimes.

It was during this setting up of the new camp that she began to really understand the use of the tepee. She watched the women carefully align the doorway to face the east.

"Must it always be so?" she asked Swan. "A thing of the spirit?"

"Oh, yes," assured the woman, "but only if you want the smoke to draw properly."

"I don't understand."

"Well, from east comes the sun, to nourish the grass and the buffalo, who gives us life. We recognize this with the door opening to the rising sun."

"But you spoke of smoke. . . ."

"Yes, that too. You have seen us adjust the smoke flaps with the poles, no?"

"Yes . . ."

"Now . . . the flaps must be cornering downwind. The opening not quite opposite the wind, but quartering. That pulls the air in the doorway and the smoke out the top."

"But why *east*?" asked Snakewater.

"Oh! You have noticed that the wind here is mostly from the south?"

"Well, yes . . . It is blowing on most days. . . ."

"Sometimes too much," agreed Swan. "This is South Wind country. There are growers north of here who call themselves 'South Wind People.'"

"Does it blow from the south all winter?"

"No, no . . . Not usually. In winter, from the north. But the smoke flaps can *still* be quartered downwind if they face eastward."

Swan reached for the smoke-flap pole and demonstrated.

"But in a storm—" Snakewater began.

"Ah, yes!" anticipated Swan. "Summer storms, usually from southwest. Winter storms, from northwest, no?"

"So, any west wind is easy. . . ."

"Right. I am made to think that the spirits explained all this to our ancestors."

"Or the smoky lodge explained it," laughed Snakewater. "But what if the wind is from the east?"

"It seldom is," Swan pointed out. "And then only for a short while. East winds bring rain sometimes. We overlap the flaps, crossed over the smoke hole, and have a very small fire for a while."

There were yet more things to be learned about the tepee. A day or so after they arrived and set up the lodges, Snakewater found the other women unrolling a bundle that proved to be an inner lining for the lodge. It was a curtain of skins, tied to each pole around the circumference at about waist height. This became a vertical wall, separating the interior of the lodge from the outer cover. She did not recall that she had seen this used before. . . .

But of course! When she had joined the lodge of Far Thunder, the weather had been hot. Lodge covers were rolled up much of the time to let the breeze flow through the cool shade.

Now they were preparing for winter. She watched the women store the odds and ends of personal possessions in the space provided behind this lining. Food supplies too . . . Cool, shielded from the fire, keeping qualities would be better.

Swan saw her inquisitive looks and explained further.

"Food keeps longer in winter, away from heat. The lodge is cold outside, warm inside. Later we can stuff dry grass in the space we're not using behind the lining. Keep the lodge warmer."

"It gets very cold here?" asked Snakewater.

"Sometimes!" promised Swan, and the other women chuckled.

33

Autumn had been a wonderful season, as they moved into winter camp. Snakewater had always loved the warm sunny days and crisp nights of early autumn, back in the mountains of the Real People. If anything it was even more spectacular here, where the woodlands met the prairie. There were trees and shrubs that she had never seen before, blazing almost overnight into glorious color. Her biggest surprise, however, was that the tall prairie grasses themselves became part of the color change. Their hues were somewhat more muted and soft than those of the trees and shrubs, providing a gentle contrast. And she had never realized how many different varieties of grasses contributed to the tallgrass landscape. Each has its place, Swan explained. Some sprout first in the spring, sheltering the more tender shoots of those coming next. Some grow low and thick, with fine leaves that carry much nutrition into the winter for the horses and the buffalo. The standing grasses also catch the snow, to provide moisture and nutrition for next season's growth.

She had been astounded at the height of the grasses. Some grew far taller than a man and, in a secluded area that had not been grazed, taller than a man seated on his horse. The most spectacular of these Swan called "turkeyfoot," from its three-awned seed-head. Another of the tall species was topped with a feathery plume of bright straw-yellow. This grew, in some places, nearly as tall as the turkeyfoot.

But the changing colors. . . . Back home grass was simply . . . well, *grass.* It died with the first killing frost, for the most part, becoming an uninteresting gray-yellow to tan until spring's new growth appeared, in the time of Greening. Here the big turkeyfoot grass ripened from bright green to a deep reddish hue almost overnight, well before the first frosts. By contrast the tall plume-grass became a golden yellow to match its own seed-head. A smaller, finer grass that grew no more than waist high became a soft pink, with feathery white seed-heads at intervals along the sides of pinkish stems.

Some of the shrubs to be found among the prairie gullies and the oak thickets of their wintering place were familiar to her. Others were new: Several varieties of sumac, some a brilliant scarlet. Another, apparently a dogwood by its leaf, was taller than her head in some places. Still another, called *wahoo* by Swan, bore scant purple-orange berries. Its leaves turned a broad range of colors, all on the same plant—yellows, pinks and purples.

Some of these plants, she thought, must be useful for teas and potions, but she had no way of knowing. She asked the women, who were some help, but not much.

"Yes, some are used for medicine. There is a flower whose root helps a cough. . . ."

"Who could tell me of these things?"

This met with shrugs and blank looks.

"What do you need to know?"

"Well . . . *all* of it! No—I understand. When the problem comes, you will show me the answer, no?"

"Yes, something like that," smiled Swan. "But, Snakewater, you are a woman with strong medicine. You do not know these things?"

"In my own country, yes. But here there are new plants. These I cannot know."

"Ah, yes! I see. But to know ours as you do those of your own country would also take a lifetime, no?"

"Yes, I suppose so."

"When we go to the Sun Dance next season, there may be a holy man who would talk with you."

Snakewater had not thought as far ahead as next season.

"When does this take place, this Sun Dance?"

"The Moon of Roses—ah, that is not how you call it? After the greening and growing moons, when the roses bloom on the prairie!"

As occasionally happened, they struck the language barrier with the word *roses.* This led to various attempts at description in hand signs. *A flower . . . Thorny . . . This tall, maybe . . . Sweet smell . . .*

Snakewater took a different approach. "Do you know how this moon is called by white men?"

"Oh!" Swan laughed heartily. "'*June,*' I am made to think."

"Good. I know 'June.'"

This struck the other women as amusing. They laughed over the circumstance of Snakewater and Swan trying to identify the season by the bloom of a flower, when both knew the white man's name for it.

But she was not satisfied. There must be some way in which she could learn. . . . *Ah!* Maybe . . .

The next time she had an opportunity to be alone, she looked carefully around her to make sure.

Then, "Lumpy, can you help me with this—the plants?"

There was a long pause, and she spoke angrily this time.

"You are no help at all! You are teasing me. You *do* know these things, and won't help me!"

Another pause, and she spoke again.

"I'm sorry. Don't cry. . . . Damn you, Lumpy, you're still teasing me! Fine Little Person you are. I should . . . oh, I don't know what!"

She shook her head sadly.

"Yes," she said finally, "I know. Everything is new here. I have to learn, though. Maybe you do too. Do you have Little People here whom you could ask? Oh, yes, I know. If you do, you wouldn't tell me. . . . Oh, all right—*'couldn't'* tell me. But I'm still not sure. Maybe you're still teasing me. Anyway, you might do a decent thing. *What* decent thing? Well, to begin with, you could stop laughing. You know how that irritates me."

With the vast numbers of oaks in the area of the winter camp, it was apparent that there would be acorns. In some adjacent woodland within easy walking distance there were also other nut trees: walnut, pecan, hickory, and an assortment of larger oaks, each bearing its own crop of acorns. It was a natural haven for any creatures that could utilize the harvest of nuts available each autumn. This season seemed to have a bountiful crop. It made Snakewater think once again of the tradition that a season with heavy harvest of nuts and berries predicts a hard winter. Squirrels store larger numbers of acorns because their instinct tells them to do so.

Snakewater had long suspected this to be a questionable assumption. Possibly, she reasoned, there was simply more food—just as, with the recent successful hunt, the prairie people had stored more jerky and pemmican. Still, it does not pay to fly in the face of conventional wisdom, she reasoned. A hard winter *may* logically follow a good growing season.

Regardless, she was impressed by the numbers and the size of the squirrels around the camp. They were of a type not familiar to her, much larger than the gray squirrels near Old Town. They were also of a different color, a reddish brown much like that of a fox. In fact, the first of these animals she had seen had deceived her for a moment. She had thought that it *was* a fox, running across a distant open space.

She wanted a chance to examine one of these creatures, and this seemed to be a good opportunity. Besides, a stew of squirrel might be a good contribution to the lodge of Far Thunder. Even with the bountiful supply of buffalo meat, sometimes a change is good. Especially when there is a chance for fresh meat rather than dried or cured.

Among these people small game was not hunted seriously by adults to any extent. A real hunter is after larger game: buffalo, elk, or deer. It would be beneath his dignity to seriously hunt the quarry of a child, such as squirrels or rabbits. It would be on such game that a youngster would make his first kill. Sometimes, however, a woman would take a bow and, for a pleasant return to the joys of her childhood, go on a short hunt. These observations had caused Snakewater to take out her blowgun and think of trying her luck.

"What is that stick?" asked Fawn, daughter of Thunder. It was she who had reminded Snakewater of Little Pigeon back at West Landing.

"That stick," she told the child, "is my weapon."

"Who will you hit, Grandmother?"

"Nobody, child. I will use it to hunt squirrels."

The little girl laughed and clapped her hands. "You cannot climb in the trees, Grandmother."

"Huh! How do you know? But, no, I would not hit them, but shoot them."

This brought an even greater laugh from the child, and the other women joined in.

"Really, how is this?" asked Swan.

"It shoots these," Snakewater explained, showing one of her darts.

This brought forth even more laughter.

"I think not, Grandmother," said Swan. "But wait—this is part of your medicine, no?"

Snakewater thought for only a moment.

"Yes!" she said. "That is it. It does not work with many eyes watching. But, look . . . I will take Fawn, here, and she can tell you how it goes. Come, Fawn. We will hunt squirrels, no?"

Snakewater and Fawn sat with their backs against the trunk of a giant old sycamore tree. Somewhere in the canopy overhead a squirrel barked, unseen among the huge leaves. It would be one of the big red squirrels that had astonished Snakewater in this new country. In the mountains back around Old Town she had known two kinds. The one most sought after was gray, and the other was much smaller, reddish, and often a nuisance, robbing birds' nests in addition to gathering nuts.

But these big red squirrels were like none she had ever seen. They appeared to be considerably larger than the grays, and easily twice the size of the little red squirrels back home.

Shoot it, suggested Fawn in hand signs.

Snakewater had instructed the girl not to speak once they arrived in the area to hunt. They would use only hand signs.

No, she signed now. *That is their scout. If he is not harmed, others will come.*

Now there was a flash of motion above . . . a glimpse of reddish fur. . . . Snakewater slowly lifted her blowgun, already fitted with a tufted dart. She could not see her target clearly yet. . . . *There!*

A bright eye poked around the side of one of the chalk-white branches high above. She carefully adjusted the aim of the blowgun and waited. Patience was important, above all. Now the squirrel moved on around for a better view, showing head, neck, and shoulder. Snakewater placed her lips on the mouthpiece. . . . A deep breath and a *puff* . . .

The fat squirrel tumbled to the ground, its upper body transfixed by the tufted hardwood skewer. *Wait,* cautioned Snakewater, as Fawn started to move toward their prize. *There may be another!* She quietly inserted another dart in the tube.

There was dead silence for a few moments, and then the sentinel resumed his scolding bark. Almost immediately another squirrel appeared, scampering with what seemed impossible agility through the branches of a big white oak nearby. There was a short jump to the sycamore, and the newcomer paused to stare. A moment too long, an almost inaudible puff . . . Another fat squirrel lay kicking, and Snakewater reloaded. The scout continued to bark the alarm.

Five in all that day Snakewater procured for the lodge of Far Thunder. There were many jokes about the prowess of the Squirrel Grandmother and her strange weapon. She had been able to furnish meat for the family with whom she lived. They all enjoyed the rich stew and picked clean the purplish bones. For her, however, it was a special time. She had made a contribution to the family, over and above her stories and her medicine. And it was good.

34

Snakewater awoke sometime in the night, unsure what had roused her. She could hear the soft breathing of the lodge's other inhabitants, who seemed undisturbed. Maybe she should go and empty her bladder, though it did not feel urgently full.

She lay there in the darkness a little while, enjoying the warmth of her blankets, thinking of recent events. She could hardly believe that over the past couple of seasons her life had changed so much. Here she lay, in a tent made of skins and poles, surprisingly comfortable. She was accepted, respected, and most of all, she felt that she was *loved.* In all her life there had probably been no one except her old namesake mentor who had actually loved her. Some had helped her, looked with favor upon her, but this was an entirely new feeling. She was part of a *family.*

Yes, that was it. There was something about being in a family group that imparted a feeling of warmth and security that she had never had before. She had often looked with scorn on people who put much importance on such things. *Who needs it?* she sometimes thought. But there was a fullness and completeness in her own heart that told her: *Everyone* needs it, and it was a warmth that she had never found until now. She smiled to herself in the darkness.

Of course, she realized, there had been a reason that she had never found such a relationship. She had not been a lovable person. It had been easier to follow the example of the old conjure woman with whom she lived—bitter, withdrawn, apparently hating everybody, and, over all, teaching her young companion to do the same. It was no wonder that the little girl had never had a friend. A tear formed in her eye and trickled down her cheek. Old Snakewater had formed in her own image, probably unconsciously, and it had not been an attractive image.

Now, this person, *Grandmother* Snakewater, had broken out of that image. She felt a mixture of resentment and pity for her long-departed mentor. Had the old conjuror *ever* had a friend? What had been in *her* early life to have made her so? Some tragedy, a disappointed love? She was only now realizing that she had known very little about her teacher. And now, never could.

Her thoughts drifted back to her own situation. She had never felt self-pity. She had been taught not to do so, to reject and deny such feelings as being unloved. And she had to admit, it had been successful. She had been unloved because she was not very lovable. She smiled a wry smile in the dark lodge. Which came first? No matter. . . . Now she had found her way, late in her lifetime. She was loved because she had *learned* to love, and was now a different person. She rolled that thought around in her mind, playing with it, enjoying the comfort in it for a little while. She was, truly, a different person, one who could love and be loved, who could respect and admire and relate to others, to have fun and face each day with pleasure, to enjoy. It was a new experience.

Suddenly the implication of those thoughts descended on her like a thrown blanket, plunging her into a despair that was mixed with something much like terror. *Where had this different person come from?*

All the stories and whispered rumors and accusations came crowding back, bringing dark thoughts that had been forgotten for a long time. *Thoughts of the Raven Mocker. . . .*

She knew that she had never intentionally tried to acquire such status, and that she was totally innocent of the charges laid against her back at Old Town. But there *had* been a time when she wondered, *Does the Raven Mocker's ability to steal fragments of other lives have to be intentional?* If not, maybe she *had* been using the life-years of others for a long time. She had been present at many deaths, and of many different kinds of people. Some had been infants, some older. Did she now have a pleasant attitude because she was feeding on the life-years of some lovable young person? Her entire attitude, her approach to life, was so different. . . . It *must* be true.

"Ah, Lumpy!" she muttered into the darkness. "What have I done?"

"Are you ill, Grandmother?" asked one of the children.

"*What?* Oh, no, child. Just thinking."

But the change was obvious. She could not conceal her worry.

"Is there something I can do?" asked Swan, concerned.

"No, no. It is nothing. Maybe I just need to get away and think a little while."

"A vision quest?" asked Swan, half joking.

"No, no, nothing like that, Swan. I don't know. . . . I lived alone for many seasons, back with my own people. This is different, among so many. It is good, but . . ."

"Ah, yes," laughed the other woman. "I feel that way sometimes. It is good to be alone for a little while. Go on, take a walk. Let your medicine work, no?"

It seemed like a good idea. Snakewater ate nothing, but brewed herself a bowl of tea with selected herbs and berries and sipped it slowly.

She took her blowgun and a pouch of darts. She did not really expect to use it, but it would give the impression of purpose, which she really lacked.

"May I go with you, Grandmother? asked Fawn brightly.

She smiled and patted the girl's head. "Not today, child. I . . . well, there are things I must do."

"It is a medicine journey," suggested Swan. "One must do such things alone."

"Yes—yes, that is it," agreed Snakewater. "I must go alone. I will be back tonight."

She wished that she had some clearer goal. She was nearly as confused as little Fawn. She put a few strips of dried meat into her pouch and started somewhat aimlessly out of the camp. People nodded or waved to her and she returned their greetings. It was a good feeling to be so accepted, but she had the sense that it was undeserved, that she was living a falsehood. Her heart was very heavy.

She headed south, for no better reason than that the geese were flying that direction. Their wild and free course across the bright autumn sky seemed a marked contrast to her mood. At the top of a wooded ridge some distance from the camp, she found a bald, rocky summit, where she could sit and see in all directions.

Back to the north was the winter camp of Far Thunder, its lodges scattered among the thickets of scrub oak. It was a peaceful scene. Lazy spires of smoke rose from the apex of each lodge—straight up for some distance, then layering out horizontally in the still autumn air. From her vantage point Snakewater found that she was looking *down* on this layer of smoke. She recalled, as a child in the mountains, that she had seen fog below her in a similar way. But that had been misty white among the treetops, and this smoke effect was gray, and much higher above the ground. It was a pleasant distraction, which in the end led her nowhere. It gave her time to be alone, to think, to worry more as she tried to solve the mystery that now seemed to hang over her life.

She wondered if it would help to fast for a day or two, and decided not. She chewed some jerky and gazed at the land, while enjoying the warmth of the sun on her shoulders. She watched a couple of bull elks in the far distance as they met in combat over a trio of cows.

The Moon of Madness. Maybe that was part of her problem. Or all of it. Was she going mad, with this worry hanging over her? Maybe it was that. Still, she was unable to escape the nagging doubt that in some way she *was* living someone else's life. Maybe more than one. If she were really a Raven Mocker, she might be living on parts of many lives. Would it work that way? Mixed fragments of life-years, so stirred together that they were indistinguishable from one another? That could explain some of her confusion. Also some of the mixed feelings she occasionally had about people and events.

But how did it happen? She still had doubts that one could become a Raven Mocker without knowing it. She certainly could not recall any one incident that would indicate a change in her status. Her life had been a continuous line. Well, except for the past two years . . . Was *that* when it had happened? No, that was when she had been *accused.* But . . . Her head whirled in confusion. Had she been accused *because* others had seen the change when she had *become* a Raven Mocker?

Assuming that there was such an entity, and that the possibility might exist that she had become one, how could she tell? When the transfer to the lifetime of another occurred, how would it *feel*? Would the Raven Mocker simply wake one morning to find that he/she was someone else? Would there be any memory of a previous lifetime, a different person in the same body? She surely had no such memories, and that was encouraging.

What could be expected to happen, though, if a Raven Mocker died suddenly, or was killed? Would some of the life-years available to the Raven Mocker transfer spontaneously, or must they be invoked? And again, would there be a memory?

What if she threw herself from this red boulder where she sat, down the face of the hill, to land on the jumble of rocks below? If she were the Raven Mocker, would her life as Snakewater be replaced by another? Would she be aware of it? That would certainly answer her questions. . . .

"What?" she spoke aloud. "Why, no, of course not! I could never do that." Her voice became softer. "But thank you, Lumpy, for your concern. . . . Yes, I'd better be getting back."

The sun was setting as she made her way back to the lodge of Far Thunder. She wondered if she had actually accomplished anything. She had had an opportunity to think and had not arrived at much understanding. She wished that she could talk about her questions with someone who could understand. Someone like her old namesake mentor, Snakewater the elder. But among these, the Elk-Dog People, there was no one who could help her. Even talking to one of the holy men they had mentioned would probably be futile. They had never heard of the Raven Mocker. No one here, as kind and generous as they had been to her, could possibly understand.

No one except Lumpy, who would usually, or at least she suspected so, rather tease than help her.

But who knows what the Little People think?

35

The first of winter's storms swept down on them during the Moon of Madness. At that time all creatures go a little bit crazy. Days are growing shorter, and there is an uneasiness that falls over everything. The beauty of autumn is behind, fallen away during the Moon of Falling Leaves, like the bright leaves themselves.

It is the rutting season for the deer. They are ranging far, searching for satisfaction of the basic urge to reproduce the next generation of their kind. The bucks rub the fuzzy covering from their antlers by attacking young trees. Their newly acquired weapons are polished and ready for combat. They go forth to fight for the favors of the most attractive females, who watch, trying to appear unimpressed. In the distraction of the primal urge safety is forgotten. It is a time of madness. The battle-ready males sometimes attack not only trees and each other, but predators, including Man. It is a dangerous situation.

The bugling call of the bull elk echoes across the land as he, too, searches for mates, only slightly less irrational than the deer.

Smaller creatures are ranging far, now separated from their mothers and searching on their own for places to winter. Larger predators are actively hunting, many of them for the first time on their own. Bears prepare to hibernate, and gorge themselves on nature's bounty, both plant and animal, to provide fat for insulation and for nutrition during the long sleep.

The last of the ducks and geese are winging southward in their migration, also somewhat erratic in their behavior. . . . *Hurry, hurry, winter comes.*

Among birds madness is not restricted to the species that migrate. Maybe the bareness of the trees in heavy timber is alarming by changed appearance. For whatever reason, quail, grouse, and smaller birds fly aimlessly, often colliding with branches and other obstacles in their flight.

In the Moon of Madness even Man is affected. Approaching the Moon of Long Nights, when the sun seems about to go out, Man, too, feels a desolation, a depression that seems hopeless. Even modern man is stricken with madness, and mental illness peaks at this time.

"Sun Boy's torch grows dim," observed Swan, as they stuffed dried grasses into the space behind the lodge lining.

It was a sunny day, but nights were crisp. Going to water, in the tradition of the Real People, was still practiced by Snakewater, but at this time of year it became a much shorter ceremony. Still, she considered it important.

"Sun Boy?" she asked Swan curiously.

"Yes . . . Sun Boy carries his torch across the sky to give us light and warmth. His torch goes dim, and this gives Cold Maker a chance to attack him. The battle goes on through the Moon of Long Nights and the Moon of Snows, into the Moon of Hunger, when our food sometimes runs low. Is it not the same among your people?"

Snakewater handed her armful of hay to Walks Alone, and stepped back out of the way to let the children hand over their contribution.

"Not quite." Snakewater laughed. "For us Sun is a woman. She crawls under the edge of the Sky Dome and travels up the side and across. She stops at her daughter's lodge for a little while, eats a meal, maybe drinks a little *kanohena*—straight overhead there, and down the other side. But tell me of Cold Maker. He is a monster, no?"

Swan laughed. "Sometimes! Cold Maker lives in icy mountains far to the north. He roars out, bringing snow and ice. That's why we move south. They battle all winter, as I said. Sometimes it seems Sun Boy's torch almost goes out. But then he always gets a new one, and Cold Maker retreats, back to the north. At least it has always been so. But maybe this time . . ."

"Ah! I see. And the new torch of Sun Boy starts your Moon of Awakening?"

"Yes. We celebrate the return of the sun, the grass, and the buffalo later, in the Sun Dance."

"Yes, I have learned of that," said Snakewater. "Is your winter hard here?"

"Sometimes. Not so bad as farther north, of course."

Some of the Elk-dog People built brush barriers around the north and west sides of their lodges. This would provide more shelter from the wind, it was said. Not only that, but it was not uncommon to encircle the whole lodge with such a barrier. Many of the men kept a favorite horse, their best buffalo runner, close to the lodge, within this barrier. This would protect the animal from predators or theft by neighboring tribes. That was a pastime to prove manhood.

Keeping a horse up by the lodge did require more work, of course. It must be taken to water each day and supplied with food. In severe weather this might be cut branches of cottonwood, whose bark and small twigs would help to supply the animal's needs. For some men the extra work was worthwhile, expressing their pride in ownership of a fine horse.

When Cold Maker did sweep down, perhaps a bit earlier than usual, the camp was fairly well prepared. There were some malingerers, as among any people, who will never be ready for anything. They will protest the unfairness of any situation, even one of their own making.

"I needed only another day!"

Yet, if that other day had been given, it would still be a day short for some.

It was a calm and sunny morning, a gentle breeze stirring from the south. There may have been a few signs, noted mostly by the old ones with more life experience: a few aches and pains in the limbs with rheumatism or old injuries; even a feel to the air, maybe, a sensation that something was about to happen.

One of the first visible signs was the approach of scattered blue clouds from the north. Not a heavy line of storm clouds, but an occasional wandering patch of shade. And it was noticeable that while the shadow of such clouds fell over the camp, the air seemed much cooler. The heat from Sun Boy's torch could not be felt. Along with the cold came a restless stirring of the air. The south breeze changed, not all at once, but in unpredictable directions. Now a shift to the southwest for a moment, then southeast, maybe even due east, and in a few moments, due north or south again.

There was a heavy, clammy feel to the air. The lodge skins were damp to the touch, and before long it was apparent that tiny droplets of moisture were collecting on everything—tepees, trees, shrubs and grasses, even on the furry winter coats of the horses, and the hair of people who remained outside.

The cloud cover was nearly solid now, only an occasional patch of sunlight passed swiftly by.

It would have been impossible to state the exact moment when the wind changed, but now it was apparent that it had. The icy breath of Cold Maker blew harder and harder, whipping gusts through the camp and chilling to the bone.

People scurried to bring in a last armful of fuel, and none too soon. The clammy moisture of the earlier part of the day was now slippery underfoot. It was hard to realize that it was now freezing, a thin veneer of ice on everything as darkness fell.

Morning dawned with the entire world covered with fuzzy crystals of frost. Each tree branch and twig, every leaf of grass, had sprouted white fur. It was a beautiful sight, had the cold not made it quite so uncomfortable. But soon after daylight it began to snow. The wind had died, making the chill more bearable. Great fluffy flakes of white came drifting down softly, like the breath feathers of Kookooskoos, the owl, falling on the silent world.

By noon there was an accumulation of a hand's span in depth. When darkness fell, it was still snowing, somewhat colder, and beginning to drift as the wind rose again. People left the lodges only briefly, only for absolute necessity, and hurried back inside as quickly as possible.

The next morning the snow had stopped and the sun shone brightly. It was almost blinding, even with Sun Boy's fading torch, as it reflected from the snow-covered world. Each tree and twig and each blade of grass was flocked with sparkling and shimmering white, reflecting glitters of light.

By noon the sparkle was gone, and in the warming air the melt had begun. It required several days for all the snow to melt in the shaded places where the rays of Sun Boy's torch could not reach. The days were comfortable, the nights chilling.

It was nearly half a moon before Cold Maker mounted his next sortie. It was now early in the Moon of Long Nights, and it was becoming clear how this moon had earned its name. Darkness fell appreciably sooner in the evening, and Sun Boy thrust his torch above the horizon a bit later to greet each day. His path, too, was weaker. Instead of thrusting boldly in a path straight upward from earth's rim, he seemed to seek an easier path slanting upward in a southerly direction. Never did his torch even approach the overhead position now. He reached his highest point scarcely halfway up in the southern sky, before weakly falling back toward the western horizon for a bleak, early sunset.

"Cold Maker pushes him hard," observed Swan. "The torch grows weaker. See how his light is yellow and watery?"

"How does he renew it?" asked Snakewater.

Swan shrugged. "Who knows? I suppose Sun Boy lights a new torch from the dying flame of this one. But he must use the last of it, it seems. I sometimes wish he would be not quite so frugal, no? I am ready for the new one."

The women chuckled. It was not yet time for the days to become longer, and would not be for some time.

Snakewater could see how, in this land of far horizons, it would be quite easy to become preoccupied with this struggle. It *was* depressing to see the days grow shorter and colder. Maybe this time the Cold Maker of the Elk-dog People *would* succeed, and Sun Boy's torch *would* go out. These thoughts, falling on the heels of the Moon of Madness, were quite depressing. Yet, she recalled, it had always been so, the dark days of winter. This was no different. Only more apparent, maybe, in this land of wide skies.

By the time the next storms pushed out of the north, the village was nearly ready. Even the most slovenly and the laziest had managed to prepare their lodges in some manner. They were ready for Cold Maker.

The coats of the fur bearers as well as the horses were thick and soft, and some of the men began to hunt and trap. Pelts of beaver, otter, and mink could be sold or traded to white men very profitably. Some of the men even had a few steel traps obtained from traders, and now established traplines along the streams.

Above all it appeared that to these people, winter would be a time of socializing. As the snows deepened, there were trodden paths from one lodge to another. On most evenings friends gathered to smoke, gamble with the plum stones or with the stick game, or to tell stories around the lodge fires.

These were good times for Snakewater. She was familiar with some of the games, but gambling with plum stones was new to her. An odd number of plum stones was used—five, seven, or nine. One side of each stone was painted red, the other remained the natural yellow. One player would choose, red or yellow, cup the seeds in his hands, and toss them out on a blanket, where the result could be counted. Sometimes the stones would be shaken in a cup made of a buffalo horn before the toss. Large bets would sometimes be placed on this game of chance. It was fascinating to watch the emotion that some of the gamblers invested in such games.

For her part Snakewater preferred the stories.

36

"Do you have Little People?" Snakewater asked the women one day as they prepared an evening meal.

"Little People?" said Swan, with her mischievous smile of good humor. "Of course. Doesn't everyone?"

Snakewater was startled. She had asked out of curiosity, and was not certain what reaction she might get. Among the Real People the subject of Little People was an accepted part of life. Not everyone enitrely credited the sometimes bizarre tales about the Little People, but few denied their existence. The attitude of most was much like their attitude toward the old ways. As the Real People had begun to adopt the ways of the white man, many had come to say, "I no longer practice the old ways," but few were willing to say, "I do not *believe* the old ways." To her this was a strange contradiction.

"Why do you ask?" teased Swan. "Have you seen some?"

"No . . . I just wondered. Among my people they are important. No one can admit having seen one, of course."

The women laughed, and then Swan became serious.

"I think everyone has stories of Little People. To some they are more important than to others. To us they are mostly amusing."

It occurred to Snakewater that here there were no stories about Little People, and now she began to think that rather strange. Or maybe not—One of the Real People would never wish to offend a Little Person. It might become too dangerous.

"Tell me more," she requested.

"Well," pondered Swan, "as I said, ours are amusing. They can help or hurt you. Those of some others seem more interesting. You have traveled with the trader. Did you not hear the stories of others?"

"Not much. I am made to think that to some, like my own people, it is too serious to talk about. But among the Plains people who hunt buffalo and live in lodges like this, I have met only your people."

"Ah! I see. Well, we were speaking of the Little People. . . . Somebody—I can't remember who—Their Little People live underwater, come out sometimes. They are to be feared. Who is that, Walks Alone?"

"I don't remember," said her sister. "One of those to the north. Not the Crows."

"No . . . I remember *theirs*. The Crows' Little People go into battle with them. Very dangerous fighters. They tell of fights where the Little People destroyed the enemy's horses."

"Ah!" exclaimed Snakewater. "By force or by magic?"

"Does it matter?" asked Swan. "Maybe both."

"Why do you suppose that there are few stories about Little People?" asked Snakewater.

Swan shrugged. "I don't know—I never thought about it. But . . . well, you would not want to *offend* them—ones who lived in deep water, or who could destroy horses in battle?"

The subject was becoming uncomfortable, which in itself must indicate something.

"Do you think it will snow tonight?" asked Walks Alone.

The others laughed, maybe a little nervously, and the subject changed to weather.

People are uneasy about the Little People, Snakewater realized. Maybe she'd ask Lumpy about that. Or maybe not . . . *He'd only tease me,* she thought.

It was a hard winter. There were days at a time when Sun Boy's torch was not seen at all. It would grow light in the morning, and dark again in the evening, with no apparent change in the gray pall of sky that hung over everything. Sometimes there was snow, sometimes not, but the air never seemed to become warm enough to melt the accumulation on the ground. The drifts deepened.

The people banked snow around the lower part of the lodges, piling it against the outside of the lodge covers. It was an advantage to have snow for this purpose, to shelter the lodges from the icy breath of Cold Maker as he howled outside.

There were many days when the ongoing storms were too bad to permit hunting or the running of traplines, so people stayed inside. Socializing became insufficient to rouse spirits. Everyone was irritable and glum. By the end of the Moon of Snows this became a matter of concern. Even with the bountiful harvest of meat last autumn, supplies might run short. The keeping qualities of dried meat and pemmican, while they were good, were not perfect. Even in weather such as this there was some spoilage.

To add to that . . . One evening just before darkness fell, there was a sudden distressed wail from the next lodge, some fifty paces away. Far Thunder seized a weapon and hurried outside. The wailing continued.

"What is it?" called Thunder, sprinting toward the commotion in the narrow path with snow piled high on both sides.

"*Aiee,* all of it!" came the sound of a woman's voice.

Other men were running, too, toward the source of the disturbance. The women emerged from the lodges, too, some carrying weapons, in case a defense might be needed.

"Are we being attacked?" someone called.

Now a man emerged from the lodge where the wailing continued.

"No, no," he assured them. "Our food . . . Some creature . . ." He spread his hands helplessly.

Some small animal—possum, skunk, or raccoon, maybe—had entered the storage space behind the lodge lining and had remained there, feasting on the stored food supply.

"I thought I heard something scratching!" the woman said again and again.

What food had not been eaten had been spoiled and contaminated by the animal's excrement and its digging through the packs and bundles.

"What will we do?" wailed the young wife.

"I can let you have some pemmican," offered Swan.

"I too," said another woman.

Quickly there were several offers of help. Despite this everyone knew that it was a serious situation. Most people had very little more than enough for their own families, and the Moon of Hunger had barely begun.

There was another incident of an animal raid and damage to the food of another lodge a few days later. Again, other families helped.

Everyone else now checked carefully behind their own lodge linings, and a few more cases of intrusion were discovered. Most were slight, but in the overall picture a considerable amount of food had been harmed.

A council was held in the lodge of Far Thunder, with three sub-chiefs present. It was agreed that they must have inadvertently camped in a place that harbored a great number of possums or possibly raccoons. There was a gentle jibe or two over "Who chose this place?" but it was not a serious accusation. Far Thunder brushed it aside. What was needed now was an answer, not an accusation.

To move to another area might have been a solution earlier, but by now it was too late. The lodges were heavily banked with snow and would be frozen in until the spring thaw.

"Why did the dogs not know?" asked Two Hatchets, a quiet young man who was greatly respected in the band.

"Mine did!" offered another. "Did not yours?"

"Some—but that was outside."

There was a discussion. The lodges where dogs slept inside had not been bothered. Those whose dogs found their own shelter in the brush and snowdrifts were most vulnerable.

"It is too late now to change that," observed Thunder. "Now, what can be done?"

There was silence. It was plain to see. Nothing . . .

The dogs could be eaten, it was noted.

Snakewater had been somewhat startled by this comment, and asked Swan about it later.

"You eat the dogs?"

"Of course. That is much of their purpose. Your people do not eat dogs?"

"No . . . I . . . Maybe in a time of starvation."

She had wondered at the great number of dogs that followed the camps, but merely attributed it to the great quantities of food available to dogs after a buffalo hunt.

"When the taste of dried meat and pemmican becomes stale, there is still fresh meat," explained Swan.

"Then this means no problems with the loss of food in the lodges?" asked Snakewater. "The people will eat their dogs?"

"There *is* a problem," Swan answered. "The people have counted on the dogs already. And a dog does not last long in a big family. A day or two . . .

Snakewater now recalled that she had seen a woman skinning an animal of some sort. It had been at some distance, and she had assumed it to be game that one of the hunters had brought in—beaver, maybe. But now . . . It had probably been a dog.

This whole idea was a new experience for her. The Real People had been settled in towns and depending on farming for many generations. It had never occurred to her that these nomadic buffalo hunters were far more dependent on the season and on the climate.

They had stopped to trade some of the meat and hides to one of the grower towns during the move south. They had acquired, in this way, corn, beans, and dried pumpkins.

Now supplies were to run short, unless the spring thaw came early to allow a hunt. Yes, she could see that there might be a problem.

The cold continued, with more snows. Everyone, at least the adults, began to eat less and less. On several occasions Snakewater would pretend not to be hungry, and would share her own portion with the children. She saw the others do the same, and supposed that similar events were occurring in the other lodges.

Those who were trapping no longer discarded the flesh of the fur bearers they caught, but brought them home to feed their families. Surely spring would come soon. . . .

"We could eat the horses," suggested Far Thunder.

But so far no one had done so. That was a matter of prestige. And so far no one was actually starving.

"I am told," Swan told Snakewater, "that this was once called the Moon of Starvation, before the coming of the Elk-dog—the horse. Now it is only the Moon of Hunger. At least so far."

There were a few days when it appeared that the snows might be over. A little melting actually occurred. But then Cold Maker mounted one last thrust in defiance of Sun Boy's now brightening new torch.

Dark clouds rolled in, the temperature plummeted, and once more it began to snow. People withdrew again into their lodges, carrying what firewood they could. That, too, was becoming scarce.

As Snakewater entered the lodge, she heard the sound of singing and turned to look back. There, walking straight and tall, was an old man carrying his weapons and marching straight into the teeth of the storm.

"What is he doing?" Snakewater asked in surprise.

"He goes to fight Cold Maker," said Swan, a little sadly.

"But . . . why is he *singing*?"

"That is the Death Song," Swan answered. "Our warriors ride into battle singing,

The earth and the sky go on
forever
But today is a good day
to die . . .

and his family will live. He will have beaten Cold Maker."

"Has he gone crazy?"

"No, no. There will be one less mouth to feed . . . more food for the children—his grandchildren. And life goes on."

37

At last the bright rays of Sun Boy's new torch began to show some results. Each day became visibly longer than the one before, as Cold Maker began to withdraw in defeat.

Cold Maker did not concede defeat gracefully. He never does. He retreats, snarling and snapping like a wolf at bay, striking out at his tormentor with a vengeance as he slinks back toward his ice caves in the northern mountains. He may even turn to attack another time or two. But it is easy to see, by the Moon of Awakening, what the outcome will be. Sun Boy will triumph again, bringing back the grass and the buffalo.

The people of Far Thunder's band had come through the winter thin and hungry, but alive. They had fewer dogs, but that would be quickly remedied. They had not had to resort to eating the horses.

One old woman had succumbed to pneumonia, and her body was ceremonially placed on a burial scaffold, to remain there when the band moved on.

"You do not bury in the ground?" asked Snakewater.

"Sometimes," Swan explained. "Maybe when we come this way again, there will be a few bones left. Those we would bury."

The body of the old warrior who went into combat with Cold Maker singing the Death Song was never found.

But the Moon of Awakening had arrived. The bare branches of the willows along the stream now began to show a bright yellowish color. Buds were swelling on the maples. On southern slopes the snow began to melt, the water trickling in little rivulets, joining other trickles to ripple downhill with increasing volume, flowing faster and faster to plunge into the swelling torrent of the stream.

Back on the newly exposed south slopes, sprigs of green began to push through the reddish soil and the dead foliage of last year's growth. The grass was returning.

There was a restlessness among the people, an urge to do *something*. The men began to hunt again, ranging farther from the camp.

The old urge to move was stimulated by the long lines of migrating geese high overhead. They were now returning northward, honking in derision at Cold Maker's retreat as he fled before the advance of spring.

"When will we move?" asked Snakewater.

"Ah! *You* are impatient! You are becoming one of us!" laughed Swan. "But it will be a little while—it is too muddy to travel yet. Soon, though!"

Snakewater was startled one afternoon by some sort of disturbance in another part of the camp. There were yells and people running.

"What is it? Are we being attacked?" she asked.

"No, I think someone is hurt," answered Swan.

There was a general rush toward the source of the disturbance. Some carried weapons, just in case.

A young man lay on the ground in front of the lodge, bleeding from a wound in his upper arm. Another, about the same age, was talking rapidly, babbling almost incoherently.

"Wait!" said an older man. "Slow down! Tell us what happened."

The young man paused for a deep breath and began to talk more calmly.

"We were hunting," he recounted. "Red Dog, Lizard, and I took our horses and rode to the east, looking for deer. The timber is heavier there, and we were made to think—"

"Go on!" an older man interrupted.

"Yes . . . Well, Dog killed a doe and we were deciding how to pack it back here, when we saw some men watching us."

"Osages," interrupted the wounded youth on the ground, gritting his teeth as a woman, probably his mother, bound up his wound.

"Yes, they were Osages. They told us that we should not be there, that it was *their* hunting ground. This was in hand signs, of course. We were polite and agreed to leave, but Dog wanted to claim the deer. They refused, and one of them shot an arrow. It missed Dog but flew on and hit the arm of Lizard there. We ran, leaving Dog's deer."

"There were too many of them," said Red Dog. "Five or six."

"That was wise," said Far Thunder. "You would have been killed over a deer."

"I told them we would be back!" said Red Dog angrily.

"Ah, that was not so wise," Far Thunder said. "What did the Osages say?"

"That they would be ready."

Thunder nodded. "They could not do otherwise. Now, how is Lizard? The arrow went on through?" he asked the woman who was cleaning the wound.

"We pulled it through," said Red Dog.

"It missed the bone," said Lizard's mother. "I will wrap it."

"I have some medicine," offered Snakewater. "I will get it."

"It is good," said Far Thunder. "Let it be so. But now we need a council. What is to be done?"

"Punish them!" called an angry man. "Kill an Osage or two."

"That is one plan," said Thunder, "but let us consider. . . . Let us meet at my lodge in a little while." He glanced at the sun. "It is too late today to start a war."

"They will start a *war*?" Snakewater asked Swan.

The woman chuckled. "No, I think not. Thunder does that to make them think, and gives them a little time. Always somebody talks big."

When the men gathered in front of the lodge of Far Thunder, there were some who spoke with anger and demanded vengeance—mostly young hotheads who were not directly concerned.

"We should make them know that we are not to be treated so!"

"Of course," said Thunder easily, "but let us smoke and then plan."

Very quickly the formal circle was formed and the pipe lighted. Far Thunder blew smoke to the four directions, to the sky and the earth, and passed the pipe to his left. It progressed ceremonially around the circle and back to the band chieftain. Thunder knocked the dottle into his palm and tossed it into the fire.

"Now," he began, "our young men have met the Osages, and blood has been spilled. What is to be done?"

"Kill them!" blurted a young warrior. "We must not be treated so!"

Far Thunder nodded thoughtfully. "We could easily do that. Then, of course, *they* would have to even the score."

"Let them try!"

"We could defend ourselves, maybe," agreed Thunder. "But there are other things to consider. We will be leaving soon, for summer range. The Osages will stay here."

"And it must not seem that we were frightened away!" insisted the other.

Now an older man spoke. "It is hard to defend a moving column against attack. We will have women and children, all our possessions."

"We can fight them!" insisted the militant young warrior. "Let them know our strength."

"But they know this region better than we do," spoke a calmer voice. "We would have dead and wounded."

"And so would *they*. They must be made to suffer! Even the score!"

"Let us think now," said Thunder, "about 'evening the score.' To do that they would have to give us one deer carcass, and let us shoot somebody through the arm, no?"

There were quiet chuckles.

"Now," he went on, "if we kill one or two Osages, then they must kill three or four of us. In the middle of all this we must move anyway. And that will look like retreat. . . ."

There were nods of agreement.

How clever, thought Snakewater. *It is no wonder that Far Thunder is a respected leader.*

"Let us show them that we are not afraid," Thunder continued.

A murmur of agreement went quietly around the circle, mingled with a trace of doubt.

"And how is this to be done?" asked a middle-aged warrior. "If we move, we look like cowards, unless we kill some of them."

"Then how can this be done?" mused Far Thunder. "Maybe we could *tell* them."

There were gasps of astonishment.

"*Tell* them?"

"But—"

"Yes," Thunder said thoughtfully. "A few of us go to them. That shows we are not afraid. We explain that we were preparing to leave, and that we mean them no harm."

There were thoughtful nods of agreement, more conversation, and by the time the matter came to a vote, there was no need for a vote. This was a plan.

Snakewater was not privileged to be present at the meeting with the Osages, but she heard the details later. Everyone did.

Five leading warriors, guided by young Red Dog, returned to the place of the deer kill, and then moved in the direction from which the Osages had come. It was soon apparent that they were being observed. To a dimly seen figure in the shadows Far Thunder openly raised a right hand, palm forward, in the sign for peace.

It was nearly midday when they saw and smelled the smoke of a village's cooking fires. They rode on, following a trail that was now plain to see.

They were met by a party of six well-armed warriors, who blocked the entrance to the town. Far Thunder and the others raised hands again in peace.

What do you want? signed a big man in the middle of the Osage party, apparently their leader.

We would smoke and talk, Far Thunder answered.

No, signed the other. *Your hunters kill our game.*

But our young men did not know, answered Thunder. *One of them is wounded.*

His own fault.

We have come, Thunder continued, *to say that our hearts are heavy for this, but we understand. We are preparing to leave anyway.*

There was a snort of contempt from one of the younger Osages. He was quieted with a gesture from their leader.

We do not leave because of fear, Far Thunder continued, *but to avoid any killing. We can kill if we must, of course.*

The Osage chieftain pondered a long while and then laughed aloud.

You must be speaking truth, he signed. *No one could think of a trick this stupid. Come, let us smoke.*

He turned and gestured the way as they moved on into the village.

The council was a success, and the two groups would remain allies, at least for now. The rights of the Osages to their hunting grounds were to be respected. Any of the Elk-dog People who found themselves in the area would try to contact some Osages to let their presence be known. They would kill for their own needs.

They agreed to make their winter camps farther to the west in the future.

How is your young man recovering? asked the Osage leader as they parted.

He does well, answered Far Thunder.

Good. . . . Boys will be boys, answered the other. *When will you leave?*

Maybe three days, Thunder signed.

The Osage nodded. *We will send a party to escort you.*

Is it not necessary.

It must be so, to honor our new friends.

So, three days later, the Elk-dog People took down their lodges and moved northwestward. They were accompanied by a party of mounted Osages. It might have been interpreted as an honor guard or as a security measure, to assure the honesty of Far Thunder's band. But at least for now there was no bloodshed.

38

It was the Moon of Roses now, June by the calendar of the white man. The Elk-dog People were gathering for their annual Sun Dance, the most important event of the year. Their nation was far flung, seven major bands in all. They camped from the timbered hills of the Ozarks to the eastern slopes of the Rockies, and from the scrub oaks where Far Thunder's band had wintered, northward to the Platte River.

The Sun Dance combined many of the qualities of religion, politics, patriotism, a massive family reunion, and the excitement of a country fair. The actual Sun Dance itself would last for five days, with prayers of thanksgiving, supplication and entreaty, personal vows and sacrifice, and reaffirmation of patriotism. For the Elk-dog People the celebration did not include a personal vision quest, as among some of the nations farther north. These would have a separate, a private quest, with fasting and solitary prayer. Often it would take place immediately after the Sun Dance, as the various bands parted until next season.

Some of the more spectacular events associated with the Sun Dance were not really part of the celebration. They had grown out of opportunity. It would be impossible to bring together hundreds of the world's finest horsemen and their mounts without races and contests. This logically led to wagers and to feats of skill and dexterity, encouraged by the onlookers. The entire encampment might last as long as half a moon, mostly before the Sun Dance itself.

There were visitors from other tribes and nations, who came to watch the proceedings and sometimes participate in the excitement of the contests. Swan pointed out to Snakewater a few lodges of Cheyenne and Arapaho, a delegation of Kiowas, and even an Apache family who lived with the Kiowas.

"Kiowas have their own Sun Dance, much like ours. It may be nearby this year."

"These are all allies?" asked Snakewater.

"Not really. They tolerate each other. Sometimes they fight, steal horses from each other. But not here. All are guests, and it would be offensive to cause any trouble."

There was a natural limit to how long this gathering could continue. The hundreds of horses required an immense quantity of grass. Even with the lush new growth that was the occasion of the celebration, there would be enough forage for only a short while. This as well as the limited opportunity to hunt near such a big encampment placed limits on the size of the bands for the buffalo-hunting nations.

Snakewater was enjoying the excitement and the pageantry. There had been a time not too long ago when she would have withdrawn, preferring to be alone. She had changed a lot in the past two years, she realized. She had been a bitter old woman. Now . . . A shadow crept across her thoughts as she thought of the Raven Mocker. Could she have actually changed that much without having assimilated the life-years of another? She thrust such thoughts away, resolved not to let this feeling confuse her. She managed to mostly throttle such sensations, and the buzz of activity helped a great deal.

The announcement had been made that the formal portion of the celebration would begin in three days. The announcement itself was very formal. The Elk-dog People's highest-ranking holy man marched three times around the entire encampment, holding aloft a sacred bundle and chanting the announcement as he went, while his assistant beat the cadence on a drum. This brought some change in the quality of the activities, but not much. Some of the participants in the racing and gambling began to behave more soberly. But there were also those who seemed to put forth an extra effort to squeeze out every available drop of enjoyment before settling down to ritual.

In the midst of all this excitement, with people coming and going and yelling and singing, Snakewater happened to glance across the creek to a long slope that descended from a low ridge a few bow shots to the north. A faint trail meandered down the slope, and along this trail toward the encampment came an odd procession: two people, several horses or mules, heavily laden with packs. Something familiar . . . Suddenly she realized. . . .

"Fox! Rain Cloud!" she said aloud, to no one in particular.

She had all but forgotten that the trader had suggested this occasion, the Sun Dance of the Elk-dog People, as a possible meeting place. She was delighted to see them, and stifled the urge to cross the stream and run up the slope toward them. Instead she moved in that direction, intending to wait at the ford of the creek. Ah, this was good! She could hear of their season's trading, and of where they had wintered, and could tell them of all her experiences. She ignored one thought that whispered from somewhere deep within. Soon she would have to make some decisions. Would she stay with these people who had become almost family to her, or move on with the trader couple, who were also like family? She smiled wryly as she recalled that for most of her life, she had had no family at all. Now, for all practical purposes, she had two!

The reunion was a time of great joy. The trader and his wife had changed very little. They commented on Snakewater's healthy appearance.

"Where did you winter?" Cloud asked. "With Far Thunder's people?"

"Yes. And you?"

"With some Arapahos, near the mountains. A good year for trading!" said Fox.

"And Far Thunder?" asked Rain Cloud. "He recovered completely?"

"Yes. I was pleased to help him."

"You look well," Cloud said. "This is a different life, no?"

"It is, but one I like," agreed Snakewater. "It is good for me here."

"What will you do now?" asked Fox. "You are a different person from the one who left West Landing with us."

It was said innocently, humorously, and surely Fox had no idea of the effect of this joking remark on Snakewater. It struck her unexpectedly with an effect of being thrown into cold water. The remark chilled her to the bone. Her change *was* noticeable, then. The dread that maybe her accusers were right, after all, swept over her. *Maybe it is true, I could be a Raven Mocker!*

"Snakewater! What is it?" asked Rain Cloud in concern.

"Oh . . . I . . . It is nothing."

"You could join us again after the Sun Dance," Fox offered.

She could not think about such things now. "Let us talk of it later," she said.

A part of the festivities included what the Elk-dog People called the Big Council. It was a formal meeting of the chiefs and subchiefs of the various bands, to openly report on the events of the past season since they'd last met. The events of any importance were already known by word of mouth, of course, but this provided open recognition and discussion where necessary.

The chiefs were seated in traditional sequence, assigned their places by long-observed custom. The circle around the fire left an opening on the east, in recognition of the symbolic doorway facing the rising sun. Around the circle in their traditional positions sat the leaders of the seven bands, with their subchiefs behind them. Fanning out toward the periphery of the crowd were the warrior societies, families, and visitors.

The pipe was passed among the chiefs, and then each in turn would relate any significant events of the season. The presiding Real-chief was of the Northern Band, so the leader to his left, chief of the Eastern Band, was the first to speak. Theirs had been a good season, with no major events. A few minor misfortunes, greeted with chuckles as he related them. The Eastern Band was traditionally the butt of jokes about foolish people. Some of them seemed to revel in it, telling jokes on themselves, even.

Next was the Forest Band, newly restored to the tribal structure. For many generations they had been known as the Lost Band, and an empty spot in the circle was reserved in their honor. Now, only a few seasons ago, the Lost Band had returned, and the circle was complete again. They called themselves the Forest Band, out of respect for old legends.

The New Band, closely allied to the People, had joined them only a generation or two ago. Theirs was a culture quite similar, and they had assimilated well.

Next, the Southern Band of Far Thunder.

"I am Far Thunder, chief of the Southern Band," he began formally. "We have wintered well. It could have been better, but for those who find themselves alive in the summer, it must have been a good winter. We camped and hunted with a band of Arapahos on our way to winter camp. They were good allies. Our supplies were plenty, but we lost some to raccoons. We lost a few people, ate a few dogs, but no horses, so it must have been a good winter."

There were a few chuckles, and Far Thunder continued.

"I would mention one event. Nearly a year ago I fell sick with bad spirits of some sort. A medicine woman, who was visiting our band with a trader, was able to see the problem and to make medicine to help me. This woman, Snakewater of the Cherokees, then stayed with us. She is the grandmother in my lodge, and has become one of us. It is my hope that she will stay, because her medicine is powerful. Snakewater has helped many."

It was unusual for a testimonial of this sort to be aired at the Big Council. The Real-chief nodded his acceptance of the Southern Band's account of their season, and looked on to the chief of the Red Rocks Band, seated next in sequence.

But now there arose a commotion in the rear, from an area where a number of visitors from other tribes were seated. Far Thunder looked in that direction, and a couple of men from one of the warrior societies moved in to restore order. It was most impolite and rude for a guest to interrupt the ceremony of the host group. The warriors would advise the troublemakers that they were not welcome.

Far Thunder waited for the restoration of order before continuing, but it was slow in coming. People began to turn and look, to see what was going on. Some began to stand, to see better, blocking the view of those still seated.

"Sit down!" somebody yelled.

At the rear, apparently the source of the disturbance, the warriors were scuffling with some of the visitors. A couple of men were trying to restrain a woman, who was striking out at the members of the Bowstring Society.

"No!" she screamed. "I will *not* sit down! That is the woman!"

It took a moment for Snakewater to realize that the troublemaker was yelling in *Cherokee.*

"She is a witch!" the woman screamed. "A Raven Mocker! She killed my baby!"

There were few among the crowd who understood the Cherokee tongue, and there was still much puzzled embarrassment, as the woman's family tried to restrain her.

But Snakewater heard. . . . Would it never end?

39 

Snakewater had not even been aware that among the visitors was a small party of the Real People; the very individuals whose intolerance had driven her away from her home and across many moons of distance.

The ironic part was that if she had been told that there were Cherokees visiting, she would probably have sought them out to welcome them. . . . They would visit and talk and hear any news from home. . . .

But *this*! The same people who had ruined her life . . . Had they sought her out, or was this, too, an accidental crossing of the winding trails of human lives? Or . . . are there really any accidents at all? This could, however, explain her recent depression, and the return of her dark thoughts. How had she happened to be wondering and worrying about her new and changed existence, and the legend of the Raven Mocker? There must have been something. . . . Her uneasiness may have been a warning that she had misunderstood.

Now she sat alone, deeply troubled. The Big Council had certainly been disturbed. The woman's family, realizing the rudeness of such behavior, had attempted to quiet her. She screamed and fought and finally they had dragged her away. The Council resumed, with the chiefs of the last three bands reporting the experiences of the past year. These were, of course, anticlimactic after the excitement of the interruption.

Snakewater had fled into the darkness while the crowd was distracted by the antics of the screaming woman. She had to get away, to think, to try to make sense out of a very bad situation. She knew that she had many friends, who would defend her against any accusation. But should they? There gnawed, in the deepest recesses of her mind, a doubt: *Maybe the woman was right.*

Below her, in the camp, the Big Council seemed to have adjourned. The fire had been built up, and she could hear the sounds of the drums and the singing. It was a clear night. The moon, a little past full, was just rising, blood red against the black sky. That had a calming effect on her, or maybe it was only a distraction. In the presence of such majesty her own problems seemed insignificant.

Below, people were dancing now, to the steady cadence of the drums and the jingling bells and rattles. This would be a social dance, for pure enjoyment. The serious ritual of the Sun Dance would be held in a special pavilion to the east of the main camp. She could see it in the brightening moonlight, a large open-sided structure, roofed with brush and leaves, large enough for many to dance at once. She had watched its construction.

The family of the Real-chief had been responsible for obtaining the symbolic buffalo used in the ceremony. They had killed a magnificent bull, skinned it, and brought the hide, the head still attached, to the Sun Dance arbor that very day. She had watched as they constructed an effigy of poles and branches, stretching the bull's hide over it in a lifelike position, head propped up and facing the arena. Before this effigy people would make their vows, pray their prayers, and offer their sacrifices. Not to the buffalo, but to the Creator for His generosity in providing the great herds. But now the Sun Dance arena was dark. Things must happen in sequence, and the formality of the Big Council must precede the rituals of the Sun Dance.

She felt a strong attraction, a fascination with these events, so different from those of her own people, the Real People. Maybe it would help if she said a prayer or two before the Sun Dance effigy. It could do no harm, and might be of help with the worry that had inescapably dogged her for the past two years.

These thoughts were interrupted by a movement on the slope. Snakewater turned, instinctively reaching for the knife at her waist as a dark figure approached. But it moved openly and slowly.

"Aiee!" panted Swan. "The slopes are steeper than when I was young."

She seated herself on the still sun-warmed rock beside Snakewater, taking a moment to catch her breath.

"I thought I might find you here," she said finally. "Quite a surprise, the crazy woman. You know her?"

Snakewater had sought privacy, to be alone with her thoughts, but now it seemed comforting to have Swan with her.

"Yes. She comes from the town where I grew up. I left there because of this."

Swan waited a little while and then spoke again.

"No one believes her, of course. People are talking about it, and that she must have gone mad. I wanted you to know."

"Thank you, Swan. That means much to me. But—this is very hard to say—she may be right."

Swan gasped, then laughed nervously. "Now it is you who have gone mad, Snakewater."

"No, I am serious."

Quickly she blurted out the whole story, the Raven Mocker legend, the odd series of circumstances that had plagued her and followed her across the country and beyond the Mississippi.

"And you think . . . Are you serious, woman?" Swan demanded.

"I have to be, Swan. This keeps coming back again and again. Will it ever stop?"

"I don't know, of course," said Swan, a little sarcastically. "But some things I do know. One is that you could not do anything to hurt anybody."

"But harm has come to those I was helping. . . ."

"Of course. Such things *happen.* You do not *cause* them."

"Maybe I do, without knowing," insisted Snakewater.

"No, no. Look . . . you have a gift, a very powerful medicine, no? It allows you to see things that others do not, to make conjures and potions and to *help* others. You cured Far Thunder, and for this I am grateful. But . . . Snakewater, I do not know of your Cherokee ways, but among my people, one who has been given such a gift and uses it to hurt others, would die. Is it not so?"

"Yes, something like that . . . But, Swan, what if the gift is *evil*? The woman calls me a witch. Maybe I am, without knowing!"

"Nonsense." Swan snorted indignantly. "You could not use an evil gift to do good, any more than to use yours to *hurt* others. You would not do that."

"Maybe . . . I don't know, Swan. What happened to the woman?"

"Her people carried her away, kicking and screaming, about—well, you heard—Her baby."

"Yes, Swan, I remember that well. She had a beautiful child. . . . I did all I could, but could not save her. I even tried to breathe for her. . . . The mother—Spotted Bird, I think—I had no idea that she blamed *me.* That was not until later. She told that I had *sucked* the breath from the baby."

"Aiee!" said Swan softly.

"There were others too. One tried to kill me. . . ."

"Ah! We had no idea, Snakewater. But they will probably leave now. My heart is heavy for you."

"Mine is heavy for the trouble I brought to the Big Council," said Snakewater.

"No one will blame you. Will you go to watch the dancing? Or even dance, maybe?"

"I think not, Swan. I am tired. . . . Much excitement, no? I will go back to the lodge."

She rose, and the two started down the dim path.

"I thank you, Swan, for coming to tell me what happened back there. And I feel better after talking."

"It is good! Oh, yes, I forgot. One of the horse herders was looking for you—your mare has a foal."

One more thing . . .

She wanted badly to see the foal. She had enjoyed the ownership and use of the little mare, given her by Kills Many during the early part of her flight from Old Town. The animal had served her well. During this past season with the Elk-dog People of Far Thunder's band, she had had little use for a horse. Except, of course, during their few moves and the travel involved. There was a brief moment of guilt as she reflected that she had done little to assist in the care and feeding of the mare. Some of the older sons of Far Thunder's lodge had been assigned those tasks.

"Could one of the boys show me where the foal is?" she asked Swan the next morning.

"Of course!" Swan turned and called to where the youngsters were playing. "Blue Hawk! Come and help Grandmother. You know where her mare is, with the new foal?"

"Yes, I think so. With my father's horses? Coyote is herding them today. He can show us."

"Good. You are a good boy!" She patted his head.

They walked outside the camp, avoiding an area where a match race with two horses on a short straight sprint was about to begin. They passed a contest with tomahawks thrown for accuracy at a mark on a dead cottonwood bole, and moved on toward a meadow where a hundred horses or so grazed contentedly. A couple of young men lounged nearby, and Blue Hawk approached one of them.

"Coyote!" he called. "Can you show us the new foal of Snakewater's mare?"

"Yes . . . Right over there!" The young man pointed.

"Yes, there she is!" Snakewater agreed. "Ah, a fine colt, no?"

It was, indeed, a highly desirable animal—long, straight legs, foxy little ears, an intelligent face with wide-set eyes. The color was a nondescript, mousy brown, a soft baby fur. The face was marked with a white star between the eyes, a narrow race from there to the nose, and a snip of white between the nostrils.

"Our father says that a foal this color will usually shed off black when it loses its baby hair," Blue Hawk told her.

Snakewater nodded. "It is good! Thank you, Hawk." She turned and waved her thanks to young Coyote, who returned the wave.

Snakewater and Blue Hawk started back toward the village.

"A very good colt, Grandmother," the youngster assured her. "You should be proud!"

"I *am* proud!" said Snakewater. "I never had a colt before."

"Aiee!" said Hawk. "Never?"

"That is true. I never had a horse of any kind until that one—the foal's mother. Your people feel differently about horses than mine, Hawk."

"They have no *horses*?"

"Oh, yes! They are very good with horses. It is only that I never had one. I lived alone, you see, and did not travel much. *Your* people travel all the time, and they need horses."

"I see. . . ."

But she had to wonder if he really did.

"Those people last night, the visitors—someone said they are your people," Blue Hawk asked now.

"Yes, some of them."

"The crazy woman?" asked Hawk.

"Yes, someone called her that. She had a baby that died, and her heart was very heavy. She still suffers, I guess."

"Too bad," said the boy.

"Yes," agreed Snakewater. "My heart is heavy for her."

She learned one more thing that morning. The Cherokee visitors, to avoid trouble, had packed and departed at daylight. That part, at least, was over.

40

Snakewater felt a strange attraction, somehow, to the Sun Dance pavilion, the "medicine lodge." She wandered over there to watch the Real-chief's family putting the finishing touches on the huge effigy of the buffalo opposite the gateway opening. The massive head, propped in a lifelike position, overlooked the arena, dominating the scene.

She saw that the lifeless eyes had been replaced with some other objects—shells, perhaps, or shiny black stones, possibly even painted replicas. The effect was strange, lending a dreamy, surrealistic tone to the entire scene. The deep shade, broken by mottled sunlight filtering through the leafy roof of the arbor, lent a further mood that she could not understand. It was thrilling, exciting, yet calming as she stood there watching the young men prop the wooden legs of the huge effigy into position. Even though this occasion, this celebration, was completely foreign to her, she felt that it had meaning—not just to these people of the prairie, the hunters of buffalo, but to *her.* She, Snakewater, was somehow drawn to this place, this ceremonial effigy.

She would come back, she decided, when the young men were finished. She would say her own private prayers before the symbolic effigy, prayers of thanks for a season that had been good. She'd ask for a better one to come. It could do no harm. A vow, maybe . . . She was unsure what she might vow. There was still indecision as to whether she would stay with Far Thunder's band or rejoin the trader couple, at least for a season. It would be possible, she supposed, for her to return to Old Town or Keowee, now that her tormentor had moved west, But that was an uncomfortable thought. It would never be the same.

In any case, her plans would be complicated by the new foal. Not too much . . . She realized that there must be many new foals among the vast horse herds of Far Thunder's people. But . . . well, of course! A foal would follow its mother, and the pace of travel with the pole-drag or *travois* was necessarily slow. That should not be a problem, then.

When she returned to pray before the buffalo effigy she should bring some sort of an offering, she thought. That, she had been told, was customary when one offered prayers. But what had she to offer? She had virtually no possessions, beyond the necessities of daily life. It crossed her mind that she could sacrifice the colt, but the thought was repugnant to her. Swan had said that a season or two ago, someone *had* sacrificed a horse, a fine buffalo runner, leaving it tied in the medicine lodge. But that was an unusual gesture, even for these people.

No, she would burn a pinch of tobacco, a little sage, some of her other aromatic herbs. The smoke should be appealing to the spirits here, as well as anywhere else. She would come back. . . . She supposed that she could come to pray after the public ceremonies started tomorrow. That, after all, was the purpose of the entire Sun Dance. She was self-conscious about it, though. She would feel much better if she could come alone, in private, after the preparations were finished, but before the public ceremonies. Maybe tonight after dark. . . .

Snakewater spent the day restlessly waiting. She sorted her herbs and set aside the small quantities she would need for her own private ceremony. A gourd—yes, a gourd with ashes. . . . She could carry a few coals with which to ignite her sacrificial smoke offering. That was readied.

Again she visited the horse herd to watch her foal a little while, and walked along the stream. She wondered what would happen now to the crazy woman from Old Town. She was embarrassed that she could barely remember the woman's name. Maybe she had forgotten it on purpose, as she had tried to put all the unpleasantness of that other life behind her.

She had been told that after the disruption of the Big Council, the traveling Cherokees had moved on. What would happen to the woman who had lost her child? Maybe in a new setting, with fewer familiar things to remind her, life would be better for her. Snakewater hoped so. Probably the woman had been pushed too far by the experience of seeing again the person whom she blamed for her troubles. Too bad . . . Her family had probably brought her here to avoid that very thing. Well, it was over now. They had taken her on, away from the contact that had wakened bad memories. They were bound for the mountains, someone had said, and a settlement of the Real People among the snowcapped peaks. That would be good, Snakewater thought, an entirely new setting, with no reminders. She wished the woman well.

She waited until nearly dark and then made her way toward the Sun Dance lodge. She carried her gourd with the coals, bedded in ashes, and her handful of herbal offerings.

There was no one near the pavilion, which was good. She needed for this to be a deeply personal, renewing ceremony. She was not certain that the Elk-dog People would understand.

Snakewater entered from the opening at the east and walked straight to the buffalo effigy at the other end. In the semidarkness it appeared almost alive. The great head drooped forward as if it were watching her.

Someone had placed a blanket or mat directly in front of the beast's nose, and she dropped to her knees on this. With a small stick she stirred the ashes in her gourd to expose the hot coals. A pinch of tobacco . . . The fragrant blue smoke rose in the twilight, and she breathed a prayer of supplication. Then, sage, and further prayer, not in words as much as thoughts and feelings. . . . A pinch of powdered dry root of one of her healing plants, another prayer.

Suddenly, out of the corner of her eye, she caught a glimpse of motion, rushing at her from the left. There was a scream of rage and the glint of an upraised weapon.

"Die, witch! Baby killer!"

It took a moment for her to realize that the screaming was in her own tongue, that of the Real People. *The woman . . .*

Snakewater threw herself to the right and rolled, surprising even herself with her agility when she really needed it. The knife slashed at empty air. Above her loomed the figure of the bereaved woman, knife raised to strike again.

But now, another sound . . . There was a creaking, crackling sound from the buffalo bull effigy, and Snakewater could have sworn that it moved. No . . . it wasn't stirring, but *falling*. Had the woman brushed against it? Surely it was sturdy enough to withstand that. Slowly and ponderously the figure toppled forward, the shiny black horns lowering. Snakewater tried to cry out, but no sound came from her throat.

At the last moment the woman looked up and screamed again—this time without words, merely a scream of terror as the massive forehead crushed her into the mat on the floor of the medicine lodge.

Snakewater rolled, crawled quickly under the brush screen that formed the backdrop for the Sun Dance effigy, and fled into the night.

She was just catching her breath when she heard a sound at her elbow. It sounded like a hollow chuckle.

"*Lumpy?*" she asked in amazement.

The relatives of the dead woman turned up the following morning. She had left their camp unnoticed the previous night, a day's travel west, and they had, too late, realized where she must be going. There were expressions of regret on both sides, and wonder and confusion as to what she might have been attempting to do in the medicine lodge.

Snakewater stayed out of sight in the lodge of Far Thunder.

Our hearts are heavy for her deeds, said the leader of the Real People in hand signs. *Maybe now she can rest.*

It is to be hoped for, answered the leader of the Northern Band, the Real-chief of the Elk-dog People. *May our next meeting be happier.*

Epilogue

Among the paintings on the Story Skins of the Elk-dog People is a record of the year when the Sun Dance effigy collapsed in the medicine lodge. The event seemingly was related to the presence of a woman from another nation, who was said to have been mad, but the exact connection was unknown. No defect was found in the construction of the effigy, and the reason for its fall was never determined.

The omen was not a bad one, as they had suspected at first. A successful Sun Dance and a good season followed. Many attributed this to a skilled medicine woman, an outsider who became one of the members of the Southern Band. She was reputed to have had great powers, and lived for many years in the lodge of Far Thunder as a Grandmother.

Author's Comments

Readers who have discovered other books of the Spanish Bit Saga will recognize the Elk-dog People as the major culture included in the series. This tribe is a composite, created because in the early books it was impossible to identify the tribes and nations with whom Coronado might have been in contact. In the interests of historical accuracy the People became a theoretical nation of buffalo hunters. They have cultural traits of Kiowa, Cheyenne, Arapaho, and a bit of Comanche.

In *Raven Mocker* the major figure is Cherokee, and I have attempted to depict Cherokee history, customs, and legends to the best of my ability. I have tried to keep my story line within the realm of possibility in depicting the "Real People," the Cherokees, for whom I have great respect and admiration. I apologize in advance for any errors or offense committed by this humble *yoneg*.

DON COLDSMITH